THE CHALLENGE

THE CHALLENGE

by
Robert F. Lundrigan
and
James R. Borchert

NORTH RIVER PRESS
Croton-on-Hudson
New York

For more information on the concepts presented in this book please contact:
Focus Management
Suite 4
644 Humphrey Street
Swampscott, MA 01907
Tel: (617) 595-7160

For additional copies of THE CHALLENGE please contact your local bookstore, Focus Management, or the publisher:
North River Press
P.O. Box 241
Croton-on-Hudson, N.Y. 10520
Tel: (914) 941-7175

Manufactured in the United States of America

Library of Congress Cataloging-in-Publication Data
Lundrigan, Robert F., 1928–
The challenge / by Robert F. Lundrigan and James Borchert.
p. cm.
ISBN 0-88427-077-7
I. Borchert, James R., 1950– . II. Title.
PS3562.U556C47 1988
813'.54—dc19 88-5331
CIP

2 3 4 5 6 7 8 9 10

INTRODUCTION

During 1942 American industry changed overnight from a peacetime manufacturer to a manufacturer of war goods. It was that tremendous change that won the war and it was the ability and willingness to effect that change that made it all possible.

Now we are in another war but this time it's not as simple as the good guys wearing the white hats and the bad guys wearing the black. It's a war being fought both here in this country and overseas simultaneously. The weapons being used are not guns and ammunition but products and productivity. It's an all–out war nonetheless, with no holds barred. The winners will survive to become the leading industrial powers on earth.

There are two things other than death and taxes that are certain in this life. They are change and competition. Life is all about change and competition. "The Challenge" is also all about change and competition. Americans are a breed of fiercely competitive individuals for whom there is no second place. Who can remember the names of the horses that finished second in the Kentucky Derby?

"The Challenge" deals with the principles and theories of synchronized manufacturing first set forth by Dr. Eliyahu Goldratt in his book "The Goal" and in his outstanding computer based scheduling tool, OPT®. It takes the theories and combines them with some of the strengths of the Japanese Just-in-Time systems to develop a better common sense approach to scheduling the shop floor, one that doesn't require the outlay of large sums of money.

I chose the novel form to make the creation of the model more palatable, easier to understand and more enjoyable to learn. I call the format Business Fiction and I hope that the readers see the tremendous potential for improvement that the constraint management concepts can bring to them.

I want to thank my co-author, Jim Borchert, for his vast and valuable technical contributions, without which I never could have finished the book. Jim was an associate of Dr. Goldratt for six years before leaving to start his own consulting firm, Focus Management. He is considered to be one of the leading experts in the field of constraint management.

In summary, I want to say that we can meet the challenge both here in this country and abroad by taking the salve of American ingenuity, otherwise known as common sense, applying it to our wounds, getting into the fight for industrial supremacy and following the principles of constraint management to the finish line and the fruits of victory.

THE CHALLENGE

CHAPTER 1

It is precisely 1:55 P.M. as the sleek black limo proceeds through the massive wrought-iron gate emblazoned with the crest of Connecticut Yankee Farm. Marty Connolly is seated beside me. The chauffeur guides the limo through the tunnel formed by the double line of tall oak trees just starting to burst into bloom.

The flight to Lexington has done nothing to diminish my feeling of apprehension. Why would the president and majority stockholder of ConnYankee, the country's leading manufacturer of precision machined parts, invite his vice presidents in charge of manufacturing and finance to spend the weekend at his home? The action is out of character for Arthur King, a man who has never been known to mix his professional and private lives. Even those of us closest to him at corporate headquarters, especially relatively new staff members like myself, know little of his private life except what we hear in the media. Marty is a ConnYankee veteran, but he too seems puzzled.

Marty's voice breaks into my thoughts. "I understand that Vickie Barlow will be here at the farm to greet us today. Have you met her yet?" He pulls a dog-eared snapshot from his wallet and hands it to me. It shows Arthur King with his arm around a pretty young blonde.

"I not only never met her, I didn't even know she existed," I say, surprised. "I knew that the Connecticut Yankee Farm was started by Arthur as a Christmas present for his wife, Cynthia, and that just as it was becoming an important breeding farm for race horses, Cynthia died—but I didn't think he was in any hurry to replace her, let alone with someone young enough to be his daughter."

"Hold on," Marty says. "You've got it all wrong. Vickie is the only child of Ed Barlow, one of Arthur's earliest and most trusted employees. I go back a long way with ConnYankee, but Ed went back even farther. A few years ago, on an inspection trip to one of the western plants, Ed Barlow was killed in a plane crash. It was a terrible blow for Arthur, and of course an even worse one for poor Vickie. Her mother had died several years before that, and there were no close relatives, so she was all alone in the world. Her mother's long illness had been very costly, so there wasn't much money left for her, either. Arthur took her under his wing—made sure she could continue at Radcliffe, and welcomed her to the farm during her vacations. After a while, I believe he and Cynthia came to think of her as the daughter they'd always wanted, but never had."

"Arthur King is full of surprises, it seems," I say. "He has a warm heart, as well as a great head for business."

"Yes," Marty agrees, "but Vickie has more than repaid his kindness. When Cynthia became ill, Vickie was great comfort to her, and now that Cynthia is gone, Vickie has made Arthur's life less lonely. She's smart, too—she's learned so much about horses that she can be a real help to him in running the farm, and now she's going to graduate school at Harvard as well."

As I ponder this information and the new light it sheds on Arthur King, I notice that the limo is passing several small cottages and barns, all painted white with crimson trim. Rows of white post and rail fencing seem to surround us on all sides. I notice several horses grazing in the enclosures formed by the fencing. The beauty and peacefulness of the place numbs my senses. "This is some layout, isn't it, Marty?"

"That it is," answers my companion, "but I'm sure that we weren't invited here to admire the scenery. Something mighty important is up. Something damned important."

As the limo rounds a curve, I notice the main house. With its huge white columns, it looks like something out of *Gone With The*

Wind, but that's not Rhett Butler and Scarlett standing in front of the main entrance. I recognize Arthur King even though I've never seen him without a suit and tie. He is dressed in faded dungarees and a grey sweatshirt. Somehow, despite the informality of his attire, I find him no less imposing a figure. Standing beside him is a young girl, also clad in dungarees and a sweatshirt.

As Marty and I leave the limousine, we are greeted with a warm smile and a punishing handshake. "Hello, Marty. Hello, Larry. Welcome to Connecticut Yankee. Marty, I think you've met Vickie Barlow."

The attractive young girl takes a step toward us, a pleasant smile lighting up her blonde-framed face. Arthur gestures to Marty first. "Vickie, you remember Marty Connolly, my main manufacturing man. The old mustang's been with me forever, thirty years anyway, and a better manufacturing man can't be found."

Vickie shakes Marty's hand lightly.

They turn their attention to me. "This is Larry Jones. We call him the boy wonder down at the office. He's our chief bean–counter, but don't let his young looks fool you. He's getting old fast, dealing with the likes of Marty and me."

Vickie takes my hand. "Arthur, I'd like to show Mr. Connolly and Mr. Jones around the farm after they've unpacked."

"I had planned a short meeting, but I suppose that it can wait until after dinner—yes, that might be best," replies Arthur King.

Marty glances quickly my way, as annoyed as I am at the further delay in discovering the reason we are here.

Vickie proves to be a delight, however. Her love of horses and of the Connecticut Yankee Farm in particular shows as she drives us around the farm in an electric golf cart. It is a fabulous place. The pastures, well defined by the ever present white fencing, the immaculate barns, and the training track with the stocked trout pond in the infield are impressive, but the horses are really something. Vickie shows us mares in foal and mares with offspring and the stallions. Ah, yes, those stallions. They remind me of Arthur King —strong, virile, and a bit heavy in the middle.

Before I know it, the evening meal is upon us. The anticipation of what is to follow, although a mystery, ruins the meal for me. Marty is barely touching his food. I am not doing any better. Vickie makes small talk, but I hardly hear what she is saying. I hope that she doesn't think me rude, but she probably does.

As the coffee cups are refilled Arthur King breaks the awkward silence. "Vickie, darlin', will you excuse us? We've got to get down to the business at hand. I've been keeping Larry and Marty on a string long enough."

"OK, Arthur. I've got to get to bed early tonight. We're schooling King Arthur tomorrow morning at five. You'd better be there." Vickie bids us goodnight and leaves the room.

Arthur likes the old hammer over the head approach to starting his meetings. Tonight is one of his best. "Effective immediately both of you are relieved of your present duties."

I look at Marty. There is no color in his face. A weaker man his age would have had a stroke. I feel the way Marty looks.

Arthur senses our plight. "Damn it guys, loosen up. I'm not firing you. You'll have a job with ConnYankee for as long as there is a ConnYankee."

A bit of the color returns to Marty's face as he leans forward in his seat preparing to say something.

Arthur waves Marty off. "For the time being, let me do all of the talking. It'll be easier on all of us." He takes a long gulp of coffee before continuing.

"I started this company during the Second World War, as you both know. I was just a kid fresh out of trade school and didn't know enough to be timid about going into business. I only knew that I could never take orders—never could. My father left me a small inheritance—enough to start something. All of the big companies were going full blast working on the war effort, and what they couldn't handle—mostly small, short-cycle jobs—they subcontracted to small machine shops. It was easy to set up a machine shop and get work. In fact, the hardest thing was deciding which jobs to turn down. It really was something back then. No scheduling problems. The cost of money was about one percent, and profits were sky high. Even inventory was a good investment. I got all the work I could handle and then some. I kept pouring all of the money right back into the business and expanding. The most profitable work turned out to be precision work—the tighter the tolerance, the bigger the profit. I was lucky, in a way, to be born when I was. I also poured my heart and soul into my business, and the more I poured the luckier I got.

"When the war ended I found myself with several well-equipped machine shops and several hundred employees to take care of. The concentration I had placed on precision work paid off. I bid on bearings for the automotive industry and parts for turbine and later jet engines, among other things. I got business. I made good parts. I worked hard and I grew." He drains the rest of the coffee from his cup, beckons to the maid for a refill, and continues.

"I've always had the knack of surrounding myself with the best people available. I don't know whether that's the secret to my success or whether it's this terrible competitive nature that I'm cursed with. I must be the best at everything that I do. You fellows know that. God knows you've spent many sleepless nights because of it."

Arthur pauses for what seems to be several minutes to gather himself. He takes a deep breath and continues. "Somewhere along the way—way back when—I met and married Cynthia, God rest her soul. I've never told anybody this before, but my biggest mistake was allowing the company to come before Cynthia. Oh, I loved her—and I know that she loved me deeply. Everything she did, she did to please me."

Arthur hesitates again. He is having a great deal of trouble getting the words to come out. "I didn't realize it until it was too late, but she always came in second best to the company. She never seemed to complain, but looking back now, I know that she must have suffered terribly through all of the years that I was consumed with a terrible need to make the company as big and as powerful as I could possibly make it.

"We started this farm—or should I say she started this farm. I only know that this place *is* Cynthia. There is something of her in every corner. She loved it here. When she passed away a couple of years ago I wasn't even here to tell her the things that are in my heart that I'd never told her."

There is a hint of moisture in the corners of Arthur's eyes as he pauses to look out the window. I feel uncomfortable.

Arthur turns from the window. "I miss Cynthia very much. Gradually, over the months, the painful sorrow I felt has let up. Vickie has helped a lot. I still miss my wife, but now the sorrow is mostly gone, and I still have the fond memories—pleasant memories of the times when Cynthia and I were together years ago, and then of the time when Vickie came to stay with us. Cynthia passed her love for the farm on to Vickie. When I'm here, and when Vickie comes, I feel I'm with Cynthia—and this is where I'm going to stay."

Having said it, Arthur regains his composure. "I'm going to retire from the active end of running the company and spend what time I have left right here running Connecticut Yankee Farm for Cynthia, with Vickie's help when she has time off from school. And if you haven't already guessed at the reason for your being here, here comes the punch line. You, Marty, and you, Larry, are the two finalists in a contest that you were in but knew nothing about. One of you is going to run ConnYankee for me!"

CHAPTER 2

Daylight finally arrives. I haven't been able to sleep a wink. My mind is still spinning from the enormity of it all. Imagine me, a thirty-year-old financial wizard—that's what I've been called—a candidate for the job of CEO at ConnYankee.

I stumble about the room acting like a robot whose programming has gone sour, as my body goes through the getting-up routine while my mind is still trying to comprehend what's happening to me. Arthur is going to get together with us again this afternoon, when he will let us in on his plan to make the final selection. He did say that most of the selection routine was over with and that some kind of competition would enable us to control our own destiny. He said that the final decision was going to be in our hands, not his. I feel like a man in over my head.

I look at my watch. It is ten before five. Arthur invited Marty and me down to the training track at five to watch a horse school. I think that Vickie mentioned it too, but I'm not sure. I put on a sweater and head down to the kitchen for some starting fluid. I just can't get it together without that first cup of coffee in the morning.

Marty is already there. He looks like he didn't get to bed last night either. We exchange morning greetings. I see Marty in a different light this morning. He is no longer my co-worker. He is something of an adversary, but not in the usual sense. Whatever the outcome of this so-called competition, whatever it is, one of us will be working for the other when it's all over—better not burn any bridges.

We take our morning coffee without conversation. I feel a bit awkward.

It is a beautiful April Kentucky morning as we stroll down the lane toward the training track. The farm is a beehive of activity. There are grooms tending to the horses—feeding, brushing, or hosing them down. From a large truck hay is being unloaded, and a horse van is making its way up the main road.

We arrive at the track. Arthur and Vickie are already there along with another man and a groom trying to keep rein on a colt. We form a kind of circle around the colt. It's not a very tight circle. The colt is not behaving himself, and his hooves look like deadly weapons the way he is rearing up and pawing the air. We all take turns ducking out of the way. The groom is being lashed about almost to the point of being airborne by the gyrations of the nervous animal.

Arthur introduces us to the other man. He is Mike Roberts, the chief trainer at Connecticut Yankee.

"Every time I see King Arthur he looks more impressive to me. He is really something," says Arthur.

Mike Roberts replies, "I think we've really got something this time, boss. He's royally bred and his conformation is perfect. I'll stake my reputation that this is going to be a runner."

They say that one can sense greatness in a person. I have that feeling about this colt. I'm no judge of horseflesh, but this one oozes class. His shiny chestnut coat glistens in the morning sunlight with the sweat brought out by his nervousness.

The groom is fighting a losing battle trying to keep King Arthur straightened out as Mike Roberts tries to get a saddle over the horse's back. It seems hopeless.

Vickie walks up to the animal and takes the checkrein from the groom. I am horrified. The colt is so powerful and Vickie so fragile looking, I'm sure that she will be hurt. To my complete surprise nothing of the sort happens. As soon as Vickie takes hold of the colt he simmers right down and stands perfectly still as she talks to him and strokes his neck. Mike is able to get the saddle on and straps it in place with no trouble at all.

"Either we're going to have to teach this horse some manners or Vickie is going to have a full time job as a groom when we go to the races," chuckles Arthur.

"He loves you, Miss Barlow," says Mike as he starts to remove the saddle from King Arthur. "After all, you were right there when he was born. He probably thinks that you're his mother. He'll learn to behave in due time."

"If he doesn't kill somebody first!" exclaims the groom.

"Is that all there is to it?" I ask as Mike removes the saddle.

"Not by a long shot," returns Mike. "These things must be done right the first time. The King has about eight months to go before he's two and his race training begins. He has a lot to learn before then—things like getting used to the saddle and then getting a boy on his back. He must be galloped, and then there's the little matter of getting him accustomed to the starting gate. Oh, there's plenty to do, all right, but I've seen many a promising colt ruined because he wasn't properly schooled. These are dumb animals we're dealing with. Once you train them one way, that's the way it's going to be. They're not like people. You can tell people the right way to go and they'll change—not horses."

"Not people either," laughs Arthur. "I've dealt with a lot of them during the past forty years, and the most difficult thing I've encountered in those dealings is the damned resistance to change. People don't accept change any better than King Arthur here. They get in a rut, a comfortable rut. It doesn't matter whether something is better. The fact that it's different turns most people off."

"Amen," chimes in Marty. "I remember the old days when we used spread-sheet scheduling at our plants. Production control and the supervisors used to come in two hours early every day to develop machine loads, mostly by counting what they had. When MRP came along the schedule was there. The counting was done for them by the computer. Most of them kept coming to work two hours early and going about doing their job as if MRP didn't exist. I don't know how many false starts we had before we finally got going with it. Now we couldn't find anyone willing to go back to spread sheet."

Arthur laughs. "If I remember correctly, you were pretty slow to embrace MRP yourself. It was only when I took the bull by the horns and made it clear to you that it was a condition of your employment that the trouble stopped."

Marty's face colors slightly before he answers, "You had to bring that up. Damn! Everyone is entitled to a mistake now and then."

"True, and as long as you learn from those mistakes we will continue to make progress."

"MRP sure has cut down on the time that PC and the supervisors spend in the plant, but it hasn't made much of a dent in the hourly people's overtime," answers Marty.

"Maybe we need to look at something else in that area," says Arthur.

Mike and the groom lead King Arthur back toward the barn area. "Let's go get some breakfast," offers Arthur as he turns back toward the main house.

CHAPTER 3

I spend the time between breakfast and lunch alone with my thoughts. It is peaceful, walking about the farm; there is a lot to think about. I'm proud of what I've done in just nine years. From a kid selling papers on a street corner in Lynton, Massachusetts, to manager of finance for a Fortune 500 company is quite an accomplishment.

My mind takes me back to my high-school days as I stand gazing at a mare with her colt. Dad was a sports nut. His dream was to see me playing in some varsity sport. I can remember all of my birthday presents—balls of all shapes, gloves, bats, and even a hockey stick. I disappointed him—too short for basketball, too small for football, and I couldn't hit a curve ball worth a damn.

High school came easy for me, especially math. I've always been good with numbers and solving problems in logic. The partial scholarship award and a no-interest educational loan Dad got from the plant got me through Harvard. The one thing Dad drilled into my head when he was pushing me toward sports still drives me. He told me, no matter what I did, to give it my best shot, and if my best shot wasn't good enough I would have no regrets. Dad still works at the ConnYankee plant in Lynton.

I gave it my best shot at Harvard—graduated high in my class—

cum laude. It was great that last semester, all the wining and dining and trips to prospective job sites. There were some attractive offers. I chose ConnYankee, partly out of a sense of family but mostly because it seemed to be a company on the move—keeping ahead of the competition—my kind of outfit.

Things happened fast. I was lucky to be in the right job at the right time, and influenced some timely investments that made significant profits in less than a year. Up the ladder I went, making the right moves—some lucky, but all based on a lot of research, common sense, and guts.

The move that got me to the top is a good example of what I mean. Our precision magnet plant was booming. The highest priced, most critical ingredient in the magnet recipe is cobalt, an exotic metal that was selling for four dollars a pound. Ninety percent of the world's supply comes from copper mines in Zaire. Word got to me that there was going to be trouble there. The blacks wanted the top jobs held by whites from the Netherlands. The price started to creep up. I made the decision to buy all of the cobalt I could get my hands on to protect the magnet business. It seemed to me to be a low-risk kind of deal, because we could unload the surplus at a profit if the price stayed up. Trouble is, my agent took me literally and got two hundred tons of the stuff—all he could get his hands on, like I told him. The bill was two million dollars. When the corporate manager of finance found out, he was furious, but his timing was terrible. I got fired the same day that the Africans flooded the mines. The world's supply of cobalt was cut off cold, sending the price of cobalt shooting up to forty-five dollars a pound overnight. Trouble is there was none. The two-million dollar investment I had made for ConnYankee was worth eighteen million in one day! Talk about a fast track—I replaced the guy who fired me within the week. Arthur King moves fast when he moves.

My first official act in my new position was to unload half of the cobalt for nine million dollars. The other half was two years' supply. My decision to buy cobalt had netted ConnYankee seven million dollars in pocket and another nine million cost avoidance—not bad for a kid who used to sell newspapers for a dime.

I'm still doing a solid job of managing ConnYankee's purse strings. I'm good at what I do. Leaning on the rail of the training track and seeing my reflection in the trout pond, I'm feeling pretty damned good about myself.

The room is just what you'd expect an Arthur King study to be. Mahogany-paneled walls and floor-to-ceiling bookcases on both sides of a massive stone fireplace are the background for a quartet of leather chairs surrounding a huge round coffee table. The fire's warmth is just enough to take the late afternoon chill from the room.

"How do you like Connecticut Yankee?" asks Arthur as he settles into one of the chairs, beckoning us to do the same.

"There's no machines, no smell of lubricating fluid, but other than that this place is really something," answers Marty.

"Spoken like a true manufacturing man. Damn, Marty, I'll bet that when you cut yourself shaving, you bleed lubrication fluid," laughs Arthur.

Marty nods his head in agreement. "You're right about that."

I tell him that I could get used to the place without too much trouble.

"Well, guys, let's get down to business," Arthur begins. "As you both know, we have started a new direction with the company. We're going more and more to small satellite plants."

"So far the satellites have proven to be far more productive than the larger plants," I add.

Arthur nods, "Exactly! It's the way to go. In the smaller plant, say one with three to five hundred workers, people have a first name relationship with the plant manager. They feel like part of a team, and when push comes to shove, people make the difference.

"Let's get something to drink. What would you gentlemen like?" asks Arthur as he gets up and starts into the next room.

"Make mine scotch and water," says Marty.

"When in Kentucky do as the natives do. Make mine bourbon and ginger," I say.

The drinks arrive in a few moments and we settle back into our chairs. Arthur continues. "I would feel comfortable with either one of you at the helm of ConnYankee. You are both outstanding individuals who have done an absolutely outstanding job for me. I've wrestled with this decision for a long time, but every time I weigh all the pluses and minuses you come out dead even. There's no doubt in my mind that you both want the job. As the King of Siam said, 'It is a puzzlement.' It really boils down to which one of you wants it most, and being competitive by nature, I've come up with a plan that will determine that.

"I'm going to let y'all decide." Arthur smiles. "Listen to me, will you? A dyed-in-the-wool New Englander using y'all. As you said a few minutes ago, Larry, when in Kentucky do as the natives do.

"We've just completed construction on two plants—one in Salem, New Hampshire, and one in Murfreesboro, Tennessee. These plants were constructed from the same plans. They are identical. We are going to move our turbine blades into them. All indicators tell us that these two locations are prime areas for the development of successful satellite operations.

"Each of you is going to run one of these plants. At the end of next year, the one who has done the best job will become the CEO of ConnYankee." Arthur pauses.

My first reaction is that I've lost. Marty is considered to be one of the best manufacturing men in the country. I'm just a pencil pusher —a bean counter.

Arthur continues, "Larry, I know what you're thinking. You think that this competition is rigged for Marty. You think that Marty's background is too much—that you've got three strikes against you from the start."

"I was thinking along those lines."

"I don't see it that way at all," continues Arthur. "You have an awful lot going for you. Your keen financial mind is definitely an advantage. An even bigger advantage is the fact that you don't have any old habits to break. Marty, here, hasn't been in the pits for a lot of years. Things have changed."

"Some things have changed and some haven't," says Marty. "The damned computer is one thing. In my day we were allowed to screw up at a normal pace. Now we do it at the speed of light."

"I started when the computer was already here," I say. "Sure it can screw us up, but it also does things a lot faster. It all depends on how you use it."

"You're both right," says Arthur. "What you're implying is that computers are here to help people, and that people, not the computer, screw up. Computers will never replace human judgment, nor can they overcome bad input. A computer is a tool, nothing more."

"Sometimes I feel that if computers never came along we'd be better off in the long run," replies Marty.

"You can test your theory if you want to, Marty," Arthur continues. "You can run your plant any way that you see fit."

"Any way that I see fit?" Marty acts surprised. "What are the rules for this competition? Do I get the Murfreesboro plant or do I freeze to death in New Hampshire?"

Arthur laughs, "Let's take them one at a time. First the issue of who goes where. I think that, in deference to your longevity, we'll give you first choice, Marty. Is that all right with you, Larry?"

My pick would be Salem. "More than fair," I answer.

"I pick Murfreesboro—never could stand the snow," replies Marty.

"As far as rules go, there aren't many," continues Arthur. "The plants will be furnished with identical equipment. They will be exactly the same to start with. Each of you will be given orders for exactly half of the market demand for turbine blades. From that point on you will run your plant as if it were your own and only business. At the end of next year you will leave the plant as a going concern with no interruption in output. Short of something illegal, there are no other rules. Do whatever you need to do to beat the competition, which in this case is each other."

Arthur picks up a large brown envelope from the coffee table and takes it to a wall safe which has been hidden behind a picture. He starts to fumble with the combination.

"I have one question," I say. "What are the measurements that you are going to use to determine which one of us is the most successful?"

"The same measurement that you would use if you owned the business," replies Arthur.

"Just what is that?" I ask.

Arthur turns from the wall safe, which is now open. "I have documented in this envelope just exactly how it is that I'm going to measure you. You'll have to figure out yourself just what that is if you want to know before the competition is over with." He waves the envelope in front of him. "Shortly after next year's end we will meet right back here at which time we'll open this envelope." With that he turns and shoves the envelope into the safe, slams the door shut, and spins the combination dial.

"Are there any further questions, gentlemen?"

"Yes," I say. "When do we start?"

"You've already started. There is an account set up for each of you. You can draw from that account as you see fit. Between now and year's end—about eight months—you'll need to staff your plant, order materials and supplies, make your plans, and get into production. You'll be expected to start shipments of product in the first week of next year," announces Arthur.

Marty smiles and offers his hand to me. "I think that I'm going to enjoy this. It's been a long time since I've gotten into the lubricating fluid. Good luck, Larry, and may the best man win."

I take his hand. "Good luck, Marty. It's going to be damned interesting."

Arthur laughs, "I know that it will be an interesting period for all three of us."

The servant appears with another round of drinks. Arthur lifts his glass. "To the competition," he toasts. "I leave you with one important thought. People, not machines, not computers, not the location of the plant, but people—people will ultimately make the difference. Good luck to both of you."

CHAPTER 4

The year of decision is upon me—not that it hasn't been hectic for the past eight months. I realize just how complicated the world of manufacturing is.

I glance at the digital clock on the dashboard of my Thunderbird. It is 6:14. The first shift starts work at seven. I want to be there, especially today. I squeeze over to the right at the roadsign, ROCKINGHAM PARK BOULEVARD—1 MILE.

The thirty-minute drive north from Lynton has become so routine that it seems as if the T'bird would make it without me. Salem lies on the border of New Hampshire and Massachusetts. Mom invited me to stay with her and Dad until I got settled in. That was eight months ago, and I'm still there. That home cooking has me hooked.

The fact that Mom waits on me and takes care of nearly all of my personal needs has freed me up to spend more time working on the tremendous challenge I face. I've even had time for a couple of dates with an old high-school sweetheart by the name of Stella Powicki. Stella is on the rebound from a short unsuccessful marriage. She has been good therapy for me—a little romance with no strings.

The parking lot is about half full. I pull into the space marked

PLANT MANAGER, take my briefcase, and head into the plant through the shipping-room door, a habit that I developed quickly. It is fascinating to see the parts progressing through the pipeline, getting closer and closer to the shipping room.

The plant is not your typical manufacturing facility—at least not yet. Everything is shiny new. The walls and machines are painted powder blue—standard for ConnYankee plants. The floor is painted grey with yellow stripes marking the aisles. Here and there yellow carts and forklifts wait for their drivers to activate them. Throughout the big room can be heard the faint hum of the ventilation system. The hum will turn into a loud clamor of all kinds of noises at seven o'clock when the workday officially begins.

I make my way toward the front office greeting the early arrivals as I go. Arthur King was right when he said that I'd know them all by their first names.

The regular Monday morning staff meeting convenes promptly at eight. Four of the five members of my staff are already there when I enter the conference room. Dean Hillard comes in a couple of minutes late and puts his one dollar late fine into the cashbox that my secretary makes sure is on the table every week. Dean is the manager of facilities. He was the first person that I hired back in April. He is the "landlord" in charge of maintaining the building, machinery, and grounds as well as keeping us in janitorial supplies. Dean is a man in his late forties, thin on top and thick in the middle. I was lucky to get him. He was the unfortunate victim of a plant closing in Lynton and came highly recommended. He is proving to be extremely sharp. I greet him, "Good morning, Dean. I see that you've managed to survive New Year's."

Dean plunks himself into his accustomed place at the conference table. "Just barely, boss. The New Year's party and then all that football really has my head pounding."

I greet the other four in turn.

I hired the manager of manufacturing, Joe Leonard, from the same place where I found Hillard. He is a splinter of a man, in his early fifties but looking more like a man of forty. He claims that what keeps him looking so young is the fact that he downs a case of Bud every night. He's been in manufacturing since high school, obtaining his degree from Northeastern University while working full time to support his family. In a way he reminds me of Marty Connolly. Many of his methods and ideas are the same.

The manager of materials and production control, Gary Niles, comes from an aircraft-engine plant in Connecticut where he held the same kind of position. He is young—in his late twenties. He played football at Duke but still maintained an excellent academic record. He is a certified member of the American Production and Inventory Control Society and is a firm believer in MRP. His track record at his prior job was outstanding. Joe calls him "the rookie." Joe calls most people "melonhead."

Ernie Gibbons was manager of engineering at a Boston instrument plant that was bought out by the Japanese. When the new owners moved the operations to Atlanta, Ernie went on the job market. His interview went extremely well and he showed in-depth knowledge of planning, fixturing, routing—the whole bit. He's done a great job getting machines and fixtures up and running.

The final member of my staff is a young lady fresh out of college, my manager of finance. I became one of the winers and diners at Harvard in my effort to find another Larry Jones. There were some good candidates but the chemistry wasn't there. One of the guidance counselors suggested that I try this gal from Radcliffe, Antoinette Rossi by name. The wining and dining experience was really a pleasure with Toni. She is some good-looking gal. Joe Leonard rides me when Toni isn't around. He accuses me of hiring her for things other than her brains. She reminds me of myself in a way. She's not only a ten physically, but she's proving to be a ten on the job as well.

"Well, people," I begin. "This is it—the first week that parts are due out the door. How does it look?"

"The rookie tells me that the entire week's schedule was through the next–to–last checkpoints Saturday night," offers Joe. "If that's so and there aren't more rejections than normal, we'll make it—no trouble."

"Great!" I shout. "I like that. How about costs, Toni?"

"Overtime is running over budget and inventory is about at its peak, and that's all I can measure this early in the game."

Joe waves his hand as if to dismiss Toni. "That's a start-up problem. It'll be OK."

"Let's watch it, Joe," I warn him. "I don't want overtime to get to be a habit. It can be pretty damned expensive. Remember, we made sure that we had plenty of capacity everywhere so that we could avoid paying premiums for labor."

I turn my attention to Gary. "What percentage of checkpoints are on schedule?"

"We're at eighty-two percent right now," he answers.

"Let's try for ninety percent this week," I tell him. "How about efficiencies?"

Joe answers the question. "We're really doing well with efficiencies. As the people go up the learning curve, our efficiencies get higher and higher. We ended the week at one hundred seventy-four."

"Leaving the actual times that we inherited from the old plant in our planning sheets has really made us look good as far as efficiency goes. Is that a fair measurement, though?" I ask.

"It sure is," answers Ernie. "Everyone can see just how much better we are than the big place."

"Makes sense. How about rejected material and scrap?" I ask.

"Six percent," Ernie answers.

"That's a point higher than last week," I warn. "But it's still nine percent lower than the big plant. Keep up the good work and keep it down there. Inventory should start peaking out about now as we start shipping. How's it look, Toni?"

Toni frowns, "It climbed another fourteen percent last week."

"That's to be expected," says Joe. "When you're filling the pipeline, inventory will go up. It'll level off this week when we ship parts out the door."

"We do have some early material on the dock. The vendors are really doing a bang-up job for us," offers Gary.

"All in all, the measurements look OK so far. Keep working on them," I say. "Does anybody have anything else to contribute?"

"Yes," says Joe. "We'll be shipping our first parts on Wednesday. It would be nice to have cake and coffee for everybody in the plant—a ceremony to let everybody know that we appreciate the great job that they're doing."

"Good idea, Joe. Set it up," I answer. "If there's nothing else, we'll break up. Just remember to keep working on the measurements. If we can optimize those we'll have one helluva year."

CHAPTER 5

As I head into my office and pass my secretary's desk, she looks up from her typing. "There've been a few calls for you," she says as she hands me three slips of paper.

"Thank you, Helen. How was your holiday?" I ask.

"Had a friend over for home-made Chinese food. It was quiet but nice," she answers.

That statement sums up Helen in a nutshell—quiet but nice. She's OK—does her work quickly, quietly, and efficiently, as an old-pro secretary should do. I'll bet her friend was a female. Helen's an old maid, never been married, never raised anything but a Siamese cat or two. I get the feeling sometimes that she tries to mother me. She's working out well, though.

I look at the call slips. The top one is from Marty Connolly, the next one from Arthur King, and the other, to my surprise, is from Vickie Barlow. I figure that I'll take them from the top. I have no trouble getting right through to Arthur King.

"How's it going, Larry?" he asks.

"Pretty good. The plant's on schedule. We'll ship on time."

"Glad to hear that. Keep it up. Marty tells me that he's on track too."

"You yourself said that we were dead even. Would you expect it any other way?" I ask.

Arthur laughs, "Not yet—but the real reason that I called was to ask you a personal favor."

"Anything. What is it?" I ask.

"It's about Vickie. As you know, she's working toward her MBA at Harvard, this being her final year. She was having trouble coming up with a good subject for her thesis. I told her about the competition and suggested that it would be one helluva subject to write about, if she'd just disguise the company and cast of characters. She loves the idea, and she'd like permission to visit both plants from time to time to observe and learn. Do you think that you could squeeze her in?"

"Don't see why not, Arthur."

"Good! I've given her a couple of orders, though. First, she is to call before she visits. Second, she is not to talk to Marty about what you are doing, and she is not to talk to you about what Marty is doing. Now, since she goes to Harvard, she'll most likely be visiting your place a lot more often than she does Murfreesboro. I hope that you'll be patient with her."

What can I say? "No problem," I tell him.

"Great. Well, good luck, Larry. Keep shipping. Remember—output is like shaving. If you don't do it regularly you'll look like a bum."

Next I call Marty. He wants to wish me good luck and may the best man win. I do the same. After talking to Arthur I know what Vickie wants. There is no answer at the number on the slip. She's probably in school—I'll call her later.

Twelve months to go, I think, staring out the window into the snow. It'll be over before we know it. I decide to walk out into the plant to see what's happening. I pass Helen. "I'll be out on the floor if anybody is looking for me. If Miss Barlow calls, page me," I tell her.

As I pass through the door separating the office area from the factory I am nearly run over by a forklift. Sounds descend on me from every direction—the rattles, roars, bangs, and hums that make up the symphony of the factory floor. The place seems to be a beehive of activity. I walk along the aisle, glancing from side to side, and notice that not everyone is busy. Two girls are half-heartedly dusting a machine, but they are so engrossed in their conversation that they are unaware of my presence until I speak. As I start to speak the girls begin wiping with newfound energy. I smile, "Good morning, ladies. Is your machine down?"

The girl with the name Dutie Wallace on her badge answers, "No, the machine is fine. There's never anything to do on Monday."

The foreman of the area notices me and hustles over. Lennie Seboy is a tall, good-looking man with a perpetual tan and not a hair on his head. For obvious reasons the workers call him "the onion."

"Anything wrong, Larry?" he asks.

"Maybe, maybe not. These girls claim that they never have work to do on Monday. Do you agree with that?"

"I've been complaining about that since parts started to flow through this operation," says Lenny. "We don't get parts from the drills until Tuesday or Wednesday and then we get buried. It's either a feast or a famine."

"Interesting," I say. "Let me look into it."

As I continue my tour I notice the same apparent shortage of work at several other points along the way. It disturbs me. I make a mental note to discuss it at next Monday's staff meeting.

As I make my way along the main aisle I hear a familiar voice above the other noises. Helen is paging me, "Larry Jones, report to your office at once."

I hurry back to find Dean Hillard and Joe Leonard waiting for me.

"We've got troubles, boss," says Dean. "The adjusting rod on the laser welder broke for the second week in a row. I called all over the Boston area. Nobody has a spare."

"Did you call the factory?"

"I've got Gary working on it," he answers. "We did place an order for another spare last week when the first one broke. We have a confirmation of shipment in five weeks."

"Joe, how long can you stay on schedule without that machine?" I ask.

Joe answers, "It's a checkpoint operation four weeks into the cycle. All of our parts go through there. We've got six weeks worth of output already past it so we'll be OK on output for awhile.

Trouble is, we'll start drying the line up. I'd say, if we can get that welder back up inside of two weeks, we'll work overtime and hand-carry parts to get on schedule."

"Damn it, Dean," I swear. "We should have had more than one spare."

"The manufacturer recommended only one, and we have no history built up to go on. I guess that Mr. Murphy has struck."

"I want you to stay on the problem until we get a new rod, Dean," I tell him. "Put some pressure on the manufacturer. Get that machine back on line as fast as you can. Do whatever it takes. Keep me informed."

"Will do, boss," says Dean as he makes a hasty retreat from my office.

CHAPTER 6

It's Thursday. We shipped our first part yesterday and the cake and coffee were enjoyed by all. I told them what a great job they were doing and got a round of applause for it. Feels good.

I've scheduled the first "round-table" session for this afternoon. The Japanese have had great success with quality circles, but they discuss things other than just product quality when they meet. They talk about quality of work–life also. I'm going to try it.

I have Helen page Dean Hillard.

"How's the laser rod situation coming?" I ask him.

"Bad news, boss. Gary's buyer called the factory in Cincinnati. It's a five-week lead time item. We offered them premium and got it down to four weeks, but they won't budge any more."

"Have the buyer call the factory back and get a list of everyone who has bought rods lately. Then call and see if you can separate somebody from one of them," I tell him.

"OK, boss, but this laser welding technique is so new that I'm afraid that there won't be too many on the list."

"It's worth a try," I say.

During lunch break I call Vickie for the fourth time this week. To my surprise she answers the phone. "You're a hard person to get hold of," I begin.

"I'm in and out between classes," she answers. "Did Arthur call you?"

"Yes, he did. Everything's all set. When would you like to begin?"

"The sooner the better." She sounded enthusiastic. "How about next Monday?"

She takes me by surprise with her apparent eagerness. "That will be fine. You can sit in on my weekly staff meeting if you can be here by eight."

"I'll be there," she answers. "See you then. Bye-bye."

Promptly at two o'clock I go to the conference room where there are ten direct–labor employees waiting. There is a tray of crackers and cheese in the middle of the conference table and a pot of coffee on a small side table. Helen has done her job well, as usual. I invite the workers to help themselves to coffee. When they are all settled into their seats I begin. "This is the first of what I hope will be many meetings of this kind. Each week I am going to hold a meeting with factory people, one on one. There will be no members of management, except myself, involved. I'd like to make this a better place to work and at the same time make it the most productive organization that ConnYankee has. It takes teamwork to accomplish a goal such as that. I'll be glad to answer any questions that any of you might have regarding this plant, and I'd like to listen to any ideas that any of you might have to make this a better place to work. You people know more about what's going on out in that factory than anybody."

They all nod their heads in complete agreement.

I review the business plans and the organizational chart as a means of breaking the ice. They seem sincerely interested. There are a couple of questions about the organization, after which I throw the meeting open to general questions and ideas. There are several relatively minor things brought up. One young fellow wants to know if we can get a newspaper machine installed at the plant entrance. Another would like to see a coffee machine at the rear of the plant so that time could be saved on travel during breaks. To instill a sense of caring, I promise to follow up on each of the ideas and get back to each individual in the form of a plant newsletter.

Dutie Wallace, one of the girls that I had spoken to on Monday at the idle machine, asks the first question. "Mr. Seboy keeps telling me that I'm a key operator because I work at a checkpoint. I don't know whether to feel good or bad about it. Just what is a checkpoint?"

"It has to do with the way that we schedule our shop," I tell her. "We manufacture twenty different kinds of turbine blades here in Salem. Our customers, the turbine manufacturers, usually give us plenty of lead time so we can plan quite a time ahead and level load our shop. That creates stable employment for all of you people.

"Every blade is different. We perform an average of fifty operations on each part, but we track them through the shop by looking at every tenth operation. These operations that we track by are called checkpoints. There are five checkpoints for every part that we manufacture. To stay on schedule all of the parts need to be through the first checkpoint eight weeks before they are to be shipped, through the second checkpoint six weeks before they are to be shipped, through the third checkpoint four weeks before, the second two weeks before, and through the fifth and last checkpoint, which is the shipping dock, on the date that they are due to be shipped. The managers and production control people follow the status of checkpoints closely and meet every Monday to review and take corrective action whenever a checkpoint may fall behind schedule. The theory behind this method of scheduling the shop is that parts will be spread evenly and the flow of parts will be balanced. Many companies use this system to balance their plants. In fact, some of them call it 'line-of-balance.' "

Dutie snickers and whispers to the person next to her. They both laugh.

"Let us in on the joke, girls," I say. "Remember this meeting is to share thoughts and ideas."

"I just said that you should call it line-of-no-balance in this plant." Everybody in the room laughs and nods their heads in agreement.

"Why?" I ask.

"Every Monday I come in here and have nothing to do and by

the end of the week I'm buried with work," Dutie continues. "Why isn't my machine balanced?"

A fellow whose name is Phil chimes in, "If our plant is balanced, why do the same people get all of the overtime and some of us get none at all?"

The byplay gets lively. All are pitching in with examples of the lack of balance in the factory, that is all but one fellow who has been silent. His nickname is Red. I make an effort to get him involved. "Red, what do you think might be the problem?"

Red parries question with question. "What does a schedule look like?"

"We track each part on a sheet called a checkpoint sheet. On it we keep cumulative totals of progress through checkpoints, so you'd have to say that we have twenty schedules, one for each part we make," I answer.

Red seems puzzled. "Dutie says that she works at a checkpoint, right?"

Dutie nods her head, "Yes."

Red continues, "How many machines like Dutie's are there?"

"There are three," I answer.

Red frowns and shakes his head, "I just don't understand how anybody can take twenty pieces of paper, twenty piles of parts, and three machines and know what to do first. I guess that's why they pay the managers big bucks. They know something I don't. I always thought of a schedule as being something like an airline schedule. You know, it tells you exactly when it's going, where it's going including stopovers, and how long it's going to take to get where it's going. All a checkpoint sheet tells us is where we are and where we were, but it doesn't tell us how to get where we want to go," says Red.

"We depend on the experience of our production control people to prioritize the work," I answer weakly, not at all sure of my ground.

"I've got a boat over in Portsmouth," Red says. "If I used the checkpoint method when I went sailing I'd steer it by looking at the wake behind me. It wouldn't be too long before I'd hit something and drown." Everybody, including me, laughs.

I don't feel comfortable the way the conversation is going. I look at my watch. "You've got a helluva point there, Red. I'll get a better answer for you. That's about all the time there is for today. This has been excellent and I want to thank you for your participation."

As I head back toward my office, I can't help wondering if I've opened Pandora's box.

CHAPTER 7

The first week is history. Everything got shipped on schedule. I feel quite complacent as the T'bird rolls through the plant gate and glides into my parking place. I notice a white Maserati in the space reserved for Toni Rossi. It can't be hers. I know what I pay her, and it's not Maserati money. The blue Kentucky license plate tips me off that it's Vickie's—some boat!

As I pass through the factory waving to the early arrivals, I notice Red, and I think of the round-table. Damn!—He's right, I realize. Checkpoint sheets are not a schedule at all. The real schedule is in the pockets and on the clipboards of the foremen and expediters—pretty loose, but it works—has worked for years. The checkpoints are nothing more than starting points and the schedule is developed manually based on just where those starting points are. It must be a lot of work.

Lennie Seboy is bent over counting parts as I come upon him. "Good morning, Lennie."

"I'm not sure I can call it good, Larry. Sometimes this place drives me crazy." Lennie cries a lot, but he's some good supervisor.

"Problems?" I ask.

"I've got this list of things to be done today, the hot ones on top and the fill-in jobs on the bottom." He waves an IBM card at me.

"Trouble is, the only parts I have to run are the ones on the bottom. I'd be better off turning the list upside down. I'll need to do some expediting again this week, but we'll get 'em out."

"Keep plugging," I say as I hurry on.

I enter my office to find Vickie sitting there. She greets me with a warm smile and both hands. Despite her crimson blazer and grey skirt, the girl on the Kentucky farm in the blue jeans and sweatshirt shines through.

"I'm glad you came," I say. "Did you have a good holiday?"

"Yes, I spent the holidays at Connecticut Yankee. It was nice. I missed the crowd at Cambridge—and I missed having a white Christmas—but it was good to be at the farm for a few days. Did you see my Christmas present in the parking space next to yours?" she asks.

I whistle. "I sure did. That's some wagon. How does she handle?"

"Like a dream. Would you like to try her out?"

"Love to—maybe at lunch if you're still here," I reply. "It's a couple of minutes before eight—can't be late for staff. Let's go."

We enter the conference room. All of the guys are there, but Toni is missing. I introduce Vickie around the table. "It's not like Toni to be late," I say. "Has anyone seen her yet this morning?" They shake their heads. I am about to begin the meeting without her when in she comes, breathless and dollar fine in hand. "Sorry I'm late, but I had to walk the entire length of the parking lot. Some dunderhead parked in my space."

She notices Vickie and lets out a piercing scream. "Vickie! What are you doing here?"

Vickie jumps up and they hug each other like long-lost sisters.

"I take it you know each other," I say, overstating the obvious.

"Know each other?" Toni answers. "We were roomies at Radcliffe for two years, belonged to the same sorority—she's my buddy!"

"I'm also the dunderhead who used your parking space. Sorry about that. It was thoughtless of me," says Vickie.

"Seeing that it's you I'll overlook it this time, but you owe me one dollar," replies Toni as she deposits her fine in the cashbox.

"Before we begin, I'd like to fill you in on why Vickie is with us," I start. "She's working on her MBA, and her thesis is going to be a comparison of the start-up of our shop with that of Murfreesboro. As you all know, both shops are set up identically and make the same products. She will be here more or less regularly to do research. Please help her in any way that you can. Is there anything you'd like to say, Vickie?"

"Only that, up to now, it has been all theory and books for me. I'm looking forward to seeing just how it is in the real world."

"You'll get a whole new education," cracks Joe Leonard.

"Let's begin," I say. Vickie takes a notepad from her briefcase. "First—has anybody made headway with the laser rod problem?"

Gary Niles answers, "Good news, Larry. We think we've struck paydirt with the list that Dean got for me. An outfit in Silicon Valley thinks that they can part with one of their spares. They won't commit themselves until their plant manager returns from a business trip on Thursday. It looks good, though."

"That's great," I say. "Stay right on it. The minute that plant manager comes back I want an answer. Keep pushing Cincinnati as well. We're going to need another spare."

I open my logbook. "The output for last week was one hundred percent—twenty for twenty. Good start. How's it looking this week, Joe?"

"We'll make it. Some of the parts are further back than they were a week ago at this time, but we moved some people from the grind operations to the final end to take up the slack."

"That won't put us behind schedule at grind?" I ask.

"No," replies Joe. "We looked at the workload and can easily spare them this week. No problem."

"Toni, how does the overtime look?"

"It got worse again last week. We're working fifteen percent overtime with a budget of eight."

I grimace as I jot down a big fifteen percent in my log. "How about inventory?"

"Inventory dollars are running ten percent over budget. We received twice as many parts as we shipped last week, and labor input was higher than output."

"I told you—the vendors are doing one helluva job," smiles Gary.

That smile irritates me. Here he is, proud of the fact that the vendors are ahead of schedule, and he has no real concern about the inventory budget. I'll fix that. Inventory will be one of the key measurements on that paper in Arthur King's wall safe.

"Why do you think that vendors shipping early is good, Gary?"

He senses my displeasure and takes a defensive posture. "I'm judged by whether or not material is here on checkpoint at dock. If even one of the twenty parts is not here when it's supposed to be, all hell breaks loose. I spend all of my time expediting—can't get anything else done."

"Is anything late at the moment?" I ask.

"No, nothing," he answers.

"Just how do you accomplish that?"

"It's a combination of two things," Gary replies. "First, we schedule material in, in monthly drops—two weeks before the start of the month. That gives us a two-week buffer."

My number-crunching mind goes to work. "Seems to me that is more than a two-week buffer."

"How do you figure that?" asks Gary.

I get up from my chair and go to the greaseboard at the front of the room. "Let's take two four-week months." I write the numbers 1 2 3 4 5 6 7 8 on the board. "Weeks one through four are the first month and weeks five to eight are the second." Directly below the first row of numbers I write another.

1	2	3	4	5	6	7	8
		6	5	4	3	6	5

"Your ordering rules bring in four weeks' worth of material whenever you fall to your buffer level. Is that right?"

"Yes," he answers.

"Then look at these numbers," I say pointing to the second row. "On week three we have five extra weeks' worth of material, on week four we have four weeks extra, and so on. In any four-week period we have an average of four and one-half weeks' buffer on hand. We occasionally get the buffer down to three weeks, but not often."

I sense a feeling of embarrassment on Gary's face as I press on. "What is the second thing?"

Gary seems reluctant to continue—a bit green about the gills.

"Our standard purchasing contract allows our vendors to ship up to two weeks prior to the wanted date."

"Another two-week buffer. No wonder our inventory keeps climbing. Where did you get those standard contracts?"

"They come from corporate headquarters. They're used throughout the company," Gary answers.

I shake my head. "How much is six-and-a-half weeks' worth of material costing these days, Toni?"

"The material cost in one week's average output is nine hundred thousand," she answers.

"We can't afford a six-million-dollar material buffer," I say, thinking about the paper in Arthur's wall safe. "Gary and Toni, set up a meeting with me for later this week with my secretary and come armed with a plan for material input that won't break us."

"While you're on a roll, Gary, give me a checkpoint report," I continue.

Poor Gary is about to die. His head goes back and his eyes roll toward the ceiling. "We came in at sixty-two percent last week," he says in a near whisper.

"We were at eighty-two percent. What happened?"

"It was that laser rod problem. We missed twenty checkpoints on account of that alone," Gary says.

I can't let him up when I've got him down. "Let's see—we were at eighty-two, lost twenty to the laser rod problem, leaving us at sixty-two. Wasn't there any improvement at all anyplace else in the plant?" Nobody says a word. "I'm going to see these checkpoints improve even if we have to come in every morning at six o'clock to go over all hundred of them one by one."

Vickie is deeply engrossed in her notepad, taking it all down.

Efficiencies are the next thing on the agenda. Joe is quite proud of himself. "Our efficiencies are over one hundred eighty percent now," he says. I check the item in my log. It bothers me to think that Joe is getting two pounds out of a one-pound bag. I've got to think about this one later, but the measurement looks good.

"How are we doing with scrap?" I ask Ernie Gibbons.

"Between six and seven percent," he answers quickly. "It's holding steady."

"Let me sum up," I say. "Output is one hundred percent on. Overtime is running fifteen percent—too high. Inventory is ten percent over and rising—unacceptable. Checkpoints are at sixty-two percent—awful. Efficiency is one eighty and scrap is six plus. We've got a lot of work to do in three areas—overtime, inventory, and checkpoints."

I close the logbook. "There are a couple of other things. Dean, see about having a newspaper-vending machine installed at the main gate and a coffee machine put in down at the back of the plant —requests from employees."

"OK," says Dean. He makes a note.

"Joe and Gary, I want you to take a hard look at the overtime. Don't work any that is not absolutely necessary, and I've got a complaint that it's not being evenly distributed. Also, I feel that our factory is getting out of synch with the parts flow. Some people are working Saturdays and have nothing to do on Mondays. See if you can find out what's causing it."

The meeting breaks up.

CHAPTER 8

Vickie disappears for the balance of the morning to wander about the plant observing, asking questions, and taking notes, as she puts it. She takes a lot of notes, that gal.

I drive the Maserati to lunch. It's some piece of machinery—the closest I'll ever come to manned space flight. The bean-counter inside of me is tempted to ask her the price tag, but I stifle the urge.

The Red Carpet is a small Greek restaurant next to Salem's only fire station, and the best place to eat in town. Steve Zetes serves the best Greek-American food in North America. We go in to find Steve with a handful of menus, as always. "Welcome, my friend. I've got a nice table over by the fireplace," he says as he leads us to a cozy spot next to a warm, crackling fire. It's perfect to take away the January chill. "The specials today are the beef stew and spinach pie. They are both very good."

We both order the spinach pie. The waiter brings us coffee. "Tell me about your horse, King Arthur. Is he still as unruly as he was last April?" I ask.

Vickie's eyes light up. "Oh, he's much better now, but still hard to handle at times. He's got a mind of his own, but Larry, he's the most magnificent animal I've ever seen—so big and so strong."

"How's his training coming along?"

"They've got him galloping now, and does he ever love it out there on the track. The plan is to begin serious training in March and get him into a maiden race at Keeneland in April. I'm looking forward to it."

"I take it, you plan to be there," I say.

"Wouldn't miss it," she answers as the waiter brings our food.

Lunch is perfect, as usual. We thank Steve and he thanks us for coming.

I get back behind the wheel of the Maserati as if it's mine—I wish. "What do you think of my plant so far?" I ask.

Vickie ponders the question before she answers.

"Frankly, Larry, I'm not terribly impressed."

I'm shocked. She's been so nice 'til now. What does she know about factories? "Oh, I'm surprised to hear that. Tell me why you're not impressed."

Unlike most people, Vickie has a habit of thinking before she speaks. After a few moments she asks, "Would you get into a home-run hitting contest with Babe Ruth?"

"Of course not," I laugh. "I can't hit a curve ball."

She smiles and continues, "Would you shoot baskets against Larry Bird?"

"Not if I want to win," I answer. "That's his game. An amateur can't beat a pro at the pro's game."

"You're playing Marty's game, Larry," she says.

CHAPTER 9

It has been said that a wise man profits from his mistakes. I've got the opportunity to be a wise man. There are plenty of mistakes from which to profit. We missed shippers for the first time—about a half-million dollar's worth if Toni's numbers are correct, and here it is only March. I'm digging a hole.

Ordinarily the parking lot would be mostly empty on Saturday, but today it's nearly full. Joe and Gary meant what they said—that they'd work everybody until they drop to get back on schedule.

I get a cup of coffee and a doughnut from the vending area and go into my office to enjoy them. I no sooner settle into my chair and take the lid from the cup when the phone rings. It's Vickie.

"I'm glad I caught you, Larry. Are you going to be there long?" she asks.

I tell her that I'll probably be here until noon.

"I'd like to come up and talk to you," she says. "I'm still in Cambridge and it'll take about an hour for me to get there."

"OK, take your time. It's slippery up here from last night's snow squalls." I hang up the phone. Vickie has been a regular at the plant since that first day, dropping in two or three times a week. To tell the truth, I've been kind of cool towards her, partly because I've been so damn busy trying to keep the plant on the shipping schedule and get the measurements up where they belong. Maybe Houdini could do it. I haven't had much luck. Besides, Vickie kind of turned me off that first day when she implied that this factory wasn't as good as Murfreesboro. She didn't exactly say that, but she might as well have—and after a measly four-hour visit—smart-ass kid!

I've got more important disasters on my mind. The measurements are still floundering around. When one gets better, two get worse. The only ones that have been consistently good have been output and efficiencies, and now output has gone to hell. Damn it, my guys are good! What's the matter? This factory is difficult to analyze. There are so many things going on at once—some I can control and some I can't.

A mathematician, with nothing better to do, calculated the different possible chess games that can be played. I can't remember the number, but it was a big one. The mathematician said that the number, if written out, would be several miles long. A chess game consists of sixty-four squares, thirty-two pieces and two players calling the shots. In my factory, I've got a hundred machines, fifty thousand pieces in process, and three hundred players calling the shots. The possible manufacturing games that can be played must be a trillion times more than chess, and for every one of those possible games there is a different schedule. Checkpoint balancing is just one of the countless number of possible schedules. The laws of probability dictate that some schedules are better—but what are they? Is MRPII the answer? Gary is an MRPII nut, but he says it won't work much better than checkpoint scheduling in a process shop such as ours. I believe him.

Joe comes in, bringing me out of my daydream. "Good morning, Joe."

He nods and hands me a brown paper bag. I open it to find coffee and a doughnut—thoughtful of him. "Chilly out there this morning," he says as he removes the lid from his cup. "Supposed to go down to five degrees tonight."

"Thanks, Joe. We can't do anything about the weather, but I hope that we make some headway with our problems. What happened this week?"

"It was that damned laser rod problem that we had six weeks ago," answered Joe. "The loss of throughput for the two weeks that the welder was down filtered through to the shipping dock this week."

"But you told me that two weeks' down time could be made up with overtime and hand-carrying. Apparently, you were wrong."

"I wasn't wrong. It's just that it's taking longer than I first figured. We work the hell out of laser and grind every Saturday and really compress the cycle at the final end. It's just that we gain only about ten percent of the backlog per week, max—sometimes a little less. We'll get there in two more weeks if we work laser and grind on Sundays."

"That's double time—pretty expensive," I say.

"Nothing's more expensive than missing shipments to customers, and I don't know of a better way to catch up than overpowering the problem with people," Joe replies.

"Two weeks, you say?"

"Two should do it, if Murphy doesn't hit us again," Joe answers.

"Go for it," I say, knowing that if I don't make schedules on time the other measurements won't mean a thing when the day of reckoning comes.

It's ten o'clock when Vickie arrives. She hands me a brown paper bag. My kidneys are full of coffee and I'll be burping doughnuts for a week, but I thank her and pretend to enjoy.

"A lot of people working today?" she asks between sips of her coffee.

"Too many," I answer.

"You missed shippers this week, didn't you?" she says.

Damn her all to hell. She's too pretty to be such a smart-ass. "How did you know that?" I ask.

"That's the reason I drove all the way up here this morning, to show you how I know. Come out into the factory with me," she says.

She leads me back to the laser weld machine. It is a large powder-blue monster that bangs and spits sparks as it does its thing. As we arrive the machine is banging and sparks are flying while attendants are busy loading a fixture with fifty blades. The machine is fast and it takes four people to keep it going, but it does an extremely accurate job. One attendant removes the fixture that is in the machine and another worker slides the companion fixture into place, shuts the door and pushes the button that starts the machine through its cycle.

"Great idea, those dual fixtures. We double the machine's output this way," I say.

"Just watch what happens," says Vickie.

The loaders unload the fifty turbine blades from the fixture that has been removed from the machine but make no attempt at filling it with new parts. In a few minutes the machine finishes its cycle. The operator opens the door and slides the fixture out onto the unloading table beside the other fixture which is still empty. The loaders unload the new fixture leaving two empty and nothing to load into the welder. The four workers head off toward the cafeteria, leaving Vickie and me standing there alone.

I notice that it's not the regular break time. "What the hell is going on?" I ask no one in particular. It really upsets me to think that the workers have so little respect for authority that they would walk off and leave the plant manager standing there. They could have at least waited until I was gone. I'm furious—I start after them, but Vickie retains me by the shirtsleeve.

"Don't blame them, Larry. They ran out of work," she says.

I look at the mountain of tote pans full of blades queued up in front of the welder. "Baloney! Look at that pile of work," I say pointing to the queue.

"The welder is set up to do C7 blades," says Vickie. "There are no more C7's in that pile. They must either change over by setting up for another part or wait for more C7's from grind. Set-up takes a half hour, and the machine is fast. It can process a week's worth of C7's in two hours. Come on," she says as she walks toward the grinding center. I follow.

The grind center consists of ten identical powder-blue machines arranged in two rows of five. There is a tall rack against the outer wall where jigs and fixtures are stored when they are not in use. Every one of the ten machines is manned and running. The grinding of turbine blades is a slow process. We watch for a few minutes, but not much is happening. The machines are making their slow, monotonous passes back and forth across the surface of the blades, removing a tiny bit of metal with each pass. Small CRT screens indicate progress at each pass. When the correct dimension is reached the grinder stops automatically, whereupon the operator unclamps the parts in the fixture, assembles ten new ones, resets the machine, pushes the start button, and checks all of the finished parts with a micrometer before placing them in a tote pan. I glance at my watch. It is ten before noon and I'm getting hunger pains. "This area is running like a well-oiled Swiss clock," I say as I turn to leave.

"I want to show you just one more thing," says Vickie, "And then we'll go to lunch on me."

She hurries toward the rear of the grinding center where the material waiting for grind is stored. When we get there I'm shocked. There are tote pans of turbine blades everywhere—on the benches, in the racks, and on the floor. My financial mind calculates this queue as being in the million-dollar range.

Vickie doesn't say a word for a few minutes. She senses that I am shocked, and she's absolutely right. What caused this pile-up to happen? I'll bet that Miss Smart-Ass knows. Why else would she show it to me and then watch me suffer?

"Let's go to lunch," she says finally.

As we head out of the grinding center, it's empty. Everybody has gone to lunch.

Driving the Maserati to the Red Carpet isn't as much fun this time—neither is the luncheon. Stuffed grape leaves are the Saturday special, but my mind isn't on the food. I'm thinking that just when I imagine that things can't get any worse, they do. "Did you come all the way up here in this weather just to show me how screwed up I am?" I ask.

Vickie laughs. "I suppose it might look that way, but that's not what I have in mind. In the past six weeks I've been to this plant quite a few times—maybe twenty. I'm fascinated by it."

I manage a grim smile. "Easy for you to say. From what you've shown me this morning we'll never get out of the hole that we dug for ourselves when the laser welder went down for two weeks."

Vickie continues, choosing to ignore my comment. "I've decided to concentrate on this plant. Instead of comparing Salem and Murfreesboro I'm going to document the startup of just one plant. It will make a much more interesting and comprehensive tale."

"What will you call your paper? The Chronicle of a Failure?" I ask.

My remark hits a tender spot with Vickie. "Oh, Larry, it's too early in the game to quit!" She fumbles in her purse, throws some money on the table, and marches out, putting on her jacket as she goes.

Since I have the keys to the Maserati, she has to wait. I get into the car beside her. She is staring straight ahead. "I'm sorry, Vickie, but you, of all people, know just how much this means to me. There's so much at stake. I said the wrong thing. Sure, I'm down right now, but I won't quit—never have, never will. My dad taught me always to give it my best shot, and that's what I intend to do—right to the end," I say.

"The end is a long way off. You've still got ten months. That's a long time; anything can happen," Vickie says.

"You were so right six weeks ago when you told me that I was playing Marty's game, and I though you were being a smart-ass. Do you think that he would have handled the laser weld problem any better than I did?"

"There's no doubt about that," she answers.

"How?"

"He would have stayed on schedule despite the setback."

I don't agree with her and tell her so. "My guys did one hell of a job getting the part and getting that welder back on line in two weeks' time. Marty couldn't have done any better."

"Larry, he probably wouldn't have done as well, but he would have stayed on schedule" she repeats. "It wasn't the two weeks' down time that hurt you. What did we see in the factory this morning?"

I visualize, "There were welders running out of work while a queue of the wrong parts sat in front of them, and there were grinders working productively with enough work in front of them to give them long-time job security."

"Would you call it a problem with parts flow?" she asks as I take the turn that heads us back toward the factory.

"You could say that."

"Do you remember that day when I first visited the plant—the staff meeting I attended?" she asks.

"I remember you attending one, but I can't be sure which one it was. They all run together after awhile," I answer.

"I took notes," she continues. "First thing you discussed was the weld-rod problem, and Gary told you he found one in the Silicon valley."

"Yes, I remember."

"The next thing you discussed was output. Do you remember what Joe said when you asked him how it was going?" she asks.

"Not exactly," I say, trying to separate that particular staff meeting from all the others.

"Well, he said that he'd make it but he had to put extra people in the final area—remember?" Vickie says. "He got those people from the grinding center, figuring the parts couldn't go anywhere, so he could spare them."

A light goes on in my thick head. This is what Vickie has been driving at all day long. If that huge mountain of inventory had been through grind, as it would have been if Joe had left the people where they belonged—grinding parts—laser with its capacity could have got us back on schedule quickly. Now we are forcing weld to work at the same slow speed as grind. The extra capacity is being wasted. That melon-head Joe screwed us up, not the welder.

Vickie tightens the screw. "Marty would never allow Joe to move those people out of grind."

Her words hurt, but they are true. My inexperience cost us. The blame is more mine than Joe's.

As I pull the Maserati into the parking slot next to my T'bird, I glance at Vickie with a new-found respect. She's not the smart–ass that I thought she was. She knows her stuff.

"I think that you can still win this game, Larry. Can I be part of it?" she asks.

"You said it before. We can't beat a pro at his own game," I say.

"We can if we change the rules," she answers. "I'll call you Monday. We saw a lot more today than we've talked about."

She waves and is gone before I can say goodbye.

CHAPTER 10

Monday's staff meeting is rough. All of the measurements are down except efficiency. Good old efficiency—just keeps going up. I'm beginning to wonder how bad off we'd be if we weren't so efficient—makes me shudder.

I tell Joe what I found out Saturday about the laser weld recovery plan and why he isn't out of trouble yet. He's critical of himself, so I let him squirm for a couple of minutes before I take him off the hook by telling him that we all missed it because the plant is so new. Gary has the idea that if we make grind a checkpoint, it won't happen again. I fail to understand how moving checkpoints can solve a problem. Can it be that simple? I think not.

I cancel Joe's plan to work grind and laser weld the next two Sundays. I tell him that he can work grind but not laser. He doesn't like it much, but he can't argue with my logic that working laser will allow the crew to stand around waiting for parts or take extra coffee breaks all during the week. I give them the old pep talk about the need to get back on schedule.

Most of the afternoon is spent on the phone with central marketing. We go over the list of customers whose orders we missed last week and develop new promises. I give my word that we'll be back on schedule in two weeks. I hope Joe's right this time.

It's late in the afternoon when Vickie finally calls. She apologizes for the time of day and asks me if I can meet her at the WurstHaus this evening so she can wrap up our Saturday tour. I figure, with all the help she gave me on the laser weld problem, what have I got to lose. And the WurstHaus brings back pleasant memories of my undergrad days at Harvard—used to go there regularly for lively conversation, huge German-style sandwiches, and that good heavy beer they serve. I tell her I'll be there at seven. It seems that every time I meet that gal we end up at some eating establishment. It must be coincidence. She's not fat, but some people are like that. Joe Leonard is a typical example. Imagine—a case of beer a night, and he's a splinter.

I arrive in Harvard Square a bit before seven. It's always difficult to find a place to park, but I'm lucky tonight. It's only three blocks from the nearest parking spot to the WurstHaus. I find a table in a corner out of the traffic to wait for Vickie and enjoy a stein of that good German beer. As I quench my thirst with the heavy brew I look around. The place hasn't changed, but the customers look so much younger than during my day.

When I see Vickie coming I flag down the waiter. I hold up my stein. "Care for one of these?" I ask her.

"You bet, thank you," she says as she drapes her jacket over the back of her chair and sits down.

The waiter brings the stein promptly. I order a bratwurst sandwich and Vickie orders knockwurst. My image of that smart-ass spoiled kid is disappearing—after all knockwurst and beer ain't exactly caviar.

"How did your staff meeting go today?" she asks.

She really wants to know what I did with the information we gathered on Saturday. I tell her about Joe's request for Sunday overtime and how I handled it.

"Great," she laughs. "You'll get just as much output at less cost."

"Thanks to you," I tell her.

"I know of a couple of other ways to improve the situation in that area," she says.

Now she's got my attention. "How's that?"

"Remember when we left the grind center to go to lunch? Everybody else had done the same thing. We were the last ones out."

"Yes," I answer. "It was noon. The whole plant goes to lunch at that time."

"That's my point," she says. "The whole grind center stopped producing parts for thirty minutes. Ten machines down for thirty minutes adds up to five hours lost output. Can you afford to lose that much output at that resource right now?"

"People need to eat," I answer.

"What if you were to organize the workers so that the machines adjacent to each other were a team? That is, there would be five teams of two workers each."

"What would these teams do?" I asked.

"The machines take an average of forty-five minutes to run a fixture full of parts. Lunch lasts thirty minutes. One worker from each team can start her machine, say, at eleven-thirty and go to lunch while her team mate watches both machines for thirty minutes. The machines are automatic once they start. The roles would be reversed at noon when the first worker comes back. You would gain five hours output every shift. It's better than working Saturday, and it's free," she says as the waiter brings our sandwiches.

I'm dumbfounded. Either this gal is a genius or my managers aren't as good as I think they are. What a great idea.

She's not finished yet. "And if you apply the same thinking to coffee breaks, you'll gain an additional five hours of output per shift."

"Wow!" I yell. "Great!" I can't wait to get to the plant in the morning to tell Joe to set it up. I hope the workers go along with it."

"They will," says Vickie. "Those are good people you've got out in the factory. Just lay your cards on the table and tell them how important their jobs are to the future of the business. Tell them how much you need them. People need to be needed." She turns her attention to her sandwich and beer for awhile before continuing. I'm developing a different attitude toward Vickie. Where did she pick up all this stuff?

"I've got something else," she says, as she wipes the last of the sandwich from her lips.

"I'm all ears now."

"Remember what the operators of the grinders did after they started up their machines?" she asks.

"Sure, they checked the parts that they had just finished."

"You're paying attention," she says. "But do you also know that the only rejected parts that they ever find due to the grinding operation itself are the parts done on the first run after a setup? The process controls on those grinders are so good that you could consider them perfect once the machine is set up correctly. Oh, sure, the operators find more bad parts as they go along, but the parts are already bad before they get to the grinder."

"Go on," I say.

"You can't afford to have grind working on parts that are already bad before they get there," she continues. "Once the first run is checked and found to be OK, start checking the parts before they are ground—not after. You'll increase throughput because you won't be grinding bad parts. That means more output, and it will cost you absolutely nothing."

I can't believe it. "Your ideas are great, Vickie. You're really something else. I guarantee you that they will be implemented the next time you come calling, even if that's tomorrow." I stare at her for a long time. How can I thank her? I feel as if I've discovered buried treasure.

"I'm puzzled," I say. "How can you, never having worked in a factory, see these things? You must be a natural."

"No," she answers. "My never having worked in a factory is a tremendous advantage, as I see it. I've read a lot by Dr. Ohno and Dr. Goldratt. Their ideas make so much sense that I assumed that their way was the right way. I guess everybody else assumes that the old way is the only way. Their minds are cluttered up with what they're used to. Mine isn't. In your factory you have the latest technology that money can buy to process turbine blades. Everything is new, but your shop–floor scheduling system is more than thirty years old."

She's got a point there. "I'll bet that Marty Connolly doesn't come up with this stuff," I say.

"You can be sure of that," Vickie answers. "You see, what we're doing is changing the rules we play by. He won't."

For the first time since we started shipping parts I have hope. There is a chance. "Are they any more rules we can change?" I ask.

Vickie laughs, "There are plenty, but they will be radical and you will fight with your managers."

I've always loved a good fight. "Hey, you've sold me. I can't win playing Marty's game, but I've got a feeling that we won't be playing his game much longer." I'm really excited. It slips out before I know what I'm saying—"I love you."

CHAPTER 11

I got carried away last night, but the only words that seem to convey my appreciation for her and the things she's done are "I love you." I hope that Vickie took it the way it was intended—a super thank you for a superb job. That's really all I meant. After all, she's just a kid. Probably got out of high school when she was eighteen—four years of college and another two studying for her master's would make her about twenty-four. I'm almost thirty. There's five years difference between us.

The smell of bacon lures me to the kitchen. Mom always makes sure that Dad and I get a good start. She must have heard me coming. My coffee is in the cup and my plate of bacon, eggs, and pan fries is already set out. Dad doesn't have as far to go as I do. He's still catching some Z's.

"Mornin', Mom," I greet her.

"Did you work late again last night?" she asks. "I went to bed before you came in."

"No, I had some business to take care of in Cambridge. Mom, how old were you and Dad when you met?"

"I was just turned twenty and your father was twenty-seven. Why do you ask?"

"No reason, just wondering," I answer

The drive to Salem is more enjoyable this morning. I'm looking forward to letting the guys in on the good ideas. My foot pushes down a bit harder on the accelerator.

"Helen, track down Gary and Joe. Have them come to my office as soon as they can break free," I tell my secretary before I take my coat off.

Maybe I expect too much. Gary and Joe don't stand up and cheer when I tell them about the changes. They just sit there looking uncomfortable as hell.

"Do I detect an air of hostility here?" I ask lightly.

Joe speaks first. "It's not that, Larry. I'm just afraid that your ideas won't fly with the workers. Take the staggered lunches and breaks—certain people like to eat with certain other people."

"That's easy to fix," I tell him. "Let them select their own teams."

"I don't think that the union will go along with your idea for a minute," adds Gary. "It's too different."

"Bullcrap! We're not asking anybody to work harder and we're not taking their breaks away from them," I say.

"The union's answer to that would be that if we get more parts out, somebody must be doing more work," says Gary. "They're extremely protective when it comes to jobs. They see an increase in output as a threat to the labor base."

"Another thing," Joe says. "If we ask the grind workers to inspect parts before they work on them they'll start a rebellion."

I'm getting upset. "Why the hell is that?"

"I'll tell you exactly what they will say. They'll say that they don't want to inspect somebody else's junk."

"I'll be damned." My enthusiasm is being dashed by my own managers. Our people can't possibly be so polarized against change. "I want to do this, guys."

"You are the boss," says Gary. "We'll try it, but we're in for labor trouble."

I turn my back and stare out of the window. What was it that Vickie said? Of course, she said that people need to feel needed. I turn from the window. "We are going to try it, guys. I'll take full responsibility. There will be a special round-table session this afternoon. Notify all of the grind workers and the union steward from that area—make it two-thirty and bring the second shift in an hour early."

The closer it gets to two-thirty, the edgier I get. It might be a good idea if I'm in the conference room when the people show up. The room has been set up nicely by Helen. I take a cup of coffee from the large urn.

The first one to arrive is Teresa Lockeridge, the union steward. I like her; she's aggressive, but smart as a whip. She looks good—as though she's lost weight. "Hello, Teresa. You look nice."

"I'm so proud. I've lost twenty-one pounds in little more than a month," she says, doing a spin. "I feel good too."

As the operators arrive I greet them one by one and offer them coffee. They're all girls. When they settle into the chairs I begin.

"Some of you have been to round-table before and you know how it usually works. I ask for your ideas for ways to make this plant a better place to work, and may I add that there have been many excellent ones. We've implemented most of them, and they really have made this plant a better place.

"This round-table is a little different. Usually I take a random sample of the work force. You are all from the same work center. This time I'll be the one with the ideas. First, let me give you a little background so you'll know where I'm coming from.

"Some of you know that this plant is one of a pair. There's another plant exactly like this one in Murfreesboro, Tennessee. Like it or not we are part of an experiment, a sort of competition. During this first year of operations one of the two plants is going to establish itself as being better than the other. I want Salem to be that plant. Do you?"

How can anyone disagree with my logic? They all nod their heads in agreement—even Teresa. "The plant that wins this competition will get the bulk of the work in the future, and work means jobs—security for you and jobs for your children. I think that's worth going after, don't you?"

They keep nodding their heads in agreement. So far, so good.

"We missed some shipments last week for the first time. Missed shipments are the quickest way I know of to get into trouble. We don't make any money if we don't ship parts, and we end up with unhappy customers. Now, don't get me wrong. You people in the grind work center are in no way responsible for what happened."

"You could fool us, the way everybody is on our case to get parts out. Why, they look at us like we're criminals if we don't work overtime every weekend," says Teresa. "We have families to take care of."

"The reason that there is so much pressure on your area is because you people are the key to getting us back on schedule. You didn't cause the problem, but you can fix it. You are the most important people in this plant," I say.

One girl claps her hands. "We've known that all along, and we're proud of it." The other girls join her in giving themselves a round of applause.

"You should be proud of the job you are doing," I add. "I'm going to lay my cards on the table. You girls are doing a super job, but the machines are slow. We need to look at ways to get more output from those machines. Do any of you have any ideas?"

I get no response—don't expect any.

"How about checking parts?" I ask.

"Once the machine is set up right it's a complete waste of time," say Teresa. "These girls never make bad parts."

"They do find quite a few bad parts, though," I reply.

Another girl chimes in, "Those parts are bad before we get them."

"Exactly," I say. "If all of the parts you put on the grinders were good parts, then only good parts would be processed through."

"We have no control over what they send us," says one of the girls.

"I can show you a way that you can control it. What do you think of checking the blades before you grind them—not afterward?" I say.

Joe was right. Teresa comes right back. "Why should we be responsible for checking other people's junk?"

"It's simple economics," I answer. "We need to increase throughput from the grind area. This is one way. You know, I'll bet that when the people working on the parts before you find out that you're not going to accept junk, there will be fewer bad parts coming to you. There may well be a time when the parts coming to you will be so good that you won't need to check them at all. Think about it."

The girls mumble to each other. I wait for them to finish before going on. "I have another idea. Let me ask you a question. When during the day is your machine not running?"

One girl says, "When we are loading and unloading."

"When we take our breaks and lunches," offers another girl. This is leading in the right direction.

"Can anyone think of any way to get the machines to run more of the time?" I ask.

"If we load and unload faster?" one girl asks.

"From what I've seen, you girls work hard enough now. I don't want you to work harder, just smarter," I answer.

Teresa is sharp. "You want us to double up and stagger breaks and lunches, don't you?"

"That's exactly what I have in mind, Teresa. You're sharp. Would you try it for me?"

None of the girls speaks. They look toward Teresa.

I continue, "I need your help. I want to make this plant the best one that ConnYankee ever had. Plants are made up of people—people like you—and any plant is only as good as good as the people make it. I know you're the best. Let's show everybody else that I'm right."

The girls start whispering to each other. "Excuse me, I need a drink of water from all this talking." I make a retreat from the room to let them caucus.

When I return they are all looking to Teresa again. "We'll give it a try, Larry. Most of us are tired of working overtime anyways," she says.

"That's good enough for me. I'll leave it up to you people to work out the details. I'll handle your supervisor. Remember—the goals are to keep the machines productive for eight hours every shift and to make sure that you grind only good parts. That's about it for today. I'd like to add that this has been an excellent meeting. Thank you for coming."

I return to my office feeling good again until I think of Joe and Gary. My first reaction is to get them back into my office so I can go up one side and down the other, but I think better of it. I'll wait a few days. If this works out the way I think it will, it may be the breakthrough that makes future changes easier. Vickie was right about the people, but I didn't have a fight with my managers—at least not yet.

CHAPTER 12

It's not your romantic type date. Vickie called to invite me to go to a basketball game with her. It seems that one of her chums at Harvard, whose dad was a friend of the guy who runs the Celtics' front office, gave her two tickets at center court for tonight's game. Celtics tickets are hard to get.

I pick her up at six so we'll have plenty of time to get a bite to eat before the game. We have lasagna at Joe Teschi's. It's superb.

Now we are stuck in a tremendous traffic jam trying to get into the parking lot in back of Boston Garden.

"We goofed," I say as I inch the T'bird another foot toward the gate, which is still about two hundred yards in front of us. "We should have parked here before we ate and walked to Joe Teschi's. It's only a couple of blocks."

"We've got plenty of time. It's still forty-five minutes before the game starts." She looks ahead toward the parking lot gate. "It's those two fellows collecting money and making change. You'd think that they would put on extra help during the rush."

I inch forward ever so slightly. "This bottleneck probably only lasts about an hour and they'll fill the lot regardless. They can't make any more money by adding more help."

"You'd think that the Celtics management would care more about their customers," she says.

"The Celtics don't have anything to do with the parking. It's a private company that just happens to have landed in the right place at the right time. If they could only schedule the cars to arrive at a more even pace, there wouldn't be any traffic jam, but that's impossible."

"You mean something like advanced reservations?" she asks.

"Yes, something like that. If they knew who was coming and they could tell them what time to arrive, there would be a nice steady flow right into the parking lot—no strain, no pain."

Vickie laughs, "That would be impossible—too many unpredictable factors involved, like traffic lights, driving distances, routes taken, stopping to eat and other traffic jams—all kinds of things."

Suddenly the car in front of me moves forward two full lengths. Before I can close the gap, a vehicle from my right squeezes in front of me. I slam on the brakes to avoid a collision, stopping no more than a centimeter from disaster. "Son of a bitch! This is the right lane. Where did that jerk come from?"

Vickie opens her window to look back. "They're coming up the sidewalk. Keep close to the car in front or more of them will get ahead of you."

"So much for the Boston drivers," I mutter. After my heart slows down to a fast trot I say, "Yes, but what if they scheduled some cars as standbys—in case somebody was late, one of them could fill the gap. That way they could always maintain a nice flow."

"Then they'd have a traffic jam again," Vickie answers.

"But it would be a controlled traffic jam. They could assign just so many to be there ahead of time."

By this time we are closer, maybe one hundred yards to go. It's getting near game time. The snarl at the lot gate looks like a hopeless mess. Cars coming from every direction, six rows of vehicles, including the ones on the two sidewalks, trying to squeeze into two openings. I can see the lot clearly now. It is only half full after all this time. There's plenty of room and there's no confusion once one gets by the entrance. Two cars at a time drive through the entrance toward an attendant with an orange flashlight and pull right into their assigned parking spots.

Suddenly, as if from nowhere, a white cruiser with flashing red and blue lights and the large blue letters BOSTON POLICE painted on the side pulls up to the gate. "Now we'll get someplace," I say. "The law has arrived on the scene."

Two police officers get out of the cruiser. One of them walks toward the cars on the sidewalk, citation book in hand and pencil at the ready. "Good, that'll teach those jerks." The other officer positions himself directly in front of the lot gate. He blows his whistle and holds his white gloved hand in the air to stop all movement of traffic for a moment. He calmly looks over the situation before deciding to start the far left-hand lane into motion first, blowing his whistle and waving his arms furiously to keep the cars moving. With both attendants concentrating on one row it moves right along. In a few minutes the entire row is gone. The officer holds up stragglers with his left hand and motions to the second row with his right hand. I look at the dashboard clock. It is nearly tipoff time.

"We'll miss some of the game at this rate," says Vickie.

"Probably the first five minutes," I answer. "Watching the first five minutes of a basketball game is like watching grass grow." In a few more minutes the second row has been depleted, but most of the cars in that row came from behind us.

"This isn't fair," Vickie says. "If we had arrived at the back of this jam thirty minutes later, and stayed over to the left, we'd be in our seats by now. He's letting too many from the same row in at a time."

By the time the police officer starts the third row in motion it is past game time. We watch impatiently as cars from behind us go zipping by. There is still a long line of cars left in that row when suddenly it stops moving. "Now what?" I ask.

"I think that there's a car broken down up by the gate," answers Vickie.

"Oh, great!" I say.

"The policeman has started our row. The broken-down car has the third lane blocked and there's no way around for the ones behind him," says Vickie gleefully.

We begin to move, herky-jerky style, toward the gate. By this time the first quarter must be half over. We are the third car from the cash attendants' position when they put their hands up and proceed to pull a long traffic barricade across the opening. There's a sign nailed to it which reads "PARKING LOT FULL." I can't say what I'm thinking in the company of Vickie, but she says part of it for me, "Those bastards!"

Everybody tries to turn around at once and now we're in the back of the fleeing mob. Finally, we are free. We find a parking space about five blocks away. It is half time when we finally get settled into our seats. The Celtics are leading by two points, but their lead is short–lived. They come out flat in the second half. They don't lose very often, and almost never in Boston Garden, but they do tonight.

On our way out of the Garden we walk by the parking lot as it is emptying out. It's worse now. There are no attendants, no policemen, and cross–traffic compounds the problem. It's cold out, but the five-block walk back to the T'bird is a lot quicker and less of a hassle than fighting that traffic around Boston Garden.

As we drive through the North End toward the river and the Longfellow bridge that links Boston to Cambridge, Vickie says, "We missed half of the game and the Celtics lost, but dinner was great and I especially enjoyed the traffic jam—it was fascinating."

That's what she said. "How in God's name can you tell me that you actually enjoyed being in that horrendous traffic jam?" I ask.

She laughs. "Long after everything else that happened tonight is forgotten, you and I will remember that mess we were in," she says.

She's really not making much sense and I try to change the subject. "The thing that I'll remember is the Celtics losing. This is the first game that they've lost at home in two years. The Celtics and losing just don't go together. It's a contradiction in terms—Celtics lose. It's like saying pretty ugly or airline food."

She laughs. "How about military intelligence or inventory control?"

"If you mean my inventory control you're absolutely right," I laugh.

"I was thinking of inventory in general. Manufacturing people try to control inventory by edicting all sorts of crazy rules and actions. They call them innovative approaches, but inventory is not something that can be directly controlled," she says.

I laugh. "My innovative approach would be to fill up a huge dump truck with turbine blades and drive it off a pier over in Portsmouth."

"That's been done," she smiles and continues. "Production

scheduling is the control, and inventory is the direct result of how well production control schedules the shop—which gets me back to the traffic jam."

I give up. "Tell me what you found so damned fascinating about a lousy traffic jam."

"It's a perfect example of how a typical factory controls, or doesn't control, production—something I've been looking for as a lead-in for my thesis," she begins.

"You mean to tell me that you actually saw a factory in that chaos?" I ask.

"Yes, I saw it all—bottlenecks, batch processing, buffer control, and much, much more. It would be hard for me to think of a potential problem that exists in the factory that I couldn't relate to that traffic jam."

She's really into it, so I encourage her. "The bottleneck was obvious—the two attendants," I say.

"That's right, and the cars waiting to go through the gate were the telltale sign of any uncontrolled bottleneck. Inventory always piles up in front of any bottleneck when production control disregards the fact that bottlenecks control plant throughput," she says.

I'm starting to get into the swing of the thing too. "I suppose that the due date would be game time. That's the time that the lot should have been filled, but the attendants couldn't keep up with the demand. They should have put on a couple of more attendants to open up the bottleneck—like me adding workers."

"Not necessarily. When you told me that the lot would be filled without adding extra help, you convinced me that the parking lot owners could not make any more money by adding attendants. From a pure profit point of view, adding more help to open the bottleneck would have cost money," says Vickie.

"That's not all there is to it," I offer. "You've got to look at the customer's side of it too. If enough people get pissed off, pretty soon there won't be enough customers to fill the parking lot, and the company that owns it will go broke. I can see a plant manager making decisions like that every day. He must strike a happy medium between costs and customer service—one that maximizes profit for both the immediate future and over the long haul. That's tough!"

Vickie nods. "It's tough, all right, but it's a decision that can be made with both eyes open if the manager knows the circumstances that cause the problem. How would you like to be a plant manager where things are always late, inventory is too high, and you cannot get to the root of the problem? That's a tough situation."

I can see what she means. Most managers don't exist in a black and white environment, like the parking lot. There are so many things going on in a typical factory that it is well nigh impossible to separate the critical from the noncritical.

We're finally breaking free of the post-game traffic and moving along at a normal pace. Vickie continues, "Remember what you said when we were stuck back there, about how much better it would be if the cars could be scheduled to arrive at a certain time?"

I nod in agreement as I turn onto Storrow Drive. "We decided that it was impractical because of all of the unpredictable factors involved."

"Yes," she continues, "But you mentioned that some cars could be scheduled as standbys to protect against the unpredictable. Isn't that just like a factory where statistical deviations occur all the time, or where Murphy strikes when he's least expected to?"

"That's right," I say. "If we could schedule extra parts to protect ourselves against statistical deviations and Murphy, then we'd be buffered against all kinds of things external to the critical resources causing factory flow to be disrupted, wouldn't we?"

"If we buffered the bottleneck against disruption by placing a large queue of inventory just in front of it, then the only thing that could possible hurt plant output would be the bottleneck itself going down," Vickie says.

I see her point. "And then, if we concentrate more on bottleneck maintenance and training, the possibility of it going down would become more remote and we'd be way ahead of the game." I think that Vickie is right. The traffic jam is the highlight of the evening.

"Even the car that cut us off reminds me of something in the plant. Can you think of what it is?" she asks.

I nod. "I sure can—happens all the time. It's that phone call from your Mr. King or marketing, asking for a pull-in. It raises hell in the factory when Joe gets one of those edicts and he has to make a certain job at the cost of everything else. I'll think harder about those from now on, before I agree to them."

"When we got so that we could see the half-empty parking lot on the other side of the gate, it reminded me of the excess capacity downstream from any bottleneck," continues Vickie as we move across the Longfellow Bridge and into Cambridge.

"That's when Boston's finest came along and really fouled things up, wasn't it?" I laugh.

"They took over like a factory foreman. They cleaned out one line at a time—just like your foremen running big batches to save setups and putting off changing over until absolutely necessary," says Vickie.

"And we happened to be in the worst possible position in the queue, didn't we?" I say.

"From our point of view we were, but the parking lot got filled a lot quicker that way," she answers.

"It got filled quicker, but with the wrong cars," I say. "It reminds me of a business where the warehouse is filled with all kinds of things that cannot be sold while the things that can be sold are late. Maybe setups and efficiencies are hurting us just like they hurt us in that traffic jam."

Vickie nods in agreement. "And when the parking lot filled up we were on the outside looking in, just like being stuck with a lot of work in process that has no place to go—no market demand."

"We could go on all night with this thing," I say. "The deeper we dig, the more we'll find. I think that I'll send all my people to a Celtics game with the stipulation that they park in that parking lot. It will do them a world of good." I reach to turn on the car radio. "No more business tonight," I say as I locate some good music.

We get back to Cambridge after midnight. I pull up in front of her house and turn to tell her how much I enjoyed being with her away from work. She takes me completely by surprise as she leans over quickly and kisses me. "Good night, Larry. I can't tell you how much I enjoyed tonight."

"Not as much as I did," I tell her as she gets out of the car. "Call me tomorrow."

"I will," she answers as she heads toward the sorority house door. I watch her until she is safely inside, feeling like a schoolboy on his first date once again.

CHAPTER 13

It's Monday morning. My first thought as I enter the shipping room door is about the queue that was in front of grind last week and how it looks this morning after two regular days and a full weekend. I figure that if none of the machines acted up, everybody worked all four days, and Murphy stayed home, it should have shrunk considerably. I'm not disappointed. The big mountain is now an organized pile. I get the feeling that things are finally starting to go my way when Teresa Lockeridge stops me.

"I want to show you something you'll enjoy, Larry," she says as I follow her to the grind center where she stops at grinder number 1050. It's in the process of being set up by three operators at once. Our planning sees it as a one man, or should I say, woman, job.

"What's this?" I ask.

"This is my gift to you, Larry," says Teresa. "What used to be a one-hour setup is now a fifteen-minute setup. When one girl lines up the fixture while another girl sets the controls and the third girl tightens the lugs, it takes fifteen minutes—not an hour—and you'll get better quality at the same time."

"I'm impressed, but what happens to the other girls' machines while they're over here helping with the setup?" I ask.

Teresa points toward the other nine machines. They are all running. "The same thing that happens during breaks and lunch," she answers. "The other operators watch them. The girls like it this way a lot better. Setups with one person are hard work—with three it's a breeze for them."

This is what it's all about. "Tremendous! These girls are tremendous—you are tremendous," I tell her.

"Whoa there, not so fast, Larry. Everything carries a price tag, and there's a price on this one. Can we continue this discussion in your office—out of the noise?" she asks.

When we arrive in my office I offer Teresa a seat. "What's this price tag you're talking about?" I ask.

She begins, "It's not normal union policy to allow what you saw out there this morning to go on. We have enough trouble holding on to the labor base without voluntarily cutting jobs."

I'm prepared for the other shoe to drop. "Why the sudden change of heart?"

"For two reasons, Larry. The first one is that we—we meaning the rank and file—believe that you are sincere when you tell us you want to make this a secure place to work for a long time. The union wants to work with you on this one."

"You don't know how good this makes me feel, Teresa. This is a significant step that will go a long way toward my goal of making us number one, and personally, it's the best compliment I could ever hope for. There's going to be other places where we can apply some revolutionary new ideas, and the union's support will make the transition a lot easier."

She brings me up short. "That brings me to the second reason. It's not a one-way street." Teresa gets up from her chair and closes the door to my office. She sits back down. "I want a direct line to you whenever I see something that needs fixing—no board meetings, no employee relations honcho from corporate—just you and me, one on one."

I see a new side of this girl. Her ambition is showing. She probably wants to be president of the union. "You're pretty damned ambitious, aren't you?" I ask.

"Yes, I am—just like you," she answers defiantly.

She's got me there. I probe deeper. "Just what kind of relationship do you have in mind here?"

"Strictly business, Larry. I bend over backwards to cooperate with you as you do the things you want to do, and you do the same for me," she answers.

This girl is a lot smarter than I thought she was. "Can you give me an example of the kind of thing that I can expect from you?"

"I'll do better than that. I want to start with something spectacular. We've been at odds with management ever since this plant opened about the way that you handle overtime assignments. It is unfair, and I want it stopped immediately—and I want you to accept my proposal to equalize it."

I let out a long, low whistle. I've been on my managers constantly ever since that first round-table when Phil brought it up, but they haven't showed me any improvement in the situation. "We've been working on that for a couple of months, Teresa, and it isn't easy. It may take some doing. When do you expect to see this happen?"

"It should take effect today," she answers.

"That's impossible," I say quickly.

"Bull!" she snaps. "It's not any more impossible than what I agreed to let you try in the grind center. How much time did you give me on that one—five minutes?"

Oh, this girl is sharp. "Let me hear your proposal," I say.

"Here goes," she starts. "Number one—I want an open log kept in an accessible place for anybody in the plant to see at any time. The log will be a tally of the overtime charged to each employee."

"That sounds fair enough," I say.

She continues, "Number two—the overtime rules are: Each employee will be charged for all overtime worked. If they are asked to work over a particular day, and if that request is presented to them before lunchtime and they refuse, they will be charged as if they had worked. If they are asked after lunch, they will have the right to refuse without being charged. On Saturday work, the employee must be asked prior to lunchtime on Friday or they can refuse without penalty. Sunday work can be refused at any time without penalty. The workers with the lowest tally who can handle the job to be worked will always be asked first."

"There will be times when I need somebody with a particular skill or somebody who is halfway through a job where it wouldn't be practical to call another person in," I say.

"I'll give you five wild cards per week, no more," Teresa answers.

I get up and walk around my desk. I stop at the window and look out. How in the hell am I going to do this? My managers haven't been able to. What the hell—the stakes are high—I've got to take a shot. "It's a deal," I say offering my hand—and perhaps my head.

As she grasps my hand she says, "One more thing."

"Oh noooo!" I exclaim.

She laughs before continuing. "It's just that I want full credit for this when it's announced."

As she leaves my office I can't help admiring Teresa. She knows what she wants and she's going to get it.

I call Vickie's sorority house number before I go to staff in the slim hope of catching her in. To my surprise, she answers the phone. I ask her to come up as soon as she can—it's a matter of life and death. She is on her way out the door to a class but says she will cut it and get up here as soon as she can.

Everybody's on time for staff today. Output is up and Joe assures me that we will be one hundred percent on schedule by the end of this week. Toni reports that overtime is in the twenty five percent range and inventory is climbing through the roof. Gary says that he hasn't yet fixed the clause in the purchasing contract that lets the vendor ship early. I tell him that there will be no purchase orders leaving the plant with that clause on them. Efficiencies are still up in the stratosphere, while rejected material is under ten percent. Checkpoints are back up to fifty percent. I carry on about that for a few minutes, telling them that it is probably the most important measurement. All in all, a crappy performance, and I tell them so.

I break the news on the new overtime policy I agreed to. Toni will keep the open tally. Joe and Gary are extremely upset, but I couldn't care less. I'm getting sick of the pair of them always telling me that things won't work, and I tell them that I expect the negative attitudes to stop. More for punishment than anything else, I tell the entire staff that this meeting will readjourn at five this afternoon and tell them to come prepared with concrete plans to get the inventory and overtime down and checkpoints up. They don't like it one bit, but damn, I'm not in business to make them happy, just to make them productive. The meeting turns out to be short, but not so sweet.

Vickie looks good to me when she walks into my office. She is wearing a trim navy-blue slacks and blazer combination that sets off her blonde hair nicely. "What's so important that it can't wait?" she asks.

I tell her about the grind center setup improvements and the deal I had to make with Teresa about the overtime.

"Good, I don't see anything but progress in any of it," she tells me.

Her answer doesn't faze me. I've already grown accustomed to her surprises. "All of it?" I ask.

She answers quickly. "You must agree that the setup development is a tremendous breakthrough."

I agree.

"And you've got to agree that Teresa's willingness to cooperate with you can only work in your favor if you handle it right, even at the price."

Again, I agree.

"That leaves the little matter of equalizing the overtime. Your decision to do that may be the best one you've made since you took this job," she says.

"I don't think it will help get my measurements where I want them. How do you figure that it's so important an issue?"

"Because it's going to force you to take a long, hard look at how you schedule the shop," she answers.

"Do you think that how I schedule the shop and unequal overtime are related?" I ask.

"I know they are, without a doubt," she answers.

I look at her for a minute. She is waiting for me to ask the next question so she can pounce on it. "Do you have any idea just how I can accomplish it?"

"Get rid of checkpoint scheduling," she answers, completely sure of herself.

"What! I can't believe it." I'm shocked.

Vickie finds my reaction amusing. She laughs and repeats slowly for effect, "I said get rid of checkpoint scheduling as your shop floor control tool."

All I can say is, "Why?" Even from Vickie this is unexpected.

"Because it's the cause of all your problems, that's why," she answers.

"All of them?" I ask.

"Yes, all of them. It's causing unequal overtime, too much overtime, too much inventory, and it's even affecting quality."

I can't comprehend how checkpoint scheduling can cause all of these problems, and we have nothing else to use for a scheduling tool. I ask her, "Even if we do away with it, as you suggest, what would we use in its place?"

"One alternative is a common-sense approach to factory control —one that looks at the plant as a unit, not a collection of disjointed centers and operations. Remember when I told you that your scheduling system was thirty years old, Larry?"

"I remember everything you tell me," I answer.

"There have been so many improvements in thirty years! Do you trust my judgment?" she asks.

"Implicitly," I reply.

"If I need to spend the entire day with you, I'm going to prove to you that what I say is true, and then you've got to prove the same thing to your managers. Without their support you can't get to first base with the changes you need to make, so they've got to believe, really believe, that checkpoint scheduling is completely inadequate for the needs of this plant," she says.

"But why has it worked for all these years throughout the company?" I ask.

She shakes her head slowly. "Larry, you've got to be convinced first before we can sell anybody else. You could drive from here to Lynton in a horse and buggy. Why do you use a T'bird?"

I shrug my shoulders. She's got me.

"There are thousands of manufacturing organizations in this world of ours," she continues. "They all schedule their shops and stay in business. There are thousands of scheduling systems—some good and some bad. Some shops don't even have a formal scheduling tool. They just establish a cycle time, launch parts at the beginning of whatever they've established, and expedite like hell. They're still in business, and they'd tell you that it works. Would you want to run your shop like that?"

"No way," I tell her.

"What I'm trying to say is that any scheduling tool or even no scheduling tool will work, because it has to work for the company to stay in business. It's just that the ones with the superior scheduling tools are the ones who remain number one. That's what you want for this place, isn't it?"

There's a fire in Vickie's eyes. This is an emotional issue with her. What can I do?

"OK—you win—Show me what you've got."

I tell Helen that I am not to be disturbed under any conditions. We don't even think to go to lunch. All that I have left to do now is convince that bunch of negative hardheads that I call my staff. It won't be easy. All the telling in the world won't convince them of a thing. They must be shown, and I don't have time for that.

I'm going to try something different when the staff gets back together this afternoon, but any successful gambler makes sure that he has an edge—I think they call it vigorish. Vickie and I are going to that meeting with an edge.

CHAPTER 14

"OK, let's have some ideas that will get our measurements back where they belong," I say, turning to the greaseboard and writing three words across the top—INVENTORY—OVERTIME—CHECKPOINTS. "There's one minor detail that I forgot to mention this morning. I won't allow any ideas that improve one of these measurements but drive one of the other two in the wrong direction. Since I didn't tell you this ahead of time, I'll give you a few minutes to think about it."

Fifteen minutes later, after much writing, erasing, and crossing out, I ask them, "How about it?"

Joe shakes his head and drops his pad on the table. "Nothing on my list fits into your guideline."

"I've got one," says Gary. "My first item—stop vendors from shipping early."

"That doesn't count, Gary. You were supposed to do that two months ago," Toni says. Everybody laughs except Gary.

Dean offers one. "Cut all of the manufacturing cycles."

"That won't work," says Joe. "We've got those cycles screwed down as tight as possible right now. If we make them any tighter, we will miss shippers and work more overtime."

"Why don't we make shorter runs?" says Ernie. "It seems to me that a lot of our inventory is stuck because it can't get into one machine or another while other parts are being run."

"No way. We'd be setting up more than we'd be running parts. Our efficiencies would go to hell and we'd never get anything out the door," says Gary.

That one sounds like it makes some sense to me, but for the time being, it is better if I let it go. "Come on, people, there must be something we can do to get our measurements in line."

"Your rule is unfair. There doesn't seem to be anything that fits," says Joe.

"Did you rig it this way on purpose?" asks Dean.

"Do the rest of you agree with Joe and Dean? Am I asking for the impossible?" I ask.

Nobody says a word or indicates anything. Vickie gives me a quick wink.

"What have I been asking for ever since we opened the doors? Tell me, Joe."

Joe laughs. "I have that engraved on my shorts. Get output up, inventory down, cut down on overtime, raise efficiency, make all checkpoints on time, have no scrap, and ship on time."

"You've been paying attention. When I called this meeting, what did I ask you for?" I ask.

Ernie replies, "The same thing—except that you've thrown a hooker at us. You're forcing us to consider all of the measurements simultaneously."

"That's the word," I shout. *"Simultaneously.* Toni, do you think that any one of our goals, when taken by itself, is bad for the business?"

"Aren't those the goals of every manufacturing organization in America?"

"Most of them," I reply.

"Then I'd have to say that they look like the good measurements to me," she says.

Joe supports her answer, "They're the same goals that every plant manager that I've ever heard of uses."

"If these goals are the proper ones for us it should be fairly easy to come up with ideas; yet when I asked for some, not one of you could come up with even one that didn't have a negative effect on one of the others. Even more ridiculous, if I ask you to come up with ways to make the measurements *worse,* you will have a hard time coming up with ideas that don't make some other measurement better. Think about it. Joe was right when he said that there is nothing we can do that fits. Dean was partially right when he said that I rigged it that way. But I didn't rig it that way tonight. I rigged it that way on the first day that we opened this plant, and we're been trying to do the impossible for nearly a year. There seems to be a conflict between the goals. It doesn't work, does it?"

All of my staff look as if they've been eating some bad mushrooms. Vickie is smiling. I press on. "Let's take them one at a time and see if we can determine which of the goals is the culprit. Maybe there's more than one." I turn and write the goals on the board.

"Output," I begin. "Does anybody care to comment?"

Toni says, "If we don't get output on time we won't make any money, and if we don't strive to ship on time we won't have any customers."

"Does anybody doubt that we must continue to measure output to schedule?" There is no answer so I wipe the word OUTPUT from the list.

"How about overtime? Does anybody in this room think that we should not measure overtime and try to keep it as low as possible? Does anybody think that it's a bad measurement?" I don't wait for an answer before I wipe it out.

I erase the word INVENTORY next. "We must keep inventory under control and we must measure it. We could go bankrupt if we don't. It's the largest single investment that we make. Does anybody disagree with me on this one?"

"Maybe our goal is too tough," say Joe.

"Maybe it is, but I doubt it," I say. "You do agree that we must measure it, don't you"

"Of course."

"That leaves only three," I continue. "How about quality?" "Quality is mandatory if we hope to be better than the competition. We've got to make good stuff," says Ernie.

I wipe out the work QUALITY. "This leaves us with only efficiency and checkpoints. How about efficiency?"

"That's absolutely necessary," says Joe. "We must know if we're getting the most bang for the buck with our people."

Toni shakes her head. "I don't like the way we do it. Everybody in this plant is nearly two hundred percent efficient. That's impossible. Nobody is two hundred percent efficient."

"That only means that we're twice as good as the plant where this job came from," says Ernie. "It makes us look like heroes at corporate."

"Corporate knows that we have new equipment, robots, and the latest technology everywhere. We should be twice as good as the old plant. That's why we're here," says Gary.

"Why can't we fix the planning so that the times used to measure productivity are based on what *we* can do, not what somebody else did? Then we'd know which workers are not productive and which workers are?" says Toni.

"It's not that easy. Some people have tougher jobs than others, and some people know how to use the clock to make them look more productive, even if they're not. It turns into a game of who is more clever, sometimes," replies Joe.

"Now we're getting somewhere." I put a big red circle around the word EFFICIENCY. "There seems to be a difference of opinion on this one."

"That leaves only CHECKPOINTS." I point to the last word on the list.

"Checkpoints are the most important thing of all," says Gary. "They tell us where we need to go, where we've been, and where our problems are. They enable us to keep a balanced flow of parts in the factory."

"If the parts are balanced throughout the factory, why do my people complain that they have no work sometimes?" asks Joe.

"And those people are the very ones who seem to work the most overtime," says Ernie.

"If we know where we're going, why is it that every time I take a fixture for preventative maintenance, somebody seems to need it back in five minutes? I've asked for a list of when fixtures will be available several times, but haven't seen one yet," complains Dean.

"You say that checkpoints tell you where you've been, but I've always been taught that there's no future in history," says Toni.

"He needs to know where he's been so he knows who to blame when we miss a checkpoint," says Joe. Everybody laughs.

I look at my watch. "It's getting late. Do you all agree that our problems seem to be with checkpoints and efficiencies?"

They all nod their heads in agreement.

"I think we're getting someplace here. We've got a lot of work to do and not much time to do it. I'm going to let you go, but first I want to set up a little experiment. I want you to break off into two teams. Let's see—there are five of you—that doesn't lend itself to two teams. Vickie, would you mind taking part in my experiment?"

"I'd love to," she answers, just as we'd rehearsed.

I try to act as if I'm selecting teams without premeditation. "Let's put one pretty girl on each team to make it even. Toni, you are on a team with Joe and Gary. That leaves Vickie with Ernie and Dean. We are going to have a debate. Ernie, your team resolves that checkpoint scheduling is the best tool for us. Joe, Gary, and Toni must resolve that it is the worst. I think that we'll have some fun, and we might even learn something. Prepare anything that you want, and we'll meet back here at this same time Thursday. I'm going to make it worth your while. Members of the winning team, if there is a winning team, will be awarded dinner for two at the restaurant of their choice. Remember—Ernie's team can say nothing bad about checkpoint scheduling, while Joe's team can say nothing good. I'll have something to eat brought in.

"That's about it for this evening. I hope that you all got as much as I did out of this get-together. Good night, everyone."

I take Vickie over to Salem Depot for pizza.

"You did a great job tonight. They're really confused now," she tells me.

"I wonder if they suspect that we've rigged the teams," I say.

"No way," she says. "They didn't suspect a thing. Imagine Gary and Joe trying to shoot their own baby, and with Toni helping them. I love it."

"Don't forget to get together with Toni. It's the key to us pulling this off." I take a bite out of the combination pizza. "Mmmm, this is good pizza, especially when one misses both lunch and dinner."

"It is good," she says. "But eating this late makes me sleepy. I've still got a long drive back to Cambridge. The only thing that I don't like about coming here is that long drive back and forth, especially in the dark."

Several months ago I was toying with the idea of leasing a condo, partly because the hotel accommodations around Salem are sparse and partly because I too hate the drive back and forth, especially on the nights when I work late. "How would you like to use the company condo when you don't have early class the next day?"

Vickie is surprised. "Oh, I didn't know that the company has a condo up here," she says.

"Well, it really hasn't, but the final papers will be passed in a few days," I lie.

"That will be fantastic. Let me know when it's available so I can bring a few things up," she says.

CHAPTER 15

There's no weather more miserable than a late March nor'easter in New England. The cold wind blows the sleet almost parallel with the ground. The driving is horrendous and the walking is worse. The icy dampness sinks into my bones. That's the kind of day that Tuesday is. I skip walking through the factory this morning; instead I park the T'bird as close to my office as I can. The heat of the building feels good as I stamp my feet to rid them of the slush. My coat is soaked as I remove it. Helen is already in her chair, looking as prim as ever.

"Good morning, Helen. Would you please get Gary Niles for me. Ask him to come see me right away."

In a few minutes Helen pops her head into my office. "Gary hasn't arrived yet. I called his wife and she told me that he had a deuce of a time getting out this morning. Seems that the plow went by his street before he could get away and piled two feet of slush right in his driveway. I left a note on his desk telling him that you want to see him."

"OK, thanks, Helen. Oh, will you see if Toni's in yet."

Toni comes into my office still shivering. "It's really miserable out there this morning," she says.

"You know New England. By this afternoon the sun will most

likely come out and melt all the crap that's on the ground. It'll be gorgeous out there," I answer.

"If you don't like the New England weather, just wait a minute— Isn't that how the saying goes?" she says.

"That's right. Toni, be sure that you set up that overtime log. If you have any questions talk with Teresa Lockeridge. I'll have a formal announcement out later today."

"I'll take care of it right away," she says.

"Oh, one more thing before you go. I don't know if Vickie will be able to get up here this morning in this weather, but I want you to be sure that you get in touch with her first thing. Maybe you'd better call her. It's important."

"I'll call her right now. She's probably still in her room."

Toni is turning to leave when I say, "What did you think of our meeting last night?"

"It was good," she answers. "You've really got the guys thinking —me too. I don't know where you're going with this thing, But I can hardly wait for Thursday. It should be fun."

I smile. "You'll know a whole lot more about it as soon as you talk to Vickie."

Gary arrives looking like the last snowman of winter. "This damned weather is obscene, especially for a good ole North Carolina boy like me," he shudders.

"I've got a couple of things I'd like you to get right on," I say.

"Sure thing. What are they?" he asks.

"Do you have any catalogs for jackets—you know the kind— jackets we can give out as awards to people who do something above and beyond?" I ask.

"Oh, sure," he answers. "We get those things in the mail all the time."

"Good. I want you to select something appropriate—let's say powder blue with a small ConnYankee emblem over the heart. I want quality, something that the people will value and be proud to wear. Get about three dozen for starters."

"Any particular size?" he asks.

"The first ones will go to the workers in the grind center. Use them as a guide," I answer.

"What else?" he asks.

"This next item may take a bit of doing, but I want it done this week, if possible," I continue. "I want you to look at leasing a condo for company business. I'll approve all the paper work. Make it nice—a two-bedroom with a good-sized living room where we can hold meetings. Look at that new section across from Rockingham Mall."

"I'd better get right on it if I hope to get it done this week. Do you want final approval before I sign an offer?" he asks.

"No. You know what I'm looking for. I'll trust your good judgment."

It's nearly noon and the fickle New England weather has turned to rain, washing all of the sleet and slush away. I'm on the phone with Les Walsh, my representative in corporate marketing, when Vickie arrives. I motion her in as I continue my conversation with Les. "I told you that our cycles are ten weeks in this plant, and that's the best I can do. Any other time I might be willing to try to push something through in less time, but right now I'm fighting to get back on schedule. We had a serious breakdown on our laser welding equipment last month that put us in a hole."

Les makes one last bid. "How about nine-week delivery? I think I can get the contract if I promise June delivery."

"Hold on for a moment, Les." I put my hand over the mouthpiece. "Marketing can sell five hundred extra S3 blades if we can ship in nine weeks. It's about a quarter million dollars."

"Take it," Vickie tells me. "You're about out of the woods on schedule delinquencies, and from what I heard last night, things are going to get better. Take a chance."

What the hell, it's only a week and we've got all kinds of extra material. I take my hand from the mouthpiece. "OK, Les. It's risky, but I'll take it on with a nine-week promise."

Les sounds like I've made his day. "That's great, Larry. I'll telecopy the req to you just as soon as it's entered. Thanks."

I put the phone back on the hook. "Good morning, Vickie. Did you have trouble with the weather?"

"It's all rain now—not too bad," she answers. "Toni called earlier and I filled her in on the plans, but it will be better if I talk to her in person. She understands that her job is to keep Joe and Gary on the path that we want them to be on, but she needs jacking up first." She waves to me as she heads toward Toni's office.

It's four o'clock before I realize it. I have a meeting with Joe and Larry to tell them about the rush order for the five hundred S3 blades, and they think that they can beat nine weeks by a day or two if they push hard. I tell them to push—no holds barred.

Vickie comes back. "That was some good session I had with Toni. She's so easy to talk to. I wish that everybody could see things as easily as she does," she says.

"She's like you," I answer, "no bad habits to break." It seems as if things are going right for a change, and I feel a need to celebrate. "How about going to Pier Four for dinner with me tonight?" I ask her.

"You dog, Larry. That's my favorite place in the whole world to eat, but I've got another date tonight," she says.

"Oh?" I mutter.

"Joe has called a meeting of the debating team at his house for this evening. I've got to go."

I laugh. "That is great!"

"Ernie is doing the same thing, so Toni tells me," she continues. "Both teams are taking this seriously."

"That's what we want them to do. Thursday is out. How about Friday for Pier Four?" I ask.

"I'm sorry, Larry, but I'm flying to the farm for the weekend. Arthur tells me that King Arthur is coming up to top form for his first race, and I want to see him. He's my baby, you know."

"Some other time, then." My disappointment shows.

CHAPTER 16

Helen's usual good job manifests itself with the Thursday evening refreshments. There is a relish tray, potato chips, coffee and soft drinks, and the crowning touch—a foot-long cheese and pepper steak submarine sandwich for each of us. It's fattening, but delicious.

The conference room is set up with an overhead viewer and an easel of paper sheets. The teams are lined up on opposite sides of the conference table. The meal is over and we're ready to go.

"All right," I begin. "I hope that we can continue with the progress that we started to make the other night. Ernie, you start. Say something good about checkpoint scheduling."

Ernie goes to the front of the room. "For more than thirty years checkpoint scheduling has been the system for ConnYankee and many of the top companies in the country. It has worked because it is straightforward and not complicated to understand. It breaks large tasks into several smaller ones which are much easier to visualize and work with. These small tasks are called checkpoints. The theory behind them is that if all of the checkpoints are on schedule, then work will be evenly distributed throughout the plant and the flow will be smooth and even."

Joe then goes to the easel. "Those small tasks—checkpoints, if you will—are one of the main reasons why checkpoint scheduling is not the tool for us." He writes down the word OVERTIME. "In the past four weeks, seventy-four percent of the overtime that has been worked by direct labor operators has been charged to a checkpoint operation or to the operation immediately preceeding that checkpoint operation. We are working overtime just so we can look good on checkpoints."

"I don't see anything wrong with that," says Dean.

"What's wrong with it is that the same people who work on those operations are the people who have nothing to do on Monday. We work them Saturday and clean all of the work out of their areas, leaving no buffers for them to work on at the beginning of the week. This is also the reason why our overtime is so far out of whack." He marks an up arrow and an equals sign with a line through it on the easel beside the word overtime.

Ernie says, "But you have to admit that working to get the checkpoints where they belong distributes inventory all over the plant and smooths the flow."

"How can flow be so smooth when people have nothing to do on Monday and are buried by the time Friday rolls around?" asks Joe. He goes on, "In fact, because of the heavy emphasis on checkpoints, most of our operators work without any schedule at all. The foremen and PC people are so busy expediting parts through checkpoints that they never get around to the noncheckpoint operations. I asked twenty people, at random, today where they got their schedules. Thirteen of them told me that they knew what to do—didn't get a schedule—didn't need one. Is that any way to run a railroad?" He writes the word FLOW on the easel and draws an uneven looking line through it. "And I've got one more thing to say. You mention small tasks." He writes SMALL TASKS on the easel. "It's bad enough that we have twenty different parts with twenty different schedules that compete for capacity, but the small-task syndrome changes twenty schedules into one hundred separate schedules, all competing for capacity, overtime, and management." He makes a large red 100 over the words SMALL TASKS.

Joe's apparent zest for what he is saying shocks me. "You've come with your guns blazing," I say to him.

"I've learned a lot out there in just two days," he answers.

It's Dean's turn. "Checkpoints, being static, take the nervousness out of the schedule. Purchasing can place orders on vendors and be fairly certain that they won't change much on the near horizon. The vendor can plan for a nice even flow in his factory. The stockroom has a static schedule, and our ship schedule can be level-loaded over a long period of time, yielding a static schedule through every checkpoint.

Vickie and Toni have done their work well. It's Gary's turn to answer. "The real world is dynamic, not static, and any schedule that cannot model real world conditions is not realistic. I feel as if I'm about to shoot myself in the foot, but here goes. As y'all are painfully aware, our input performance from vendors has not been a spectacular success. Due to poor inventory practices and vendors shipping early, we have about five million dollars too much material on our dock right now." He takes a packet of checkpoint sheets from his folder. "I've calculated that we are averaging twenty percent ahead of the issue checkpoint for the first quarter of the year—another inventory problem."

"You got a static schedule, why can't you issue parts to it?" asks Dean.

"The big problem for the stockroom is priority. Let's suppose that on Monday everything is even to checkpoints. What are we supposed to issue first?" Gary says.

"Does it make any difference?" asks Vickie, playing the devil's advocate.

"Oh, yes," he continues. "The static checkpoint sheets say that each part has two weeks to get from issue through the second checkpoint. We are busy down on the dock. It takes us a week to issue a week's worth of work. We start Monday with the first part and issue the last part late Friday. The parts that we issue on Monday have a full two weeks to get through the second checkpoint, but the parts that we issue on Friday have only one week. It's the parts that we issue on Friday that eventually get the overtime work on them. In other words, we are letting the stockroom establish our priorities for us. To make matters worse, what they usually do is start with the top checkpoint sheet and work their way down through the packet. The secretary who staples the packets together is really setting the priorities for this plant. Everybody in the plant goes by the way the packets are stapled together. To prove my point, if everybody will look at the bottom sheet of the packet—"

He waits while we take out our checkpoint sheets. "You will not find a worse-looking sheet in the entire packet. Everybody makes commitments from top to bottom. Part T9 has been on the bottom of the pile since day one, and it has the worst record of conformance to checkpoints of any of our parts. It's no coincidence. Put another part on the bottom and put T9 on top and you'll see what I mean."

"Good job, Gary. Did you realize this was going on before now?" I ask.

"Not at all," he answers. "We stumbled on it when we were getting ready for this meeting."

"But I don't understand why you are twenty percent ahead of checkpoints," says Dean.

"It's because we don't always issue parts the way that the factory would like, and we try to get ahead so that they'll stay off of our backs."

I turn to Vickie. "It's your turn."

"Because we have a tendency to start parts through the factory in batches of a week at a time, our efficiencies are way up there. Our incidence of setup is so low that we have ninety-seven percent of the time available to run parts. We set up only three percent of the time, on the average."

Toni takes a package of overhead transparencies to the overhead viewer and turns it on. The first slide is what looks like a small flow diagram.

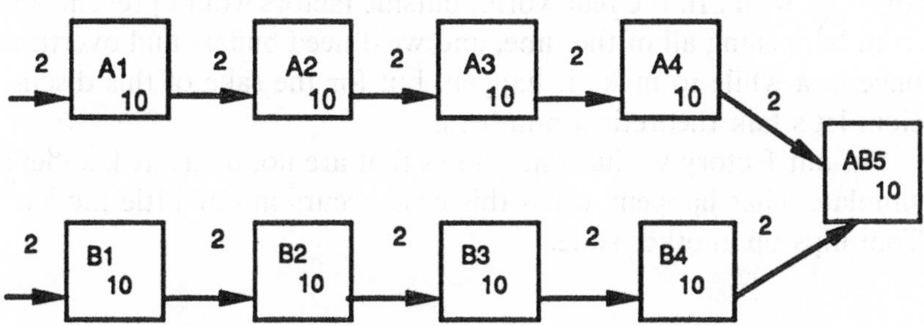

"I want to show you how saving setups causes inventory to rise dramatically. It's difficult to diagram the entire factory, so I've purposely oversimplified my example," says Toni. "Looking at the diagram, we have a simple factory that manufactures one thing called

AB5. There are nine dedicated operations that make up this factory. Part A goes through four operations. Each one takes ten minutes to perform and there is two minutes' move time between each operation. The same is true of part B. The final operation takes ten minutes to assemble parts A and B into the final product AB5. All of these operations can be performed simultaneously. Can anyone tell me what the cycle time is for this kind of plant?" she asks.

"That's easy," says Gary. "It's sixty minutes."

"How did you figure that?" she asks.

"Where I went to school I was taught that cycle time consists of run time, setup time, queue time, move time, and wait time. In your example the run time along the critical path is a total of fifty minutes and the move time is ten minutes. I don't see any setup time, nor is any queue or wait time indicated, because the parts move from one operation to another as soon as they are completed. It looks like an assembly line to me."

"That's just what it is," says Toni. She puts up another slide. "This is what Gary just said, in chart form."

RUN	MOVE	WAIT	QUEUE	SET-UP	CYCLE
50	10	0	0	0	60

"Now, suppose that our perfect plant works eight hours per day, five days per week, and the market demand is two hundred and forty AB5's. Theoretically, we can ship exactly two hundred and forty per week. In the real world, outside factors would prevent this from happening all of the time, and we'd need buffers and overtime once in a while to make it happen, but for the sake of this discussion, let's talk theoretical numbers.

"In our factory we have machines that are not dedicated, so let's simulate what happens when this case occurs in our little model." Toni flips up another slide.

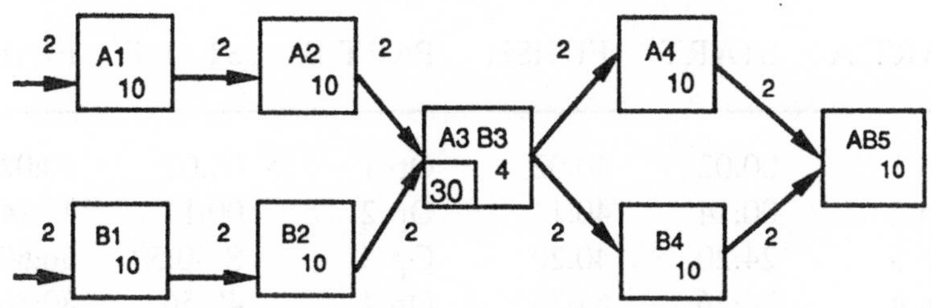

"Machine three is used to run both parts A and B now, and it only takes four minutes, but there is a setup of thirty minutes every time we change over from one part to another. Suppose that we were to run my little shop with checkpoint scheduling and drive setups down as low as we try to drive them here. Gary, you did so good on the last one, would you like to try this one?" she asks.

"Let's see," says Gary. "We like to minimize setups because they aren't productive. We'd run a weeks' worth at a time at operation A3 and B3." The rest of the managers nod in agreement.

Gary stares at the slide for a few moments before heading toward the board. "Run time through the entire factory would be six minutes lower due to the reduced machine time at operations three—forty-four minutes, and move time would still be ten minutes, but now we have wait time and queue time as well as setup time to contend with."

"It gets a bit tougher to figure," says Toni. "Can you handle it, Gary?"

He is determined to come up with the solution and takes but a few minutes to do so. When he is finished the board is completely covered with hieroglyphics, but in the middle of the mess he has managed to produce a chart of operations sequencing.

PART A	START	FINISH	PART B	START	FINISH
Op 1	00:02	40:02	Op 1	00:02	40:02
Op 2	00:14	40:14	Op 2	00:14	40:14
Op 3	24:20	40:20	Op 3	S 40:50	56:50
Op 4	24:26	64:26	Op 4	40:56	80:56

Operation 5 (Assembly) Start 41:08
First Piece Ships 41:18
Cycle Time = 41h:18m

Gary explains his chart. "Operations one and two for both parts are unaffected by the change. The first part would be available into operation three in twenty-six minutes, just as before, but since operation three is now so much faster than the other operations, and nothing can be shipped until both parts are at assembly, there would be no use in starting up the machine until 24:20. Exactly six minutes later, the first part would be ready for operation A4, and twelve minutes after that it would be at assembly. Can everybody see that?"

They nod their heads in agreement. "All well and good," says Ernie. "But the part can't be assembled. We have no B's at final assembly. Just like the typical production manager, you've got us shut down again."

Gary ignores the dig and continues. "By the time that machine three finishes all two hundred forty A's, the entire week's run of B's is sitting in a queue right in front of the new machine waiting its turn." He points to the letter "S" he has entered just in front of the start time for operation B3. "We will need to take thirty minutes to set up the machine for part B before we can continue. We can then begin running B's at 40:50. In six minutes, at 40:56, the first piece is delivered to operation four, and to assembly at 41:08. There are plenty of A's waiting at the assembly operation, so we can ship the first piece at precisely 41:18."

Joe lets out a long, low whistle. "Do you mean to say, because we are more efficient on only one lousy machine, we have actually increased our cycle time more than forty-one times?"

"That's right Joe," says Toni. "It's hard to believe. Can anyone tell me why that would be detrimental to the good of any sound business?"

Ernie answers. "It seems to me that cycle time and inventory go hand in hand—the longer the cycle, the bigger the pipeline and the higher the inventory. Once the pipeline is full, we get out one assembly every ten minutes and bring in one set of parts every ten minutes. Not only would the cycle be forty-one times longer, the inventory of work on the factory floor would also be forty-one times higher."

Dean offers, "That could get mighty expensive. That's money tied up permanently that could be invested or used on improving things in a plant. Even sitting in a bank somewhere drawing interest, the money itself would be more productive."

"Well put, guys," says Toni. "The cycle time and work-in-process inventory have gone up more than forty-one hundred percent just because one machine is being driven to run huge batches. Can you imagine what is happening here in Salem with many machines being driven to run large batches simultaneously?"

Toni's message is getting across. It's like the dawn of a new day as the lights go on in everybody's head.

"But setups are a fact of life in manufacturing, aren't they?" asks Ernie.

"The fact that we need to make setups is, but running abnormally large batches all of the time is definitely not. Let me show you what I mean," answers Toni. "Suppose that we cut the batch sizes in half. What would happen to the cycle, Ernie?"

"I guess that the run time and move time per piece would still be the same. If we cut the batches in half I think that the queue and wait times would also be cut about in half, while the setup time would double," he says.

"You've got the general idea," says Toni. "And if you do cut the batches there will be a corresponding drop in cycle time and work-in-process inventory. To save time I've calculated the results of a couple of different batch sizes." She flips up another slide.

PART A	START	FINISH	PART B	START	FINISH
Op 1	00:02	20:02	Op 1	00:02	20:02
Op 2	00:14	20:14	Op 2	00:14	20:14
Op 3	12:20	20:20	Op 3	S 20:50	28:50
Op 4	12:26	32:26	Op 4	20:56	40:56
Op 5	Start 21:08		Finish First Piece 21:18		
Cycle = 21h:18m					

"That's a dramatic improvement—about in half, just as Ernie guessed," says Joe. "Of course, we'd need to run through the cycle twice in order to make a weeks' rate."

"That's true," says Toni. "All of the operators except those on operation three would see no difference in their workload once the pipeline was filled. They'd have the same smooth flow of work that they always had. They'd do two hundred forty a week as always. The difference would be that operator three would need to make two extra setups."

This bothers Ernie. "I'm impressed, I think, but being a manufacturing engineer, I'm not sure that I like making twice as many setups. We could spend too much time making nonproductive setups and lose output."

Toni is ready for him. "How much time is needed for machine three to do a week's output?"

Ernie calculates quickly in his head. "Let's see—four minutes times two hundred forty times two per assembly—that comes out to nineteen hundred twenty minutes per week. That's thirty-two hours."

"How much time is worker three available?" asks Toni.

"Forty hours."

"If parts take thirty-two hours to run, what does the operator do for the other eight hours?"

Ernie shakes his head. "Other than making setups, nothing."

"If that's so, why don't we utilize the worker to make setups and reduce the inventory and cycle times?" asks Dean before Toni has a chance to speak.

"How would we know when setups are costing us output?" asks Ernie.

Toni continues. "If we have eight hours to play with and each setup takes thirty minutes, we could set up machine three sixteen times a week before we'd cut into productive run time. That means that theoretically we could make eight setups for A's and eight for B's. Our batch size could be as low as thirty." She flips up another chart.

PART A	START	FINISH	PART B	START	FINISH
Op 1	00:02	05:02	Op 1	00:02	05:02
Op 2	00:14	05:14	Op 2	00:14	05:14
Op 3	03:20	05:20	Op 3	S 05:50	07:50
Op 4	03:26	08:26	Op 4	05:56	10:56
Op 5	Start 06:08	Finish First Piece 06:18			
Cycle Time = 6h:18m					

"I'm impressed," says Joe. "That's a significant improvement over the original batch of two forty. It cuts the inventory about eighty-five percent."

I can see that everybody in the room is impressed. I am—but Toni is not finished yet.

"Let us take this a step further. Suppose that we wanted to lower the inventory and cycle time even more than that. What could we do, Ernie?"

Ernie ponders for a moment and then answers. "If we could reduce the time it takes to make a setup, we could get the cycles even lower."

"The Japanese do just that. They continually drive setups to a minimum so that they can cut batches. They know that it is something worth doing—something that pays them back manyfold," says Toni.

"You're damned right," Ernie replies. "There isn't a setup out on our floor that couldn't be improved if we put our minds to it. It might even be feasible to create a job where a person does nothing but work on improving setup times."

"That sounds like a good idea," says Toni. "There are some places in a factory where large batches would help us. Those places where the demand is equal to, or nearly equal to, the run time available. These are the bottlenecks or pacing resources.

"In summing up, I said that theoretically, thirty is the best batch. In real life, given the conditions of this little factory on the board, a batch size of thirty might be too tight. We need some insurance for fluctuations at machine three so that subsequent operations would never be starved for parts. We need a bit of slack in the form of a time buffer. A batch of thirty-five or forty would produce some idle time so that Murphy doesn't kill us. This is just an example to show what can be accomplished in a factory that is not all wrapped up with the big batch syndrome," says Toni.

This meeting is going better than I'd hoped in my wildest dreams. I want to push on, but nature calls. "Let's take a break," I say.

CHAPTER 17

I want the session to be one of interplay between my staff members, with my role that of an observer. It's working out better than I hoped. Toni and Vickie have the guys eating right out of their hands, and the guys don't even know it. I've learned some things myself. I wonder where we're heading next.

I enter the conference room to find all six folks on one side of the table—Joe's side. "What happened?" I ask.

"We concede, boss," says Dean. "We can't defend checkpoint scheduling. They've got too many guns for us and we never did have a strong argument. We lose, and that's all there is to it, but as Paul Harvey says, 'We want to hear the rest of the story'."

Toni continues, "We ended up before break saying that there are times when it is important to run large batches. Let me show you what I mean. Once again, to make it easier to comprehend, I'm going to work with a relatively simple model." She flips a slide onto the overhead viewer.

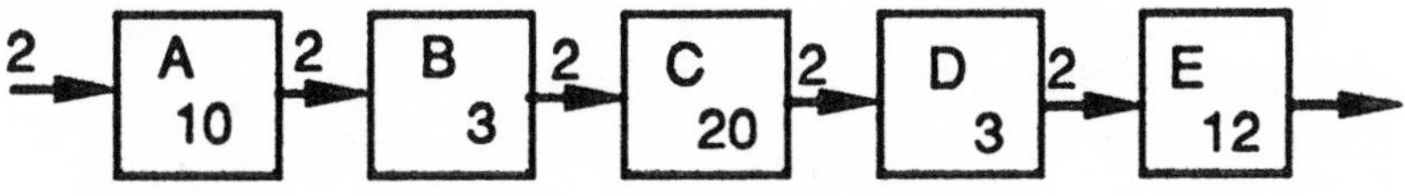

"As you can see, five machines called A through E process parts and transfer them one at a time. What is the cycle time, Ernie?" she asks.

"Fifty-eight minutes," Ernie answers immediately.

"You're doing so well, I'll try you again. How many parts can we ship in an eight-hour day?"

"I don't even need the calculator for that one," Ernie answers. "Four hundred and eighty minutes divided by twelve minutes per part is forty—forty parts in eight hours."

Gary is quick to interrupt. "You've calculated the capacity of resource E, not the capacity of the plant as a whole," he says.

Ernie frowns as he concentrates on the model. "Oh—I see what you mean, Gary. Resource C can process only twenty-four in eight hours, and that's all that we will get out of the pipeline. I assumed, incorrectly, that resource E could work productively for eight hours, but it's really limited by what C can do, isn't it?"

"That's right, Ernie," Toni says. I notice that she is peeking at her notes more and more. It's no wonder—she's only had a couple of days to get ready. She's done damned well so far.

"Output is determined by what is processed through the slowest resource in any manufacturing sequence—the bottleneck!" she says.

"Do this one together," she continues. "How long would it take to process a batch of one thousand parts, checkpoint style? In other words, the entire thousand is completed at one operation before it is passed on to the next resource."

"Wait a minute," says Vickie, once again playing her role. "That's not at all realistic. Parts will be passed to the next operation before that."

Joe comes to the rescue. "Not necessarily. In our plant, with twenty different products competing and with our tendency to run large batches, it is very realistic."

Gary finishes the problem first and goes to the board to show his answer.

Operation A =	10,000 minutes	= 167 hours		
B =	3,000	= 50		
C =	20,000	= 333		
D =	3,000	= 50		
E =	12,000	= 200		
	TOTAL	= 800 HOURS		

Dean whistles, "Eight hundred hours for a one-shift operation is twenty weeks."

"That's right," says Toni. "Can anybody tell me what the inventory profile would look like?"

Vickie says, "All thousand parts would be delivered to operation A on day one. Since nothing gets moved on until the entire batch is finished, the average inventory would be one thousand parts for twenty weeks. I would never run a factory that way."

"How would you run a factory, Vickie?" asks Toni.

I notice the smooth transition from Toni to Vickie. I catch Toni's eye and give her a quick wink to convey my appreciation for the superb job that she has done.

Vickie takes over. "Toni has shown us that the bottleneck resource, in this case C, is the one place where we should run large batches because it really controls our output. A setup or a work stoppage would cost us more than just idle time on C. It would cost us output for the entire plant. Does everybody agree with that, or am I mistaken?"

"I didn't think of it that way, Vickie, but you are absolutely right," says Joe. "Lost output at a truly limiting resource means money lost for the entire business, doesn't it?"

"A setup at a bottleneck is very expensive, then," says Ernie.

"You're thinking the way I am," Vickie continues. "Getting C going as soon as possible and keeping it going should give us better results."

"That would mean scheduling the whole shop around the bottlenecks so that we can keep them going all the time," says Gary.

"I wonder just how much difference that would make in my little model," says Toni.

"Can you draw it up for us, Vickie?" I ask her.

"I'm on the checkpoint team, so I have nothing prepared. I'll give it a try, but it will take me ten or fifteen minutes," she lies.

"Why don't we take another break for about fifteen minutes, then." I look at my watch. It's already eight-fifteen. I'm going to have one tired bunch of staff members tomorrow. "Let's reconvene at eight-thirty."

CHAPTER 18

When I return to the conference room Vickie is putting the finishing touches on a busy diagram. "Toni did one hell of a job, didn't she?" I say.

"She's a jewel—and what a memory. I crammed all of that information into her in two half-day sessions," says Vickie as she puts the marker down. She looks at her watch. "I think I can finish by ten. It's a good thing my plane doesn't leave Boston until about noon tomorrow. I haven't even packed. I'd never make it if it was any earlier."

Toni comes in followed closely by the guys. "Save me, Vickie. These guys are asking me questions that I can't answer. I told them I'd be stealing your thunder."

Vickie laughs, "You've let the cat out of the bag. I'm supposed to be on the checkpoint team, remember?"

Joe comes up short. "You melonheads, this was a setup, wasn't it?" he says.

I was going to wait 'til morning to tell them, but the damsels are in distress. "Vickie was working both sides of the street," I say.

"Do you know what they call a lady who works the street?" asks Ernie.

They all laugh. "No, no, I mean that she helped Toni," I say.

"Toni's a hooker too!" exclaims Dean, and the room is in an uproar.

"You guys are embarrassing me," I say. "I must be getting tired."

"It's no wonder," says Joe. "With two hookers anybody would be tired." More laughter.

When they calm down, I continue. "Let's get serious so we can get out of here before midnight—Vickie?"

"I've put together a rough diagram to illustrate the way I'd run my factory." She points to the board. The diagram reminds me of a herringbone.

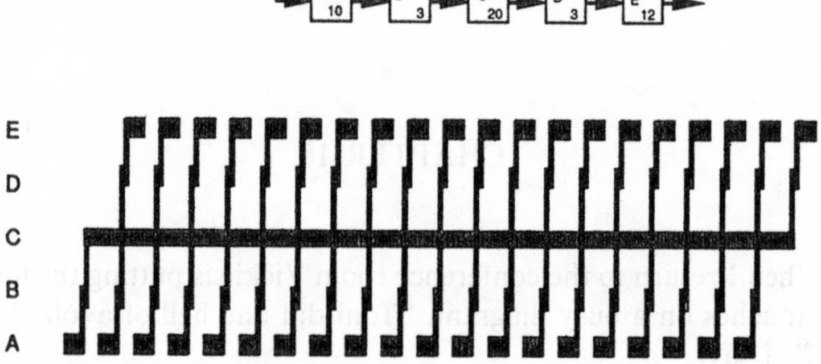

"In my factory I'd get the bottleneck going as soon as I could and then I'd schedule around it, to keep it going. The way I'd do this is run batches of fifty at a time at all of the other operations. Let's look at the diagram. You'll be amazed when you see the difference. Resource A processes fifty parts in five hundred minutes and passes them on to B where the parts are run in one hundred and fifty minutes. The bottleneck is able to begin running parts in six hundred fifty minutes. By starting another batch of fifty through resource A every one thousand minutes, the bottleneck is kept running until all thousand parts are completed. As each fifty-piece batch is finished at the bottleneck it is moved to resource D for one hundred fifty minutes and then on to the final resource, E, where the batch is completed in six hundred minutes. Ernie, if there's still some power left in your calculator, how long will it take to ship all thousand parts?"

Ernie punches numbers. "Six fifty to get the bottleneck started, twenty thousand to run all the parts through the bottleneck, and seven fifty to ship the last batch—that adds up to twenty-four thousand. Divide that by sixty to get the hours and divide that by forty to get the weeks. Ten weeks," he says. "That's exactly half the time that it took checkpoint style. I'm impressed."

"Let's take it a step further. When will we ship the first parts?" Vickie asks.

"Let me take this one," says Gary. "That would be the total time it takes to run the first fifty pieces through all of the operations." He looks at the diagram for a minute. "We'd ship the first fifty in one week!" His eyes widen in amazement.

"How about the second fifty?" Vickie asks.

Gary looks at the diagram once more. "It looks like we will ship another fifty every thousand minutes until they are all gone. Wow! That's only a little over two days."

"Very astute," says Vickie. "Once the bottleneck gets rolling, we would ship parts at the same rate that the bottleneck can do them. How long did it take us to ship the first parts with the checkpoint system?"

Joe answers, "Twenty weeks, but something is bothering me. I assume that the spaces between the black blocks represent idle time."

"In terms of the one thousand pieces, that is true. It doesn't mean that the machine and worker could not be doing something else," says Vickie.

"If we had a steady demand for parts instead of just this one lot, we could keep the other resources busy all the time, couldn't we?" asks Dean.

"No, we could not," answers Vickie. "Look at the diagram again. Resource C can process one part every twenty minutes. No matter what the demand is, resources D and E are going to get only one part every twenty minutes to work on. Can you see that?"

Dean nods his head.

"Look at operations A and B. What good would it do to run more than the bottleneck can handle? The pile of inventory in front of the bottleneck would soon resemble Mount McKinley," says Vickie.

"In other words, the bottleneck is key. If we want to get more throughput we must open up the capacity at the bottleneck," says Joe.

Vickie claps her hands. "Exactly!" she says.

"What about the inventory?" she continues. "Would anyone care to venture a guess as to what the inventory profile would look like?"

"I don't know how close to scale your diagram is—it looks pretty close. The first fifty would ship just shortly after the third batch is started, and it will continue that way. Roughly a hundred or a hundred ten pieces would build up and then we'd offset input with output," says Gary.

"How does that compare with the thousand-batch method?" Vickie asks.

"Inventory would be way down—about one-ninth," says Gary. "What would we do with all of the storage racks?" he laughs.

"One more thing before we go on. Can anybody tell me when it might be advantageous to run operations A and B ahead of the bottleneck?" she asks.

I notice Joe. He is really into this thing—he has a thought. "I've been thinking that if we worked to your diagram, and either worker A or worker B stayed home when they were scheduled to run parts, we'd shut down the bottleneck. That would be a disaster. I think that it would be advisable to have an inventory buffer sitting right in front of the bottleneck, and then we'd be protected against disruption from resources that feed the critical resource," he says.

"Joe, you've made my day. Good! How big a buffer would you want sitting at the bottleneck?" Vickie says.

"I'd probably figure things like reliability of machines and people and parts, and maybe how many operations I'm covering for, and then make a decision—maybe a week's worth," Joe says.

"That's right. The important thing is that you would control just what size buffer you want and where you want it to be so that throughput is protected, right?" asks Vickie.

"That's exactly right. I'm beginning to like this more and more," says Joe.

"We've seen two different kinds of scheduling systems. The first one, the one we call checkpoint, is a high inventory, high overtime scheduling system. The one we just reviewed is known as a low-inventory scheduling system. It's similar to the systems that the Japanese are using with so much success. They call it Just-in-Time. As I go on I'll refer to the systems as high inventory and low inventory. Other than the tremendous advantage of having low inventory investment, can anybody think of any more benefits from using the low inventory system?" Vickie asks.

I think about the call from Les Walsh and his appeal to ship those five hundred S3's and the nine-week promise. "If we were using a low inventory scheduling system, I could have promised the job that marketing wants in four or five weeks."

"That's right' " says Vickie. "Not only that, but what a tremendous advantage you would have over your competitors. Wouldn't you like to have a vendor who can respond very quickly to your schedule changes and deliver emergencies on short notice?"

"I'd give him all of the business he could handle," says Gary.

"With low inventory scheduling you could be that kind of vendor to your customers," says Vickie.

"Can anyone think about a way that quality could be improved by using a low inventory system?" she asks.

"Now, you aren't going to tell us that we'll have better quality just because of the way that we schedule, are you?" asks Dean.

"Let's just suppose that a vendor shipped bad parts, and we didn't catch them until the first piece was at final inspection, just before shipment. With the high inventory system, how many parts would be in the system when the problem was discovered?" she asks.

"That all depends on how many bad ones the vendor shipped, but there could be up to twenty weeks' worth of output in the line, and if all of them weren't bad, they'd sure be hard to find. We'd have to look at all of the work in process to find them. It's happened to me in the past, and it's a mess," answers Dean.

"I get it," offers Ernie. "With the low inventory system there would be only one-ninth of the inventory. We could find the bad parts much easier, and chances are that most of the bad parts would still be in the stockroom or at the vendor's. We could find out what the problem is and fix it before we get into deep trouble."

"That's right, Ernie. How about engineering changes? What if an engineer came up with a change that improved the product? How long would it take to get it on the market with the high inventory system?"

"It would take twenty weeks, and with the low inventory system it would take only one week. That could be a tremendous competitive advantage, couldn't it?" Ernie answers.

"You can bet on that," says Vickie. "Gary, what if you negotiated a lower price with your vendor? Wouldn't that improve the profit picture?"

"That's right," he replies. "With the high inventory system we would be shipping high cost parts for twenty more weeks, while we could get rid of the high cost parts in as little as a week with the low inventory system."

"I could go on, but I think you've got the picture. A business using the low inventory scheduling system has a powerful advantage over its competition, don't you all agree?" says Vickie.

"It sounds too good to be true. Does such a system exist and how much does it cost?" asks Joe.

"There are systems available, but I'm talking a manufacturing philosophy. All it will really take to benefit from the good things we've talked about tonight is dedication, willingness to change, and hard work. BOTTLENECKS—BUFFERS—and BATCHES. I've touched on each one of them tonight. Control the three B's, that's what you must do."

It's time to wrap things up. It's after ten. "Thank you all for a great meeting. I promised dinner for two for the winning team. I think that we are all winners this time, and you will all share in the award. I know that Vickie and Toni threw a lot at you tonight, but think about it. I like it—and how about a round of applause for my two hookers."

The guys give Toni and Vickie a standing ovation.

CHAPTER 19

It's after midnight by the time I get into bed. I'm tired, but I guess the adrenalin is flowing. My mind is filled with all kinds of silly thoughts. I can still taste the tuna sandwich that Mom left for me—The pepper steak is still with me but I don't want to hurt Mom's feelings—I'm going to be dragging my bones about the plant tomorrow—or is it today—so are the others—I'm damned satisfied at the way it went tonight—I wonder how the guys will feel about it after they've slept on it—They say that beauty and brains don't mix —There are exceptions to every rule and I've got two of them—Vickie mentioned three B's—Bottlenecks, Buffers, and Batches—I've got three more B's for Toni and Vickie . . . Beautiful, Brilliant Babes—A guy could do a lot worse than either one of them—couldn't do any better, though—They both must have plenty of guys sniffing around—I've got to get to sleep—It must be after one —I hope Vickie has a safe trip—Wonder what time it is now—Go to sleep, Larry.

It's morning. I somehow manage to get dressed, have breakfast, make small talk with Mom, and guide the T'bird to Salem. By the time I drive into the parking lot, my body clock has me in pretty good shape. I pass Teresa on my way into the plant. She's satisfied with the overtime agreement so far. I tell her that I want to be informed of any violations.

When I reach my office, the four guys on my staff are already there. They look as bad as I feel. "Good morning, gentlemen," I greet them.

Joe is the spokesman. "It might not be good, but it is morning," he says. "The four of us spent most of last night at the Bullfinch Pub over on Route Twenty-eight. We downed a few brews and talked about last night's meeting. Let's go, Larry."

"What do you mean—let's go?" I ask.

"We want to change the way we run this plant. You've convinced us that checkpoint scheduling is counterproductive."

"The first criterion I used when hiring all of you was that I wanted people who were progressive enough, and had guts enough, to explore new ground. That's the way I am, and that's the way I want my people to be. I know now that I got what I was looking for," I tell them.

"Where do we start?" Joe asks.

"I'll tell you what," I say. "Let's think about it this morning and we'll meet back here right after lunch."

Where do we start? That's what Joe said. I wasn't expecting to be thrust into this thing cold turkey. Why the hell did Vickie pick now to go to Kentucky?

The phone rings. It's Gary. "The jackets will be in Monday. They look real good," he says.

"Good job. We'll have some kind of ceremony for the people in grind. What about the condo?" I ask.

"I found a nice one over by the Rockingham Mall. We should be able to take possession immediately. When would you like to see it?"

"Can we get in tomorrow?" I ask.

"I've got the key," says Gary.

I get another call from Les Walsh for a progress report on his emergency order. I tell him everything is fine, although I haven't really checked on it. He tells me that if we perform well on this one, he has a verbal commitment from the customer for another three-million-dollar follow-on order.

It's nearly noon when Vickie calls. She's at Logan Airport waiting for her flight. "I just had to call to find out what the guys are saying about last night's meeting," she says. "Do you think that maybe we've given them something to think about?"

I laugh. "You did a lot better than that, Vickie. The whole bunch of them were waiting for me when I got here this morning. They want to get started right away."

"That's great! I can't wait 'til I get back on Tuesday," she says.

"It may seem great to you, but what do I tell them between now and Tuesday?"

"Tell them to get started. There's plenty of preliminary work to be done."

"What do you suggest that we do first?" I ask her.

"Oh, no," she says. "You figure it out for yourself. It's all laid out for you. Just remember the three B's. I've got to run now, Larry. My plane is boarding. Bye—see you Tuesday." She's gone.

After the staff is gathered in my office, I tell Helen that we are not to be disturbed under any conditions. "How does the output look for this week, Joe?" I ask.

"We're going to be all right, but we have to work final inspection over tonight. All of the scheduled shipments will be on that truck if we have to tie and gag the truck driver," he says.

"Does anybody have any ideas on how to get started? Do we drop checkpoint scheduling cold, or do we phase it out gradually?

"When a patient has blood poisoning and the doctor decides to amputate, he doesn't do it a little at a time. He makes one big, clean cut," say Gary. Toni shudders at the thought.

"But doesn't the doctor make sure that safeguards are in place so the patient won't die?" I ask.

"You're right," he says. "We will need something to use during the transition."

I don't like it, but I say it. "Continue posting throughput to checkpoints for at least another week. That's how we'll play it—one week at a time."

"There's a lot to do. The best place to begin is with the three B's—Bottlenecks, Buffers, and Batches." That's what she told me, so I say it, hoping to stimulate some action.

Joe saves me. "There may be three B's, but the whole concept centers around only one of them—the one that makes so much sense to me. Bottlenecks govern what the plant can produce. We must start with our bottlenecks," he says.

"Damned right," say Ernie and Dean in unison, as Toni and Gary nod their heads.

"That is the logical place to start. Somebody make a list of our bottlenecks on the board," I say. Nobody volunteers.

"Then we know what we have to do, don't we? All of you work on the problem and come to Monday's staff meeting with a list of the bottlenecks in our plant."

"How will we determine what the bottlenecks are?" asks Toni.

I think of that traffic jam at the Celtics game. "One way is to look for a pileup of inventory. There's sure to be a bottleneck in the immediate vicinity."

"Why don't we ask the first-line supervisors and the production control people which machines are the most trouble for them?" suggests Gary.

"You mean Pareto's law? You know—the one that states that ninety-five percent of the wealth is held by ten percent of the population, and so forth," says Dean.

"That's it," says Gary, "—the old ABC principle. I'll bet that our people spend most of their time on only a few machines. Those are the bottlenecks."

"As Joe said last night, he asked twenty people where they got their schedules, and thirteen of them said that they never got one. I'll bet anybody in this room right now that those thirteen scheduleless people do not work at bottlenecks," I say.

"I've got some pretty good ideas about where the bottlenecks are just from listening to the foremen bitch. Sometimes it's nearly impossible to get a die for preventative maintenance. They want it back in five minutes," says Dean.

"I think we are definitely on the right track. The way to find the bottlenecks is to let your imagination loose on the problem. I'll let you all go back to work now, but first, as promised. . . ." I hand each of them a gift certificate. "I hope that Helen got all of your favorite eating spots right," I say. "Enjoy an evening out with your wives, or in Toni's case, boy friend. It may be the last one for awhile. We've got a lot of work to do."

CHAPTER 20

Saturday morning is the first time in days that I've been able to sit down and go through my mail. There's the usual hodgepodge of monthly reports from corporate and the computer room, and a letter from my successor in finance, Scott Crotty. The letter is addressed to all plant managers to let them know that inventory will be a big concern this year. Attached to Scott's letter is a copy of a handwritten note from Arthur King. It says, "Scotty—Inventory is becoming a terrible drain on the company. Let's get it down."

Before I leave the plant to take a look at the new condo, the phone rings. It's Toni. "Hello, Larry. Still at it?"

"Just going through my mail. I'm leaving now."

"I just thought that if you haven't got anything planned for this evening, I'd like you to be that boy friend you told me to take to dinner," she says.

I'm surprised that she doesn't get tired of seeing me all day long, but I haven't had a better offer today—or yesterday for that matter. "I'd like that, Toni. What time shall I pick you up?"

"I'll be ready at seven," she says.

The condo is perfect. Gary has done a good job. There's a large living area, complete with fireplace, looking out over a small lake. The kitchen is small but efficient-looking, with an eating bar separating the work area from the dining table. Off to one side of the living area there's the master bedroom with bath. The other bedroom is in the form of a sleeping loft accessed by a circular stairway. Very cozy—I make a mental note to bring some of my things up Monday.

Toni is ready at seven, as promised. I always thought she was attractive, but I've never seen her dressed up before. She's a knockout—definitely a ten plus.

We go to the Hampshire House in Boston for a nice dinner, and then to a nightclub for drinks and the show. It's really good to get away from reality for a few hours, and Toni is great company. The evening flies.

During the drive back to her apartment, I ask her, "Why did you ask me out? You see me all day. I'll bet that you could take your pick of guys."

"That's what I did, Larry," she answers.

"I'm flattered, and I hope that you weren't disappointed this evening," I say.

"How could I be disappointed being with you, Larry? We've got so much in common. We're both bean-counters, we're both from Harvard, and we both love our work. We talk the same language, you and I. The only thing I'm disappointed about is the fact that I had to be the one who asked for the date," she says.

"You know how it is. We've been so busy lately, and we do have a business relationship—appearances must be maintained."

When we get to her apartment she asks me in for a nightcap. We spend a little time putting the finishing touches on a fine evening, and the temperature is rising. I get the feeling that she wants me to stay, but discretion rules. I leave just before it gets too heavy.

CHAPTER 21

Joe is not there when staff begins. We wait ten minutes and begin without him. "Gary, do you have the output results for last week?" I ask.

"We made it. We're back on schedule again, although it was pretty late Friday night when we got the last of it on the truck. We pushed so much up through the end of the line that it's going to be nip and tuck this week," he says, as Joe comes in.

"It's worse than that. I've been trying to get the X-ray technician up from Boston. We had a power outage sometime Sunday, and when they brought the lines back up, the surge blew something on our final X-ray inspection machine. Everything goes through that machine, and our output will be a fat zero until we get it fixed," Joe says.

"When can the repairman get here?" I ask.

"It's a message center. I told them that it was urgent that we get somebody up here pronto, but coming out of Boston, he's at least ninety minutes away. I've got my secretary staying right on it. She'll call down here as soon as she has something."

"I don't have to tell you that it's mandatory that we stay on schedule. Don't let happen what happened over in front of the laser weld when we had that problem. Keep the work flowing right up to the X-ray machine so that when it's fixed, the output will be sitting right there," I say.

"I don't get burned in the same place twice," says Joe. "The work will be there."

"Keep me posted. Now, back to the weekly measurements." I pause for a moment while I think. "I won't talk about the other measurements this week. I'm not sure yet which ones are productive and which ones aren't. Of course, you will all still do the things that need to be done to keep the factory going while we're in this transitional mode.

"Let's spend the rest of the meeting discussing our bottlenecks," I continue. I look about the room for a candidate to start the list. Toni looks extra nice to me this morning. "Toni, list your bottlenecks on the board, and if any of you have anything to add, feel free."

When it is finished, the list consists of eight suspected bottlenecks.

Grind Center	Heat Treat
Shot Blast	X-ray
Acid Dip	Braze Inspection
Tumble Blast	Hot Form

"Is that all of them?" I ask.

"It's difficult to be certain," says Ernie. "The pileup-of-inventory method doesn't tell us too much. There's lots of piles of inventory out in that factory."

"How can we be sure that we've got them all?" I ask.

"I think I can come up with a way using the computer," says Gary. "We have a resource planning program that we've never used, and I think it can be modified to do what we want. The program uses planned time to calculate percent utilization of a resource based on what our output schedule is. I could modify it so that I could tell it how many of everything there is in the factory and make the report tell us the utilization of our actual numbers."

"Do you mean that if the report says that resource XYZ was utilized more than one hundred percent, and we have told the program that we had eight XYZ's, it would mean that we have found a bottleneck?" asks Toni.

"That's right," says Gary. "By the same token, if the report showed utilization to be under one hundred percent, we'd have a noncritical resource."

"When we find bottlenecks, I think we should double check our data to be sure that our times and quantities are correct," says Ernie.

"It sounds like it might work. When can you have it ready to run?" I ask.

"There's a ton of data to put in. If we get right on it and work a couple of people over, I think it will be available on Thursday when we come to work," Gary says.

"We'll get back together on Thursday morning, then," I say. "Before we break up, there's a couple of bottlenecks on your list that I'd like to talk about briefly. I'm thinking about the Grind Center for one. Did you consider the fact that we're getting a lot more throughput now with the staggered breaks, quick setups, and pre-inspection?"

"Even with the added throughput, I think we should run it as a bottleneck. It's so close to one that if a person stays out for even one day, we can get behind schedule," says Joe.

"I'll buy that," I say. "The other one that's got me worried is X-ray. If you people are right and it's a true bottleneck, we are losing our shirt today!"

CHAPTER 22

We lost six hours yesterday because of that damned X-ray being down. If X-ray is a bottleneck, as the staff thinks it is, then we've lost six hours output. Thank God for Saturday and Sunday. We can work overtime and make it up, but it won't help us this week—pretty expensive, too.

Vickie calls from Cambridge. It's good to hear her voice. "I can't make it up there today," she says. "I've got to catch up on the two days I missed, but I just have to know how it's going. What have you done?"

"I took your advice and started with the three B's. Joe thought that we need to know where our bottlenecks are before we can do anything else."

"Good for Joe," says Vickie.

"We got a list of suspected bottlenecks together, and wouldn't you know it, one of the machines on our list blew up when we were having our meeting," I say.

Vickie laughs, "Murphy's law—Identifying your critical resources is definitely the right thing to do first, but it won't be easy."

"We realize that already. There are just more suspected bottlenecks out there than we expected. Gary came up with a plan that might just save us a bunch of time," I say.

"Good. I hope it works. Larry, how would you like to have dinner with me tonight at Loch Ober?"

This is the second time in just a few nights that I've been asked out by a beautiful woman. Can it be the new cologne I'm wearing? "What's the occasion?" I ask.

"There's someone I'd like you to meet. You'll be pleasantly surprised," she answers.

"Man or woman?"

"It's a man. Can you bring Toni with you to sort of even things up?"

"I'll ask her."

"If I don't hear from you, I'll assume that she's coming. Gotta run, Larry. I'm late for an appointment. See you about seven—bye."

Toni is no problem at all. In fact she seems delighted when I ask her. The only thing she doesn't like is the fact that we have to drive all the way to Boston by seven. I give her the rest of the afternoon off. You know how women are. It won't take me long. I've moved most of my things into the condo already.

Loch Ober is an elegant restaurant at the end of a hard-to-find alley, right in the heart of downtown Boston. Until a few years ago it was off limits to women. The libbers picketed the place, and management gave a little. Women are now allowed on the upper floors, but the main room on the ground floor is still barred to them. They say that wars have been fought and empires won and lost in that room. As the maitre 'd leads us to the elevator, I can't help staring at Toni. She is gorgeous tonight.

Vickie and her friend are already in the private dining room when we enter. She gives us a hug and kiss. "I've already told MX all about both of you. This is MX Cullen," she says.

A tall, thin, but ruddy-looking individual grabs my hand and almost breaks it off. "Howdy, Larry," he says with a silly grin.

He quickly turns his attention to Toni—can't blame him for that. I hope he doesn't shake her hand—he'll kill her. My worries are for naught. He takes her hand gently in his and bends to kiss the back of it. "Vickie, you didn't tell me that Toni was so beautiful. I think I'm in love."

Toni appears to be embarrassed, but it passes quickly as we settle into our chairs. The waiter comes with a large silver pot filled with coffee and the wine list. We order drinks, but MX says he'll stick with the coffee. "I've nothing against alcohol, it's just that I don't like it," he apologizes.

As the drinks are served, Toni starts the conversation. "What does MX stand for?"

"My Ma named me Matthew X Cullen. There's no period after the X because it's not an initial. It's my middle name. Ma thought it was cute, I guess. When I was at Oklahoma U., I played on the football team as a kick-return man. Some sportswriter wrote that I ran kickoffs back like an unguided missle. MX Cullen became the MX missile. It's stuck with me ever since. I don't mind it—sets me off from the crowd."

"MX is a computer geek," says Vickie. "He majored in computer science, and when he got out of college he went to work for an oil refinery in Tulsa. I want you to hear his story. Tell them, MX."

"I graduated at the top of my class," he begins. "Lexicon Oil was recruiting, and they made me an offer that I couldn't refuse. When I first saw the refinery I almost turned around and ran. Did you ever see a big refinery? It's an ugly looking collection of pipes going every which way, all rusty and dirty, running over, under, and through hundreds of tanks and buildings. Until that moment I'd never really thought much about a refinery before. Do any of you know how many products they make?"

I try it. "I imagine that there are quite a few: gasoline, both high- and low-test, leaded and unleaded, motor oil, heating oil, diesel oil, and kerosene."

MX picks it up again. "You're barely scratching the surface. There are hundreds of petroleum based products—but you get the idea. That terrible-looking maze of pipes and tanks somehow turns out all kinds of petroleum products, starting with crude oil. Did you ever see crude oil? It's black and slimy, and it stinks to high heaven. Starting with that dirty stuff, taking away this and adding that in the correct proportions, at the right temperature and pressure, at precisely the right time, that black mess gets changed into the products that we see every day.

"They wanted me to develop a computer program that would

help them schedule the entire refinery. They put me in an office with a large window overlooking that collection of pipes—kind of a think tank. I sat at the terminal. I stared out the window. I studied the specs. I changed the plant layout. I went crazy. I couldn't find the key. I felt like I was taking their money under false pretenses.

"One day I got stuck in a traffic jam at the toll plaza on the Will Rogers Turnpike. It was ridiculous—hundreds of cars trying to get through six coin booths. I watched the senseless traffic patterns, the timid and the brave drivers, and I could hear and smell all of the gas and oil being wasted by the hundreds of cars and trucks that were competing for the six spots. I thought that if they could be scheduled there would be no tie-up, no wasted energy, nothing but a smooth flow on both sides of the toll booth." He stops to refill his coffee cup.

Vickie says, "Larry and I know exactly what you mean. We were in a similar situation not long ago at a Celtics game. Remember, Larry, we were saying the same thing. We talked about scheduling the arrival of cars at the parking lot and decided that it would be impossible because of the amount of variables like stop lights, routes taken, dinner stops, other traffic jams, and so forth."

"I remember," I say. "We missed most of the game because of it."

MX continues, "It was that traffic jam that gave me the key I was looking for. The key was to control the flow through the limiting resources, and it was all downhill after that. Just by relating all of the problems of the refinery to that toll booth I was able to come up with a tool that could make millions—no, billions of dollars. It took me a couple of years, but when I was done, my program not only scheduled the entire refinery, but it told them where their problems were, where they could make improvements to increase their output. It was different from anything they expected. When I showed it to them and showed them how changing things like pipe diameters and tank capacity could triple their sales while reducing operating expense simultaneously, they didn't want any part of it. I think that they wanted to see a schedule that looked just like their manual one, but on computer paper. They told me to take my program and my radical ideas and leave. I got fired. They thought I was nuts, I guess."

The waiter comes with the menu and we order dinner.

I'm intrigued with MX's story. "What happened to that program of yours?" I ask.

"I had some contacts from my football days—alumni, you know. I pounded the pavement in search of some place to try out my ideas. I even prepared a snappy presentation. Finally, to make a long, frustrating experience short, I made contact with a company that was building a new refinery. I showed them what I had. They were impressed enough to want to buy it. We made a deal. I got company stock for my software, and I stayed on to help them until they got rolling. It took several years and lots of hard work, changing subroutines, massaging the design, and making false starts, but they stuck with me and I stuck with them."

"How did it all come out?" I ask.

"The oil company I sold my software to is Ocal," says MX.

"Ocal is the biggest oil company in America," I say.

"How about Lexicon, the company that fired MX?" asks Vickie. "That company no longer exists. Ocal bought them out."

"I made a good deal with the stock—good enough so that I'll never need to work again," says MX.

Our meals are served. My lobster Savannah is superb, although one person couldn't possible eat it all, at least not me. I look at MX's plate. He had the same thing. It's all gone. I guess that missiles use up a lot of fuel. Toni and Vickie seem to be enjoying themselves.

MX starts the conversation up again when the dessert comes. "I may never need to work again, but I couldn't survive if I'm not doing something. I got a grant to work on adapting my software so that it can be applied to industries other than oil. My theory is that all of manufacturing in this country is tied up in a huge traffic jam, and that's one of the main reasons why Japan is beating the crap out of us. My goal in life is to use my algorithms to make the good old US of A number one again."

"A noble goal, MX," I say. "You've got a long journey ahead of you."

"They say that one cannot take a long journey without taking the first step. Would you like to take the first step with me, Larry?"

"What do you mean?" I ask, puzzled.

Vickie joins the conversation. "It's time that I filled you in, Larry. I've been working with MX at Harvard, helping him with his work while I work toward my MBA. Most of the ideas that I've suggested to you have come from MX."

"No, Vickie," says MX. "Your contributions have been significant. I wouldn't be anywhere near where I am without you. If I'm what you call a computer geek, then you're a manufacturing geek."

Vickie smiles and continues, "I've taken the liberty of telling MX why you are running the plant up in Salem. I hope that you don't mind."

I'm really disturbed. Although there are no rules, I've chosen to keep the competition a secret. Vickie, as far as I know, is the only one outside of Arthur and Marty who knows. I feel that she has betrayed me, but what can I do about it? "I hope that you had a good reason," I say.

"I can't tell you the whole reason yet, but it's partly because I know that we can win this thing, and it's important that MX knows what the stakes are." she says.

I notice that she said "we can win this thing". She considers herself a part of the competition, a part of my team. Toni brings me up short.

"Am I missing something? You folks know something that I don't. What's the big secret?" she asks.

What the hell—no sense not telling her. After I explain the whole thing I say, "I would appreciate it if the information never leaves this room."

"Now that the air is cleared, how about it, Larry? I need a beta site and you need a victory. We need each other. There's no limit to what we can accomplish. We can bury Murfreesboro," MX pleads.

"Let me sleep on it, MX. Sounds intriguing, but the bean-counter in me won't let me leap before I look. I'll let you know in a day or two," I say.

"Fair enough," he says.

As we finish up our dessert and enjoy an after-dinner drink—MX has more coffee—the conversation turns to the plant.

"What are you doing now to win the race with Murfreesboro?" MX asks.

"I'm doing everything I can to make the plant more productive, but to tell the truth, some of the things I've been doing have holes in them. That's what I've learned from Vickie and you already."

"What is productivity, Larry?" he asks.

I've got to think about that one—never tried to put a definition on it before. "I guess productivity would be the tendency to produce something, and improving productivity would be the tendency to produce more of that something," I say.

"Excellent, Larry. How do you know that you are working toward productivity improvements in your plant?" he asks.

"Up until now we have been keeping track of certain goals—things like output, efficiency, overtime, scrap, inventory, and schedule adherence, but since Vickie's debate the other night, we have our doubts," I say.

"Vickie told me about that debate. That was an excellent idea on your part. You just said that productivity is the tendency to produce something. Put a word on it. What is that thing you want to produce?" he asks.

"Turbine blades, of course," I answer.

"No, that is not the answer. If you produced more turbine blades and needed to work all kinds of overtime, invest in more inventory, and create more scrap to do it, would that be more productivity?" he asks.

"That wouldn't happen. We measure things like overtime, scrap, and inventory. We would keep it under control. We would look at our efficiencies and make sure that they were staying up there too," I say.

"Then what you are saying is that if you improve efficiencies, you improve productivity," he says.

"Yes," I say. "In fact, efficiency measurements are tied directly to the corporate-wide productivity formula. We are number one in the entire group right now."

"Then you have nothing to worry about. You must be ahead of Murfreesboro," MX says.

"There's a lot more to it than that," I say. "I've sat in on countless meetings with plant managers. They review their businesses one on one with the corporate staff on a quarterly basis. They all have the same graphs to show. I can recite them in my sleep. Head count, overtime, efficiency, effectiveness, shop costs, scrap rates, checkpoint adherence, investment. That's what will determine who wins this thing. Arthur King will have some complicated formula on that piece of paper in his safe, a formula that combines all of the things that a plant is measured on into one number. I've got to keep all of those things as high as I can get them."

"The problem you are running into right now defeats you, doesn't it? You are finding that to improve one of those measurements, you must undermine one or more of the others." says MX.

"That's true," I say. "But there must be a key, like the key you discovered in that traffic jam in Oklahoma. I've just got to find out what that is."

"You are about to," says MX, confidently. "Did Arthur King tell you to run your plant like it was your own business?"

"He did," I say.

"Productivity improvements, as you know them, are fine as long as you make them in terms of your main objective for being in business. Why would anybody open a business, Larry?" he asks.

"That's easy," I say, "—to make a living."

"And in order to make a living, what is it that you must produce with your plant?" he asks.

"Money," I say.

Vickie has been waiting for quite a while. She gives me a round of applause.

"You now have the key. It's all downhill from here. Just make every decision with your goal in mind. The goal of any manufacturing organization is to make money. That is the only goal. The other things are ways to achieve that goal." says MX.

"Then efficiency may be a negative measurement. If I keep people efficient without asking myself the question, 'Are they making money?' I may be losing money. That's pretty hard to determine, though, isn't it?" I ask.

"You need a way to relate making money to the everyday operations of the plant. There are three important things to consider. Let me tell you what they are. First, increased saleable output; second, lower inventory; and third, lower operating expenses. Watch those three simultaneously and do nothing that helps one of them while hurting either of the other two, and you will make money. In fact, good business decisions will optimize all three at the same time."

I think about my checkpoint measurement and the truth of what MX is saying becomes crystal clear. "Getting on checkpoints makes me work more overtime, which is an operating expense; creates idle time, which is another operating expense; and increases the hell out of the inventory. It may not even increase output. I see what you mean."

"Then you have learned a valuable lesson tonight—so valuable, in fact, that I'm going to let you pick up the check," he says.

As we are leaving, MX asks, "Would you mind dropping Vickie off for me?"

"No, not at all," I answer. "Are you pressed for time?"

"No, but I'm going to take Toni home, if she agrees to go with me," he says.

I look at Toni. I can tell she's all for it. She's looking at MX the way schoolgirls used to look at Elvis.

CHAPTER 23

I drop in on Toni to say good morning. The girl's on cloud nine. "You and MX hit it off pretty good last night," I say.

She smiles and says, "He has some kind of charisma about him. I can't explain it, but it's like a magnet."

I could tell her what it is, but I'll let her discover love for herself. It's always better that way. "Toni, I want to remind you not to say a word about the competition."

"Don't give it another thought. Your secret is safe with me," she says.

Vickie arrives while I'm discussing the X-ray makeup plan with Joe and Gary. "All of the parts we need for the week are sitting right in front of X-ray right now," says Gary.

Joe says, "We need to X-ray, then polish and stamp before we box and ship. Polish and stamp is done by a robot. It takes the little monster exactly two minutes per part, so we know exactly how many we can get out—four hundred eighty in two shifts. We've got three days left, which will get us fourteen hundred and forty. That will leave us about three sixty short. We'll cheat a little bit, get them by midafternoon on Saturday, and ship them by premium transportation. They'll definitely get to the customers on time."

"May I ask a stupid question?" says Vickie.

Gary is ever the gentleman. "There are no stupid questions—only stupid answers."

Vickie smiles, "I was wondering how long it takes X-ray to process the parts. Don't we have it on our suspected bottleneck list?"

"It averages thirty an hour when it's running. That's tight, but it should be all right," says Joe.

"That is a manual operation, isn't it?" she says.

"Partly," says Gary. "The loading, unloading, and reading the X-rays are the manual elements, while the actual X-ray machine itself is fully automated."

"I want to be sure we get everything out. Joe, you put Lennie Seboy at X-ray and tell him to stay right there and keep a log of throughput," I say.

After they leave, Vickie shakes her head. "What's troubling you?" I ask.

"I'll bet you ten dollars that you won't ship on Saturday—unless you bring in the second shift also," she says.

"Everything adds up. What makes you think we won't make it?" I ask.

"I have a hunch," she says.

"I'll tell you what. I'll make it even better. I'll give you odds—your ten against a night on the town." This is the safest bet I've ever made. I can't lose if Joe and Gary have figured right, and if they haven't, I get to go out with Vickie.

"You're on, but I'm already making plans for that night out," she says.

So, she thinks that she's made a good bet too. I change the subject. "Vickie, you didn't tell me about King Arthur."

Her eyes shine with love. "You should see him run, Larry. We've got a champion. I just know it."

"That good, huh?" I say.

"There isn't a horse at Connecticut Yankee that's as big as he is. There isn't a horse in Kentucky that can run as fast as he can, and there isn't a horse in the whole world as beautiful as he is," she says.

I laugh at her unbridled enthusiasm. "You aren't going overboard, are you, Vickie?"

"No, I'm not," she answers quickly. "When you see him run in two weeks, you'll become a believer. You wait."

"What do you mean when I see him run in two weeks? How is that going to happen?" I ask.

She simmers down to say, "Oh, I forgot to tell you—you're invited to see King Arthur make his racing debut at Keeneland two weeks from this coming Saturday. Arthur is expecting you."

"There's so much to do here at the plant," I say. "But I would like to go. When you get a chance, tell Helen what your flight plans are so she can make the same reservations for me."

"No need of that," she says. "MX is going too, and he's flying his private jet."

"Arthur King and MX should hit it off right well," I say. "They'll make an unorthodox pair, won't they?"

"They're odd, but alike in a lot of ways," she says. "By the way, have you thought much about MX's proposal?"

"Constantly," I tell her. "I've decided to listen to what he has to say. I'll call him tomorrow and set something up." Vickie is delighted.

After a nice dinner at the Red Carpet, I spend the night at the condo to catch up on some paper work and just relax. The next morning, it's Thursday and the bottleneck reports that Gary is working on are due out. I set up a meeting with the staff. Gary brings a computer report about four inches thick.

"I hope that isn't a list of our bottlenecks," I say jokingly.

Gary doesn't think my remark is funny. "That's the way it came out. Every single resource in this plant is a bottleneck."

"Garbage in—garbage out," says Dean.

"Yes, obviously something is wrong with your data," I say. "Have you figured it out yet?"

"I just picked this report up on my way here—haven't had time," Gary answers.

"Then let's analyze the data together. Maybe we can come up with something," I say. "What did you input?"

"The file consists of every operation in the plant. Attached to each part number is our manufacturing plan, which consists mostly of orders and some forecasts."

"Did you double check the manufacturing plan to be sure you're not double dipping?" asks Toni.

"I went over it with a fine-tooth comb," says Gary. "There are two bits of information attached to every operation—the resource where the work is done, and the time per piece. It's the same data that we work with every day."

"Does anyone see anything wrong so far?" I ask.

"Where did you take the time per piece from?" asks Toni.

"Right off of the planning sheets," answers Gary.

"Then I know what the problem is," she says. "You used the same time that is making us two hundred percent efficient. The time is inflated—I'll bet the report tells us we need twice as many machines as we have."

"It varies," says Gary as he thumbs through the report.

Joe seizes the chance to ride Gary. "Your report is useless, melonhead."

"No, it's not," says Toni. "Gary, can you retrieve efficiency reports by resource from some other program?"

"I'm sure that it's readily available," he answers.

"How long would it take you to modify your bottleneck program so that the time per part gets divided by the efficiency rating for the particular resource where the work is done?" she asks.

"That will work. Great! Give me two hours," he says.

We meet again two hours later. I don't expect to see Gary with that sad look on his face any longer, but I'm wrong. It's worse. "How did it come out this time?" I ask.

"Piss poor," says Gary dejectedly. "Now there are no bottlenecks. Everything is utilized at a rate of less than one hundred percent. This report is useless."

"Wait a minute," I say. "Do we all agree that the input data is right?"

They all agree that it looks good. "Then we're not putting garbage in and we should not get garbage out—right, Dean?"

Dean nods his head.

"Let's assume that the report is right for the moment. What is it telling us?" I say.

"It's telling us that we don't have any bottlenecks in this plant," says Joe.

Ernie interrupts. "No, the bottlenecks are there. It's just that we are not utilizing them to their capacity."

"Why?" I ask. "Something is preventing us from getting the most out of this plant. What is it?"

"The bottleneck in this plant does not show on that report," says Toni. "Our bottleneck is the manufacturing plan. We don't schedule enough to maximize output. It's the checkpoint system biting us again."

"Very astute of you, Toni," I say. "What you mean is that the static ship schedule we have on our checkpoint sheets only allows so much to be done during each time period—right?"

"That's right," she continues. "We can't get the most out of the plant because we can't adapt our static schedule to the dynamic world."

"And that's why we are here right now. We know that we need something better. How can we use this data Gary has amassed for us so that we can make progress?" I ask.

Toni has taken leadership. "Why don't we figure out what the highest-utilized resources are? They should be the bottlenecks—at least for starters."

"How many do we want to control?" says Ernie.

"I don't think we need to dictate a number. Why don't we take the top one, and match it against a list of our products. Cross off all of the part numbers that go through it, then go to the second highest-utilized resource and do the same thing. Continue on that way until all of the part numbers are accounted for, and we should have a pretty good bottleneck identification," she says.

"Then we'll have at least one pacing resource for every product we make," says Joe. "Sounds like it will work."

"A lot of the parts will go through more than one bottleneck, though," says Dean.

"There's nothing wrong with that," says Toni. "If that's the way the real world is, that's what we need to know."

"It'll take me a while to get that done," says Gary. "How about Monday's staff?"

"I suppose, with our regular work and the output crunch we've got this week, Monday will be soon enough. Good job, Gary," I say as the meeting breaks up. I'm extremely impressed with Toni's input. That girl amazes me.

CHAPTER 24

Vickie and Toni are with us as I take MX on a Saturday morning tour of the plant. He carries a small tape recorder to which he speaks from time to time—beats taking notes, especially on a tour. The factory is a lot quieter on Saturday, making it much easier to talk. I conduct the tour, as MX requests, taking the same route as the parts do—from issue to ship. He says he can visualize better this way.

Whenever MX talks to his recorder, I try to see what he's looking at. Most of the time it's a pile of inventory. "Does the position of the inventory give you any ideas?" I ask.

"It reminds me of the refinery when a large pipe fed a small one. It needed fixing, but I don't have anything definite yet."

I show them the grind center, my pride and joy. It's empty this morning, for the first time in weeks. It gives me a sense of satisfaction as I explain what we've accomplished. I give Vickie most of the credit—she deserves it.

After I've finished telling MX about the changes, he says, "You left out the most important change of all. You have the workers functioning as a team. You must do more of that."

We continue our tour, following the route of the parts flow, stopping here and there to discuss machines and processes, until we arrive at the X-ray area.

Lennie Seboy is there, as I instructed, looking worried. "Are we going to make it?" I ask.

"We've got an outside chance, Larry. But we won't make it without the second shift. I've already called them and managed to get full coverage even though it's short notice—good people," he answers.

I glance at Vickie. That smart-ass has an "I told you so" grin from ear to ear. She knew.

I take the log sheets for Wednesday through Friday from Lennie's clipboard and return to my office.

Vickie has to get the first word in. "Where are we going tonight, Larry?"

"What's this?" says Toni.

"It's a bet we made about this week's output. When Lennie called in the second shift, I automatically lost," I tell her.

I look at Vickie. "You knew all along, didn't you, smart-ass?"

"I love betting on sure things," she answers as she goes to the board. "I haven't seen those sheets you've got in your hands, but I can write numbers down on this board that will be pretty close to what actually happened." She writes down sixteen numbers.

0 12 36 40 36 35 30 15 0 12 40 36 40 35 30 15

"The sixteen numbers represent output for the sixteen hours worked at X-ray," she says

I look at the log for Wednesday. The numbers are slightly different, but the zeros are in the same places. She's pretty damned close to perfect. I glance at the Thursday and Friday sheets. They show pretty much the same patterns of numbers. "Where are you hiding the crystal ball?" I ask.

"It's the way the manufacturing engineers set the job up," she says. "The flow keeps getting disrupted on a regular basis." She points to the zeros.

I'm not all that upset. There's a lesson here someplace. "You'll have to run that one by me again," I say.

"Me, too," says MX. "For a minute there, I thought you were going to talk about statistical fluctuations."

"There's some of that here too, but that isn't the main reason that we missed so badly," Vickie says. "You see, the X-ray operation is vouchered as one integral operation, although it really consists of several elements of work—load, unload, X-ray, and read. The problem is that there's only one voucher that accounts for all of those elements. If the workers don't complete all of the different elements for each piece that they start, they figure that they will be falsifying their work record."

"I can understand that," I say.

"That's why the flow is so poor," she continues. "When the first shift comes to work, there are no parts in the X-ray machine. They start loading them, but the process time through the machine is one hour. Nothing comes out until at least one hour after the shift starts. The workers keep loading the machine to keep it full, until they stop loading it about an hour and a half before the end of their shift, so that they can complete the entire operation for all of the parts that they've started. This means that the machine is once again empty for the second shift. The cycle starts all over again."

I see the solution immediately. "All we need to do is separate the X-ray job into two operations, so that the workers can leave the machine loaded with things that they can voucher as loaded. The next shift can take credit for unloading what the previous shift did not voucher."

"That's right," says Vickie. "Just separate load and unload and the problem of flow through X-ray will be eliminated. You won't see that zero output the first hour of every shift."

"The second hour isn't much better," says Toni.

"That's a different problem that has to do with fluctuations around the average, but this is Saturday—no more lessons," says Vickie. "Have you decided where you're taking me tonight, Larry?"

"Why don't you come with MX and me?" says Toni. "We're going to a club to see a show. I think that Godfrey Cambridge is appearing. He's funny."

"Oh, I like him. How about it, Larry?" Vickie asks.

What can I say? I lost the bet. "Sounds fine to me."

"It's all set, then," says MX. "Larry, you pick up Toni on the way and meet us in Cambridge about six."

Now I know what that Oklahoma sportswriter was talking about when he called MX an unguided missile. We leave my T'bird in Cambridge and use his car. He drives to Logan Airport where he keeps his plane. We see Godfrey Cambridge all right—in a nightclub on Broadway in Manhattan. We fly down, see the show, and end up back in Boston at about 1:00 A.M. That's not enough for one night. Now he's got us in some lounge halfway between Boston and the New Hampshire line. I've had too much to drink to drive the T'bird back to Salem. It's a good thing that MX doesn't drink. I'd hate to trust my life to a drunk unguided missile. I lost count of the bourbon and gingers, but if one ounce an hour is enough I'll be drunk for about a week. The last thing I remember is leaning against a piano while MX is playing an old Harvard drinking song that we all know. Vickie and Toni are on either side of me, trying to keep me on my feet while we sing.

I wake to find myself in bed in the condo. I can't remember getting here or how I managed to get into my pajamas, but here I am. My head feels like there's a Tasmanian devil in there with a hammer, trying to get out. I need coffee so bad that I can almost smell it. Wait a minute—I *can* smell it!

I get up very slowly, so as not to antagonize that Tasmanian devil, and go to the kitchen. It's Vickie. She looks lost in a pair of my pajamas. I've seen that trick pulled in the movies a few times, and the heroine always looks so cute in the hero's big 'jammies. Vickie looks cute too.

My mind just won't function without coffee in the morning. Vickie puts a cup in my hand, and I thank her for saving my life, while I hold my head with the other hand. "How the hell did I get here?"

"You were pretty incoherent," she says. "MX dropped us off before he took Toni home. He never came back." She takes a sip of coffee and smiles. "It was a great night, wasn't it?"

"The part that I can remember was," I tell her. "It's what happened after we sang at the piano that's got me worried. It's a complete blank. How the hell did I get undressed?"

Vickie winks at me and smiles, "I repeat, it was a great night, Larry." She leans across the bar and gives me a kiss.

"You didn't—I didn't—Oh, crap." That's all I can say.

Vickie seems happy as she hums that drinking song. "If you'd had some food in this place, I'd have made you breakfast in bed."

I'm embarrassed all to hell. I fumble for the right words. "Uh—I'm sorry, Vickie, for what happened last night—trouble is, I can't remember if we—"

Vickie laughs aloud. "You have absolutely nothing to be sorry about—nothing. I enjoyed everything about last night." She leans over and kisses me again.

It must have been great, but I can't remember a damned thing. What a lousy feeling.

She lets me stew for awhile before she breaks the spell. "You're funny when you're boffo, Larry. Nothing happened last night. MX carried you in and put you to bed. I slept up in the loft. I had to borrow a pair of your pajamas, though."

I feel both relieved and disappointed at the same time. "Then why did you kiss me this morning?" I ask.

"Because I wanted to," she answers.

A couple of phone calls later we realize that my car, as well as Vickie's and MX's, are all in Cambridge. We spend most of what is left of Sunday playing musical cars to get people and vehicles where they belong.

CHAPTER 25

The hangover is gone this morning. It was a rough Sunday, but I'm feeling much better. Got to let Vickie know that I'm not a drinking man. It's important.

At staff I introduce MX as a consultant from Harvard who is going to help us develop our new scheduling tool.

I start with the usual—output. "Joe, give me the output for the week."

"We made it, but it was late Saturday night. That damned robot isn't getting the parts out as fast as it's supposed to. It's not as reliable as your usual robot," he says.

That's my cue. "It wasn't the robot at all," I tell him. "We've screwed ourselves by the way we've routed the parts." I proceed to tell the staff what Vickie explained Saturday. When everybody understands the problem, I say, "I want load and unload to be separate operations effective immediately. We should never see the X-ray machine devoid of parts again."

I change the subject. "Gary, how did you make out with that bottleneck analysis?"

"Pretty good. There are only four resources that meet the conditions. It's complex though, the way that the parts flow through them at different times and from different places. The four resources are: grind center, turret lathes, shot blast, and hand deburr."

"That sounds like something we can get our hands around," I say. "Along with ship, which Toni says is the real bottleneck, we have five."

"What's our next move?" Joe asks.

"If everything we've learned up to this point is to make any sense, it seems to me that we must maximize throughput at those five resources. I think that we'll show some improvement just by concentrating on that alone, while we develop a full-fledged scheduling tool. Do you have any thoughts along that line, MX?"

"Just that I agree with you. It won't be simply a matter of keeping those five spots busy, though. You'll find that you will need to apply yourselves at the noncritical resources, where the other two B's will come into play—buffers and batches. If you don't, you'll not be able to keep the bottlenecks fully utilized."

"Then, here's the game plan," I say. "First, let's double check the time and routing data on the critical resources to be sure they're accurate. If they are, we can assume that we've got a starting point. Remember, folks, output is the name of the game."

"We'll need some new measurements, then," says Gary.

"You're absolutely right," I say. "What shall they be?"

"We must still measure output," says Toni.

"That goes without saying," I answer.

"How about inventory and overtime?" she asks.

"If we are trying to make money by increasing throughput while decreasing inventory and operating expense simultaneously, we'd better keep track of those things as well."

"Scrap is an operating expense, isn't it?" asks Ernie.

"We'll keep track of that too," I say. "Those are four of our six original measurements—that's good."

"I think that we should discontinue measuring the other two," says Joe. "But we need something else."

"What if we take the average ship rate for each product and apply it to the bottlenecks," offers Toni. "After all, we still need to average a week's work at every operation. The work isn't going to disappear."

"You mean that we measure throughput at the bottlenecks instead of the checkpoints. We could make out sheets that look like checkpoint sheets only they would track only the ship plan, the bottleneck operations and nothing else," says Joe. "I like it because it won't be much of a change in appearance from the old sheets."

"It may not look much different, but it will be," says Toni. "If the supervisors work overtime to stay on those checkpoints, they will just be increasing flow through the bottlenecks. It might just work."

"Then it's settled. Starting right now, we work on four old measurements—output, inventory, overtime, and quality—and add a new one, which will be throughput through critical resources. Is everybody straight on that?" I ask.

"It sounds good," Joe says. "I hope we haven't overlooked something."

"I'm sure that we have," I answer. "The important thing is that we've got a tool that should lower the inventory and uncover problems all over the place. When we find the problems we fix them. It should be an ongoing improvement program with no real end. In the meantime, MX will be working on a more formal system. I want all of you people to give him all the help you can. I feel that we're going to be proud of this place by the end of the year."

CHAPTER 26

"Ladies and gentleman, fasten your seat belts," quips MX as we taxi onto the runway at Logan. "Damn, there's bottlenecks everywhere we turn." He points to the long line of aircraft in front of us waiting to take off. "You would think that air traffic control could schedule better than this."

As we creep slowly toward the number one position for take-off, I close my eyes and think back on the last two weeks. It has been a hectic time. We've gone to a new system and a new measurement and have still managed to stay on schedule, while the overtime has actually dropped twelve percent—all in all, a good start. One problem surfaced in the stockroom. Gary said that there was nothing that told him what parts to issue, how many, and when to issue them. I couldn't come up with an answer on the spur of the moment, so I told him to mirror shipments, to issue whatever he shipped in the same quantities. I know that this decision is asinine on my part. It guarantees that the inventory can never decrease, but I need time to work it out.

I think about the four of us. Things change so fast. After that great date I had with Toni, I figured that there was something there that could develop, and I didn't mind a bit. She's a great gal. When Vickie called to invite me to Loch Ober and asked me to bring Toni, I assumed that she thought the same thing—except it didn't work out that way. If Vickie had designs on MX, she made a big mistake that night. Ever since they laid eyes on each other, MX and Toni have been inseparable—love at first sight. I look at the pair of them, MX piloting the plane and Toni beside him in the copilot's seat. Vickie and I are in the cheap seats behind them. I feel mixed emotions, happy for Toni and—I'll get over it.

Arthur King's limousine picks us up at the airport, which is directly across the highway from Keeneland, where King Arthur makes his racing debut tomorrow.

During the short trip to Connecticut Yankee Farm, I reflect on the major changes that have taken place in my life since I took this same ride exactly one year ago. I have a new job and a new outlook on business as a whole. Things in the real world are not at all what I imagined them to be when I sat in the ivory tower. No—they're different, but they couldn't be better. I've also got new friends, a new home, and a bright future, no matter what happens from here on in.

After we get settled, Vickie takes MX and Toni on a walking tour of the farm. I tag along. On our way back we pass King Arthur's stall, which is empty. "Where's the star of the show this evening?" I ask

"Arthur had him shipped over to Keeneland early. He's high-strung and has never been away from home before. We don't want him fractious at race time tomorrow. He'll calm down overnight," says Vickie.

"What if staying in a strange stall all night makes him more nervous?" asks Toni.

"It shouldn't. Statistics prove that horses run much better when they are brought to the track early," she answers.

The word "statistics" jogs my memory. "Forgive me for changing to more mundane matters, but you reminded me of something you mentioned a couple of weeks ago when you explained the X-ray problem. Remember? You said that statistical fluctuations were coming into play, but you didn't elaborate on it."

Vickie laughs. "Poor Larry, can't get your mind off your work, can you?"

"I'm sorry," I say. "It's just that you raised the question in my mind."

MX interrupts, "Go ahead and explain it to him, Vickie, or he won't be able to sleep all night."

Vickie takes a riding crop from where it hangs on the stable wall. I put up my hands in mock surrender. "Don't hit me. If you feel that strongly about it, forget it," I say.

My hands are about three feet too high to defend myself from the crack she gives me.

She uses the handle of the whip to draw a diagram on the smooth ground in front of the stalls.

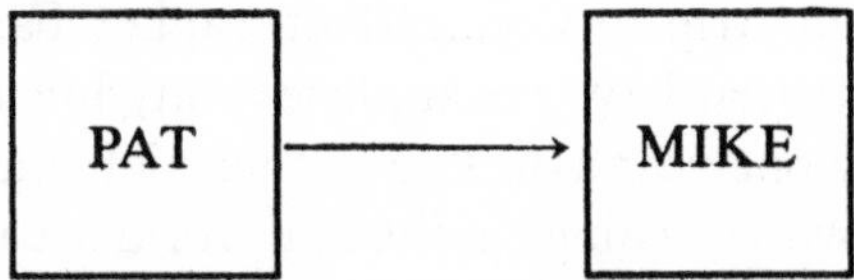

"Statistical fluctuations can kill you if you're not aware of them when you try to balance your plant," she begins. "Suppose that we have two workers, Pat and Mike. Pat performs a skilled manual operation—like hand grinding. Mike does nothing more than load the parts that Pat passes to him into an automatic machine—in other words, Mike's job is machine paced. Both of the jobs are planned for ten hours per part."

I'm smart. I've been learning all about this stuff for weeks. "That looks like a perfect situation—an assembly line. The flow will be nice and smooth," I say, but I should know better. This girl is always lulling me to sleep.

"Remember the old bell-shaped curve from school?" she continues.

Toni, MX, and I all shudder. Toni says it for us, "How I hated that subject."

"Let's look at the distribution curve for both Pat and Mike," says Vickie. She draws a couple of bells on the ground. One is much broader than the other.

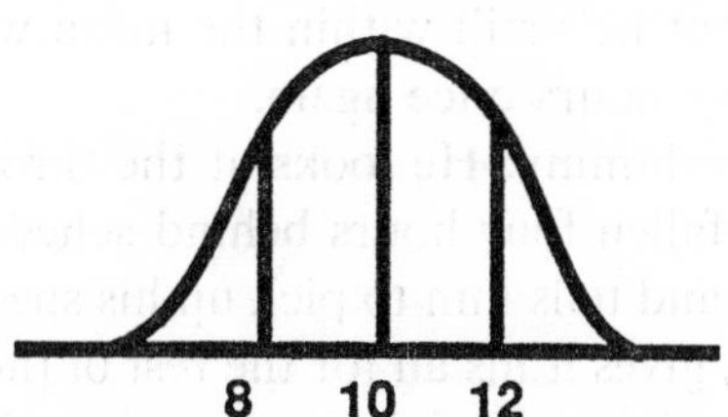

"Pat's distribution of time per piece falls mainly between plus and minus two hours with an average of ten. That's what you would expect of a manual operation," she says.

"That's true," I say. "People are not robots."

"How about Mike?" she continues. "He runs a machine-paced operation so his distribution of time is right on ten all the time."

I agree with that. Machine times do not fluctuate. "According to the principal of the bell-shaped curve, Pat will average ten hours per piece, but his time will fluctuate from as low as eight hours to as high as twelve hours. Mike will always get the parts out in exactly ten hours. I can't see anything wrong with it yet," I say.

MX is disinterested, patting one of the horses, while Toni is with us, paying close attention.

"So much for statistics," says Vickie. "What happens in the real world goes like this. On Monday morning, Pat is given a schedule for the week." We move down the shed row to give Vickie more smooth ground to write on.

Part	Pat Sched.	Pat Actual
1.	0 - 10	0 - 12
2.	10 - 20	12 - 24
3.	20 - 30	24 - 32
4.	30 - 40	32 - 40

Vickie puts the finishing touches on her chart and continues. "Pat has a bad hangover on Monday. He's probably been out with MX. It takes him a while to get going and he never does feel right all day long. Nevertheless, he makes the supreme effort and finishes that first part in twelve hours, within his allowable deviation. He goes home and has a fight with his girl friend. It's on his mind the next day and it affects his work, but he's still within the mean when he does the second part in twelve hours once again.

"Now, Pat's foreman is no dummy. He looks at the throughput sheets and sees that Pat has fallen four hours behind schedule. He makes sure that Pat knows it and tells him to pick up his speed. Pat, being a conscientious worker, gives it his all for the rest of the week. He finishes both parts three and four in eight hours apiece. What is the net result?"

I look at the chart. "Pat did one hell of a job. Despite all of his trials and tribulations he was able to get the work out on time. That's the kind of employee I want in my factory."

"I don't think that you do," says Vickie. "Let's look at Mike's situation." She moves down the shed row again and draws up a schedule for Mike.

Part	Mike Sched	Mike Actual
1.	10 - 20	12 - 22
2.	20 - 30	24 - 34
3.	30 - 40	34 - 44
4.	40 - 50	44 - 54

"Mike's machine has no personal life. He turns the switch and it's ready to go," says Vickie. "Mike goes to the machine on hour ten and turns it on, but there is no work to do. He waits until Pat finishes the first piece before he can start. The machine is reliable. When it gets the work it does it in ten hours. Mike looks for the second piece on hour twenty two and once again must wait until Pat finishes. He gets the second part on hour twenty four and finishes it in exactly ten hours. He is now four hours behind schedule. The third part is waiting for him and he is able to get it into his machine immediately. Ten hours later he puts the last piece into the machine and finishes the schedule four hours late. If you were ready to give Pat a medal a few minutes ago, Larry, you'd probably want to fire Mike, wouldn't you?" she asks.

She got me again. Will I ever learn? "The natural tendency would be to look at the results in terms of a week's work, and seeing Pat on schedule and Mike behind, the wrong guy gets the blame and the wrong guy gets the raise," I say.

MX has wandered back into our little group. "Exactly," he says,

"But it means more than that. Vickie's little example shows you something more significant than just whether a person is doing his job or not. It shows you that you cannot average out statistical fluctuations in the factory. They pile on top of one another."

"If that little example is a whole factory it would mean that all operations are a bottleneck," says Toni.

"What do you do, Larry, when you add up all the times to do all of the jobs and try to man your factory so that it is one hundred percent efficient?" asks MX.

"I never thought of it this way before, but I'm trying to balance capacity so that if I am successful every resource in my plant would be critical," I say.

"And what would happen to the statistical fluctuations if you had fifty resources that were perfectly balanced capacity-wise?" asks Vickie.

"I'd have fifty bottlenecks and fifty places where statistical fluctuations could accumulate. Nothing would ever get shipped. I'd go bankrupt!" I say.

It's starting to get dark and we make our way back to the main house. I keep thinking about what I've just discovered. I'm thankful that we've never been able to accomplish balanced capacity in our plant, and I'm thinking something else. Nobody else has either, because they'd be out of business if they had.

CHAPTER 27

The workday begins at dawn on a horse farm. It's Saturday morning, and we're in the dining room having coffee—that is, Arthur, Vickie, Toni, and I are. MX is not there.

"I wonder where MX is," says Toni. "Didn't he get awakened like the rest of us?"

"He's the only sane one—probably still sleeping," says Vickie.

"Well, he's not going to get away with that," says Toni as she heads toward his room. She returns in a couple of minutes. "He's not there."

Arthur says, "He probably took a morning jog."

"He's definitely not the jogging type," says Toni.

The mystery of the missing missile is forgotten for the moment as suddenly all hell breaks loose. Mike Roberts bursts in. He's out of breath and red in the face with excitement. "You're not going to believe this, Mr. King," he says, as he fights to catch his breath. "We've been robbed. Somebody made off with all of the buckets that we use to water the horses. There isn't a single one left."

"That's got to be the silliest thing I've ever heard," says Arthur. "Surely, you're ribbing us."

"No! No, I'm not." Mike is nearly in tears. "I know that we have security on every gate. It's impossible, but it's true. Over one hundred water buckets have vanished into thin air."

"That's crazy," says Arthur, just as one of the grooms comes rushing in. When he sees us he stops short and removes his baseball cap.

"Boss," he says to Mike. "I found the buckets. They're spread all over the place down by the trout pond, but you better come. We need all the help we can get. There's somebody guarding them."

We all run after the groom, down the lane that leads to the training track and the trout pond. There are other grooms heading in the same direction, some armed with pitchforks.

What we find is the most ridiculous sight I've ever laid eyes on. There is a pile of buckets—maybe six feet high—and several rows of buckets leading away from the high pile. The rows go in slightly different directions. Some are longer than others, but they all end in the same spot at the edge of the pond. Sitting among them, cross-legged, barefoot, and still in his pajamas, is MX. He is not moving a muscle, impervious to our presence. There's a morning chill in the air, but it doesn't seem to bother him.

I look at Arthur, expecting the worst. Arthur looks at Vickie. Toni looks at me, and suddenly we realize the absurdity of the moment and burst out laughing. Our laughter snaps MX to his senses.

He notices me. "Hey, Larry, come here. I've got it!" he shouts.

"What in the hell are you doing out here like this?" I ask.

"You know me," he answers. "I need to work with visual aids. Look, see the buffer." He points to the six-foot high pile of buckets. "Picture it. It's a dynamic buffer that ebbs and flows with the market demand, a living thing." He points to the other buckets leading to the water's edge. "Every one of those buckets is a machine that processes parts between the stockroom and the first buffer. Can't you see it? It's beautiful."

"All I can see is a lot of buckets that are needed elsewhere, one dirty-looking lunatic in his pajamas, and a bunch of very angry horsemen," I say as I try to pull MX to his feet, but end up down in the dust with him.

Arthur is nearly doubled over with laughter at our antics. It's a long hard struggle. MX is trying to show me his bucket factory while I'm trying to get him back to the house. The grooms start picking up the buckets to return them to where they belong, carefully avoiding MX, whom they look on as a nut.

Finally, the struggle is over. I feel that it's my duty to apologize for MX's actions to Arthur. I do, and tell him the story of how MX got his name, the unguided missile—that's what he is.

Arthur is not upset. On the contrary, I've never seen him enjoying himself so much. "Your friend will go to great lengths to prove a point, won't he?" Arthur says gleefully. Vickie told me that MX and Arthur King would get along. She knew what she was talking about.

After MX gets cleaned up and dressed, he becomes rational. I'm able to make a little sense out of his senseless escapade, as he explains, "I couldn't get to sleep last night—never can the first night in a strange bed. I kept tossing and turning while the thread of something kept going through my mind. I kept thinking about issuing parts. An idea came to me, but I work better when I can visualize a problem. I remembered all those buckets I saw when we walked around the farm. They were everywhere. At first I took a few of them over to the trout pond and actually tried dumping water from one to another to create a flow pattern, but that didn't do anything for me. I got more buckets, and it helped, so I got a few more. The more I got, the clearer the picture became. When I had all of the buckets I could find, I sat there and figured out how we can schedule the stockroom so the the first bottleneck gets tied to the market demand and pulls material from the stockroom. It's beautiful and simple."

My urge to strangle him is stifled by the sound of a car horn. "The girls are waiting to take us to the races," I say. "Let's continue this discussion later."

Keeneland is like most other racetracks I've seen, with its beautifully manicured gardens and large trees. There is one thing that sets it apart from the other tracks, though. There is no track announcer blaring constant messages and warnings to the bettors, and the races are run without a commentary. The only sounds are those of the racing fans cheering their favorites on. It's different.

We are seated in Arthur King's private box, which is situated directly opposite the finish line. MX is up to something. He takes a lap-top computer from the briefcase that he has brought with him.

"I've programmed this thing so that it can tell me which horse is going to win. All I need to do is punch in some data from the racing form—takes all the guesswork out of it—watch." He opens the racing form to the past performance charts for the horses in the first race. He pushes the reset button, and a menu appears on the liquid crystal screen. It's looking for things like weight, last three finishes, track condition, speed rating, class, age, and time of last race.

MX goes through the past performance chart, finds all of the data required for each horse in the race, enters it, and punches the execute button. The screen blinks a few times and a large number 3 appears on the screen.

"There's your winner!" exclaims MX.

I look at the tote board. Number three is the longest-priced horse in the race—eighty to one. "Nobody else agrees with you," I say.

"Let's put the data in for the second race now, so we can play the daily double," says Toni.

"Good idea," says MX. When he finishes putting in the data for the horses in the second race, the computer blinks the number 8.

"What are the names of those horses?" asks Vickie.

I look at my program. "Torpedero is the three and Devil's Dish is the eight," I tell her.

"I like those names. I'm going to play a double." She leaves with Arthur. Toni and I prepare to head toward the betting windows, but MX makes no move.

"Aren't you going to make a bet, MX?" asks Toni.

"No," he answers. "I want to watch a couple of races to see how this program of mine works before I risk any money."

I laugh. "You tout me on the three and eight and then you won't bet yourself. I won't risk more than two dollars on your picks if you don't have any more faith in your program than that"

The first race is a mile and one-sixteenth in distance. I look at Torpedero's past performance record and notice that he has been running in shorter races. He has a history of getting to the front and tiring. He hasn't come in the money for as far back as the record shows. No wonder he's the longest shot in the race.

Everybody is back and the race begins. Torpedero, true to form, breaks out of the gate on top, settles in along the rail to save ground, and quickly opens up a healthy gap between him and the rest of the field. As they turn into the homestretch, his lead is six lengths. "They'll need to give him oxygen any minute," I yell as the horses straighten out for the run to the wire. It doesn't happen. Torpedero actually increases his lead to win by a city block.

All of us except MX have a daily double ticket combining Torpedero with Devil's Dish in the second race. When the possible daily double payoffs are posted on the infield tote board, a loud murmur goes through the crowd. Most of the payoff amounts look like telephone numbers. They are astronomical. Devil's Dish is the favorite to win the second race, and the daily double payoff, if he wins, is the smallest on the board—a mere one thousand eight hundred dollars.

None of us leaves the box to make bets in the second race. It seems to take an eternity before the race is ready to go. Devil's Dish is a Calumet horse with a good record. We watch them load him into the starting gate, the Devil's red and blue colors easy to spot.

They break out of the gate and Devil's Dish settles into third along the rail. The girls are excited, shouting encouragement to the horse. I am too. "He's in a good spot," says Arthur as he views the race through his binoculars. "I think that he's going to make a move. The jockey's sitting down."

Devil's Dish swings around the second horse and takes off after the leader as they approach the final turn. By the time the horses are heading for home he has passed the leader and opens up a two-length lead. At the sixteenth pole he has improved his lead to four lengths and seems to be cruising effortlessly. "Yippee!" I yell and grab both of the girls. "We're home free!"

Suddenly I notice that the jockey is starting to whip and push as Devil's Dish starts to lose his lead in a hurry. It looks as if he's hit a stone wall. By the time he passes the seventy-yard pole his lead is down to two lengths. The jockey is working so hard to keep him going that I think he might get off and carry the horse the remaining distance. The lead is disappearing with every stride, and six horses rush past him right at the finish line. The photo sign is lit on the infield board.

"I don't believe I've ever seen a horse stop that fast," says Arthur.

"We won't win," say Toni. "I'm not lucky like that."

"If we did win, it's by no more than an inch," I say. "Any one of seven horses could be the winner."

We wait for several minutes while the officials examine the photograph. When the official winner's number is finally flashed on the board it doesn't sink in to any of our minds for a brief instant. Devil's Dish hung on. He won.

We all cheer and hug each other—all except MX. He's busy putting in the records of the horses for the third race. "I'm rich!" says Toni. "Vickie, where's the nearest shopping mall?"

The results of the first two races convince MX. He starts betting with both hands. I decide to bet only fifty dollars per race and save most of my daily double winnings for the King Arthur event. Toni stops betting altogether. She's planning a spending spree at the mall. The next five races are a complete washout for MX's computer.

I'm down to fifteen hundred dollars. MX hasn't cashed a ticket all day. He puts the computer back in his briefcase and slides it under his seat. "Won't work—too many variables," he says.

"And you're trying to schedule my factory?" I laugh.

He doesn't dignify the question with an answer. Instead he turns his attention to the next race, which is the big one—the one we've come all this way to see. "There are no past performance charts for any of the horses," he says to Arthur.

"That's because this is a two-year-old maiden race, early in the season. All of the horses are making their racing debut, just like the King," he answers.

"How do we get a line on any of them?" asks MX.

"By looking at their breeding, if you know horses, and by looking at workouts if any are posted in the form," says Arthur. "But this is the part of racing that I really like. These horses are the best that the farms around here have to offer right now. You don't know—one of these horses might be next year's Kentucky Derby favorite before the season is over. Just bet on King Arthur and don't worry about it," he says.

"How has King Arthur been training?" I ask.

Arthur's eyes light up. "He's a runner, that one. He does have one big problem that we're working on right now. I hope he doesn't pull it during this race."

"I didn't know. What is that?" asks Vickie.

"He's having trouble changing leads when he comes out of the turns," says Arthur. Vickie nods her head. She knows what he is talking about. I don't.

"Can you explain that to a novice?" I ask.

"When an animal as big and as fast as a thoroughbred goes around a turn he develops tremendous momentum. He must lean into the rail in order to keep his balance. When the track straightens out again he must transfer that momentum to his other side or he'll continue making an arc and go wide, right to the outside rail. Some horses have trouble learning this," explains Arthur.

"Like the feeling I get in a roller coaster?" I ask.

"Exactly," says Arthur. "The King is learning, but it will take time. He doesn't do it all the time, but he still does it."

The horses come out onto the track for the feature race. King Arthur is majestic, his coat shining in the sunlight, and the powder blue colors of Connecticut Yankee set him apart from the other horses. I look at the odds board. King Arthur is a two-to-one favorite. "Why are they betting so much on your horse, Arthur?" I ask.

"Word gets around in the racing business. The King has been beating horses older than he is on the farm."

We all leave to make our wagers. I bet all that I have left, fifteen hundred dollars, on King Arthur to win. It's house money.

We return to the box just in time to see them load the horses into the starting gate. Arthur looks through his binoculars. "This should be fun," he says. "The King hates the starting gate."

Three handlers are struggling to pull and push at the same time, but King Arthur looks like a Missouri mule. He won't budge. "They're going to have to blindfold him," says Arthur.

After a few more pulls and pushes are to no avail, one of the handlers takes a bandana out of his pocket and wraps it around King Arthur's eyes. He calms down, relaxes, and lets the handlers lead him into the starting stall with no further trouble—until they remove the blindfold. When the King realizes where he is he becomes extremely nervous. A handler climbs into the stall and holds King Arthur's head straight. When the gate opens all of the horses surge forward—except King Arthur. He surges straight up into the air. The jockey is nearly thrown out of the saddle. By the time he gets straightened out to run, the other horses are a good ten lengths up the track. It looks as if it's all over.

"Damn it," says Arthur.

When King Arthur settles into stride, he is something to behold. His strides seem to be twice as long as the other horses. The ten-length deficit is being made up, and soon he is passing the horses in the rear of the pack as if they are standing still. He passes all but the leader by the time they head into the final turn, and the distance between them is shrinking rapidly. Around the turn they go, stride for stride. King Arthur pulls up alongside the leader and they go head to head into the homestretch. We are hysterical as we cheer our champion. Then it happens. Suddenly the other horse has a clear lead again. King Arthur goes to the outside fence, losing gobs of ground in the process.

"He did it again," says Arthur as he shakes his head in despair.

I throw my fifteen one-hundred-dollar win tickets on the floor. "Easy come, easy go," I say.

Suddenly there is a roar from the crowd. Way out against the outside fence, half hidden by the fans, comes what looks like a locomotive. The jockey has done a smart thing and kept King Arthur way on the outside, not losing any more ground by trying to get him back in with the other horses. The angle makes him look like he's going twice as fast as he is, and the gap is being closed once again. He goes under the wire a half-length in the lead and drawing away. It's unbelievable. We look like a bunch of crazy people, hugging and kissing and hollering all at the same time.

Arthur starts out of the box. "Come on, everybody—down to the winner's circle to get our picture taken." They all leave.

"Wait for me!" I holler from my position on hands and knees, as I look for my fifteen winning tickets on the floor where I had stored them.

CHAPTER 28

It's just MX and me that evening, sitting on a bench near the house, enjoying the last rays of the setting sun as we talk. The girls have gone to a mall to spend their windfall, and Arthur has gone to some local horsemen's association dinner. "I'd say that this has been one exciting day. I'm so high that I'll never get to sleep tonight," I say.

"It has been memorable," says MX. "I'll remember it for a long time, that's for sure. Of course, I don't have forty-five hundred dollars in my pocket, like you have."

"Did you lose much?" I ask.

"I bet enough on King Arthur to get me even. I thought that I'd have a coronary when he bolted to the outside fence," he answers.

"It was touch and go for a minute, wasn't it. Tell me about that nonsense with the buckets this morning," I say.

"You can call it nonsense, and I guess that I did look like I'd lost all of my marbles, but I've found the key I've been looking for—the building block. It will work," he says.

He lapses into silence for a minute. It's inevitable that he'll continue, so I enjoy the brilliant sunset while I wait. He soon gets going again. "It started when I came to terms with the problem that Gary has. I thought about it for a long time, and the decision to issue the same quantities as we ship, which you think is asinine, is the key, believe it or not. There's just more work to do, is all. We must reduce inventory while maintaining flow. I thought a lot about buffers. Tell me, Larry. Why do we need buffers in our factory?"

"To protect ourselves against Murphy," I answer.

"Right. If we want to maximize output, what must we do?" he asks.

"We must keep our bottlenecks utilized all the time."

"You're batting one thousand so far," MX continues. "If keeping our bottlenecks utilized is the right thing to do, and we both know that it is, where should we concentrate our protection against Murphy?"

"Right at the bottlenecks," I answer.

"Good. Would you agree that, if we maintain—say—a week's buffer in front of a bottleneck, that nothing in the factory, outside the bottleneck itself, can stop us from making output for at least a week?"

"That's right."

"Then it would be logical to move all of our work in process into the bottleneck buffer as quickly as possible, wouldn't it?" MX asks.

"Yes, that makes a lot of sense. We wouldn't even need buffers anyplace else, would we?"

"We would have some protection at the other resources, but not in the form of inventory. We would have time, the idle time that is inherent in a noncritical resource," says MX.

"Sounds good so far. The problem would be to determine what the size of the buffers should be in front of the bottlenecks and how to manage them," I say.

"Let's visualize the operations between issue and the most highly utilized resource in the plant." MX looks toward the horse barns.

I grab him by the arm. "Don't you go get any more buckets," I warn him. "The most highly utilized resource is the grind center."

"What was the cycle time from the stockroom through grind center with checkpoint scheduling?" he asks.

"It took four weeks to get parts from the stockroom through grind," I tell him.

"We need to make one basic assumption before we go any further. Our new system must reduce inventory," MX says.

I add, "And to do that we must reduce our cycles."

"You're right on target," says MX. "So, let's make the buffers seventy-five percent of the original cycle time for starters."

I see buffers as piles of inventory. MX is talking as if buffers are cycle time. "How do we turn three weeks' cycle time into a buffer?" I ask.

"Now you're asking the sixty-four thousand dollar question," MX says. "The way we do it is to calculate the average weekly market demand for each part that goes through grind, for some period into the future—let's say thirteen weeks. We multiply the weekly average by three."

I see a vision of mountains of inventory in my factory. "A three-week buffer in front of each bottleneck and all of the work in process will send inventory to the moon." I say.

MX laughs. "Let me finish. The three weeks will be our work-in-process level, not our buffer. I call it dynamic WIP, because we can adjust it with fluctuations in the market demand."

I humor him. "OK, we've got a dynamic WIP that is three weeks' market demand in front of the bottleneck. What happens next?" I ask.

"How many parts does your average tote pan hold?" he asks.

"Fifty, plus or minus, depending upon the size of the parts," I answer.

"I'll need to calculate how many new tote pans we'll need. They will be different colors, but first, let me go on," says MX.

"We've got totes coming out of our ears now. Why would we need new ones?"

"It will become apparent to you in a little while," MX says. "We start running the parts through the bottleneck, and as each tote is emptied it is sent back to the stockroom, where it gets refilled with new parts and issued to the first operation. All resources leading to the bottleneck must run parts in the exact order that they receive them. There must be no skipping around to avoid setups. There will be a tendency on the foremen's part to save setups by combining totes into larger batches. This cannot be allowed to happen."

It's getting very dark now. We can barely make each other out.

"You mean that the stockroom is paced by the bottleneck resource, which, in turn, is paced by the market demand. Interesting, but how do we get started?" I say.

"I'd like to get some of those water buckets over here, but I'll try to struggle along without them," MX says. "Here's what we have to do. We set the original WIP level up with new, different-colored totes. Let's say we use yellow. We start filling the yellow totes with the parts that are waiting in front of grind already. When we've done that, we go back to the previous operation on the routing and put whatever parts are there into yellow boxes. We continue doing this until we run out of either pans or parts."

"That's good. If there are totes left over we take them into the stockroom to be filled, and if there are parts left over they must wait for totes to be released from the bottleneck," I say.

"That's right, Larry, and nobody is allowed to work on parts until they are put into new tote pans," says MX.

"If the yellow pans are returned from the bottleneck resource to the stockroom, there won't be new pans beyond the bottleneck, will there?" I ask.

"Beautiful, isn't it. Once the parts are through the critical resource they get processed the rest of the way in the same old gray pans that you've always used. The only difference is that like the noncritical operations in front of the bottleneck, the later operations must be performed to coincide with the parts' arrival. That should force smaller batches and speed up the flow."

"Sounds good. How do we know if we've got the correct buffer size?" I ask.

"At first your actual buffer right in front of the bottleneck will be large—on the order of two weeks or more, because the parts already in process won't have to travel the full route to get to the buffer. A short time after all the totes are going back to the stockroom, the buffer will find a level. Let's assume that we want the buffer sitting in front of grind to give us a week's protection against Murphy. On Friday we inventory the buffer. If it's more than a week's worth of inventory, we find out what parts are over-buffered and take some totes out of the system before they go back to the stockroom," explains MX.

"And the other side of the coin is, if the buffer falls below the week we want, we can add totes into the chain. I like it. We will have total control," I say.

"Nice, isn't it," says MX. "We still need to deal with the other parts though—the ones that don't go through grind center."

"We can do the same thing at the other bottlenecks," I say.

"With slight modifications," says MX. "By the way, these so-called bottlenecks we're talking about are not really limiting resources, are they?"

"Not in the strictest sense. The market demand governs what we make," I say.

"Then let's not call them bottlenecks anymore. A better word is pacer. We'll call them pacers," says MX. "We attach the market demand to the pacers by controlling the buffers."

"We have four of these pacers," I say. "How do we keep it all straight? Some of the parts may go through more than one pacer. When do we send totes back to the stockroom and when do we send them on?"

"If Gary has done his homework the way that I know he has, all we need is five different colored tote pans. Let's say gray and four other colors. Each of the four pacers is assigned a different color tote. Parts which are controlled by a particular pacer are issued in that pacer's totes. All parts between the stockroom and the pacer will be in colored totes. When a part's pacer processes parts, they are transferred into gray totes, and the colored totes are returned to the stockroom for refilling."

"That would mean that the most highly utilized resource would see only its own color, and each of the other pacers could be working on parts going to more highly utilized resources as well as its own. Parts are not transferred into gray totes until they are processed by their own pacer," I say. "It sounds complicated, but it's really quite simple, isn't it?"

MX cautions, "As long as everybody follows a few rules, it will work like a charm."

"Yes, that's right," I say. "Do you think that you can have a rough set of rules put together by Monday morning?" I ask.

"I can throw something together," answers MX.

"Good, we'll present the plan at staff and see what they think," I say, as a flash of headlights temporarily blinds us. "Let's go and see what Vickie and Toni spent their loot on."

Everybody's in a great mood on Sunday morning as we gather for breakfast. Arthur is happy because his horse has won impressively. Vickie is too, and Toni has a new wardrobe. MX is happy because he's got a system, but I'm the happiest of all because my friends are happy and I've got a pocketful of money to boot.

"I hope y'all enjoyed the weekend. I know that I did," says Arthur. We all agree.

"Larry, let's take a short walk before you leave," says Arthur.

We wander slowly down the lane toward King Arthur's barn, not saying anything for a few moments. Arthur breaks the silence. "Do you realize that King Arthur ran that race yesterday just three-fifths of a second off of the track record?"

"No, I didn't realize that," I say. "That means that he'd probably have broken the record easily if he had come out of the gate better and run on the inside all the way."

"He would have destroyed the record," says Arthur. "And when you think of the horses that have run that distance at Keeneland—Citation, Riva Ridge, Secretariat—all of the great ones. . . ."

"What are your plans for the horse?" I ask.

"We're going to ship him to New York for all of the big two-year-old races. We'll only be a shuttle flight away from you. You and Vickie will be able to come see him run," he says.

We walk some more before Arthur changes the subject. "You've surrounded yourself with some impressive people, if MX and Toni are any indication. Vickie tells me that you are ready to try some innovative approaches to manufacturing—something about synchronization. I like what I hear so far."

"We think we've got something," I say.

We're at King Arthur's stall. He knows he's something special and he shows excitement when he sees Arthur. Arthur strokes him under the chin. "I want to win the Derby with this fellow. That will make me the best. The secret of happiness is when a person is best at what he likes to do best. That's the best of all possible worlds."

Arthur gets an apple from a bucket hanging on the wall and feeds it to the horse. "Larry, I want to ask you for a personal favor."

"Anything, Arthur, what is it?" I say.

"I'm a little worried about Vickie, up in the Boston area all by herself. I know that she's grown up and all, but I still worry. Will you watch over her for me the way her own father would if he were there?" he says.

"You don't need to worry about Vickie. She's a great girl," I say. "But I certainly will keep my eye on her."

"Thank you for that," says Arthur as he shakes my hand.

CHAPTER 29

I hear commotion coming from Toni's office, and some of the language isn't fit for human ears. I hurry over to see what's going on. Clay Clayton, a manufacturing engineer, is blasting away at Toni, giving her both barrels. When he sees me coming he stops, but not before I hear the tail end of it: ". . . should get off your ass and get out into the factory so you'll find out what the hell it's all about."

I can't stand a guy like that. "Calm down, Clay," I say. "What's the problem?"

He waves a piece of paper in my face. "I've sent this damned appropriation request to Miss America here three times, and she bounces it back to me three times."

"You will address her as Miss Rossi, and you'd better calm down," I say. This guy is getting on my nerves. "What is it that you want to buy?"

"I worked my ass off on this project—nights, weekends—I can save the company a million bucks a year, and Miss—uh—what's-her-name won't sign off on it."

"Her name is Miss Rossi," I say.

"I find a milling machine that can process parts twice as fast as the ones we've got. We spend over two million dollars a year on labor with our present machinery, which runs a part in two minutes. The one that I found will run parts in one minute. That's half the time, and therefore half the cost. The machinery costs five hundred thousand dollars, and we'll save a million dollars in labor the first year alone, making the payback in six months. Only a damned fool would refuse to approve such a deal." He looks Toni straight in the eye, but she doesn't flinch.

I'm having trouble keeping myself from flying off the handle with this guy, but I hold it in. "I'm sure that Miss Rossi has a valid reason for returning the request. Let's hear her side of it—Toni?"

"There are no savings here," she begins. "In fact, the purchase of such machinery would lose the company a half million."

"I can't believe it!" shouts Clay as he slaps himself on the side of the head, for effect. "She just doesn't understand!"

"She understands more than you think," I tell him. "Now, let her talk."

"Clay, we ship all of the products we get orders for with the old machinery, and never work overtime at that resource. We can't ship more than our customers order, so where are the extra parts coming from?" she asks.

He doesn't answer her. It's apparent that he has closed his mind to anything that she says. I take over. "Will your new machinery allow us to ship more products?"

"No, but our efficiency will get much better," he answers.

"Then we can lay somebody off?"

"It would save one-half of a person per shift," he says.

"Obviously, I can't lay off one-half of a person, can I?"

"No, but that person could be freed up to work on something else," says Clay.

"Then we could lay somebody else off," I tell him.

"No."

"Will buying that machinery allow ConnYankee to make any more money, if we don't ship more products or lay somebody off?" I ask.

"No," he mutters.

"Then you must see Toni's reason for rejecting your proposal. Her job is to control the purse strings, and if we bought those new millers of yours, we would be spending a half million dollars for a white elephant."

"That's never been the way that we've looked at things in the past," says Clay.

"That is going to be the way that we look at things from now on," I tell him. "There are things out in that factory that need working on, and we've got a tool that will help us to focus in on them. From now on, I want you to look at the business as a whole before you waste both your time and the company's working on things for which there is no real payback."

Clay looks like a beaten man as he makes a hasty retreat from Toni's office—serves him right.

I go into my office to cool off before the follow-up meeting on MX's system starts. I notice a letter from the main office on top of my incoming tray. It's signed by the entire corporate staff, including Arthur.

There's a big inventory push, and all manufacturing operations are ordered to get the inventory on or under budget by the end of June. The operations that don't will be visited by a corporate task force to discover what remedial action is necessary to get inventory back in line. From my days on the corporate staff, I know what "visit from a corporate task force for remedial action" means. It means the kiss of death for the plant manager. I go to my board and write the word INVENTORY in big red letters.

MX's first meeting, on Monday, had been a long, difficult one. There are some things that manufacturing people have trouble with and resist. One of those things is change. I told them to think about it, discuss it among themselves for a couple of days, and then they could have one more shot at MX with their concerns.

MX starts the meeting by going through his rules one by one. "Parts will be processed at non-pacer resources in the order in which they are received."

"What if we get five hundred C7's, followed by two hundred H4's, and before we finish the C7's, another hundred show up. Wouldn't it make sense to jump that last hundred to save setup labor?" asks Ernie.

"That would defeat the intent of the system, which is to reduce cycle time. If making an extra setup causes parts to get to the bottleneck late, the system is designed to reveal it. We must maintain the disciplines, or people will start making unilateral decisions all over the place, and the system will collapse."

"Fair enough," says Ernie.

MX states his second rule. "Colored boxes must not be passed beyond their own pacer and must be sent back to the stockroom within one hour."

"Does that mean that we can pile the boxes on a skid and move them all back once per hour?" asks Joe.

"Yes—one hour or less, if the skid gets filled before that," answers MX.

"Pacer process batches should be as large as possible, but not exceed the average weekly market demand, is the third rule," says MX.

"Explain that one in a little more detail," says Joe.

"We want to maximize throughput at the pacing resources up to a point," says MX. "If we make a lot of setups, throughput may not be sufficient to keep up with market demand. If we run more than the market demand, we will build up inventory between the pacer and the shipping dock, with no place to send it. In effect, we will be making inventory instead of money."

Joe is satisfied with the explanation.

MX continues, "The next rule is—No work will be done at operations preceding the pacers, unless it is in colored tote pans."

"There shouldn't be any, after we get through the startup phase of this thing, should there?" asks Gary.

"Mysterious things happen out in the factory. Sometimes parts seem to appear out of thin air, but you're right," says MX.

"The last rule has to do with priorities," says MX. "Normally, it shouldn't be a problem but, in case of conflict, the first tie-breaker will be the date parts are issued—oldest date gets top priority. Any other time the top priority should be given to the parts where the buffer inventory equals or exceeds the weekly rate."

"That makes a lot of sense," says Dean. "That's the way that we can avoid making too many setups at the pacers."

"That's all the rules. Are there any questions or concerns?" asks MX.

"You mentioned that we should never run more than a week's rate at the pacers. Suppose that Dean wanted to take a die for maintenance. I think that it might be advisable to run ahead to free up the die for him," says Joe.

"Good thought," says MX. "There are exceptions to every rule, and you've come up with a good example. Basically, it all boils down to the fact that managers will make decisions to deviate from the rules, but they must be made with the interest of the business as a whole in mind. Without a good reason, such as yours, running ahead of schedule will eventually cause an inventory buildup at the most expensive place possible—at the end of the line."

"If we want to reduce inventory investment, and we process the weekly rate through the pacers, while we ship the same quantity, it seems to me that we will prevent ourselves from getting rid of the excess inventory that is already between the pacers and the ship point," says Gary.

"That's another startup problem," says MX. "One way would be to shut down the pacers for a couple of weeks, until the pipeline shrinks, but that's not advisable."

"We could taper down by reducing throughput at the pacers slightly, for awhile," says Joe.

"You don't even need to do that," says MX. "Since all of the resources beyond the pacers have extra capacity, just driving them hard will have the same effect. The only thing wrong with it is that all of the excess will pile up at the shipping dock with no place to go."

"Let's have a sale," says Toni.

"Spoken like a true woman," I say. "But we could call Les Walsh and have him contact our customers. Some of them might allow early shipment. I'll call him myself."

"The best solution of all would be to put the pressure on marketing to get more business for us," says Toni.

"I'll certainly mention that to Les while I'm talking to him," I say. There are no more questions. "I know that I can depend on all of you to give this your best shot. It's important to the future of this business. Don't get discouraged when bugs crop up. We'll fix them as we go along. Are there any other issues?" I ask.

"I found those colored tote pans that you wanted. How many shall I order?" asks Gary.

"I've got that all figured out for you," says MX, as he takes a piece of paper from his briefcase and hands it to Gary.

"I'll have them on the dock tomorrow," says Gary.

"The tote labels will be ready at the same time," says Ernie. "I'll have them put on the totes as soon as they arrive."

"Let's all plan on working Saturday to get all of the parts transferred into colored totes. Joe, bring in enough hourly people to get the job done. Use the people on the bottom of the overtime list," I say. "There will be no overtime worked on Saturday except for those working on this project. We don't want a moving target out there."

"I think that I should bring some facilities people in to do preventative maintenance on those pacer resources so they'll be humming on Monday," says Dean.

"Great idea, Dean. Go for it," I tell him.

Everybody is so up for the task at hand that I decide to hold back the bad news about the inventory push. Monday will be soon enough for that. "You have tomorrow and Friday to prepare the troops. I want every individual in this plant to be fully informed of what we are doing, before the end of the week. Let's use the 'inform the informer' approach. You people tell the people on your staffs, and they will, in turn, tell the people who work for them. We need the cooperation of every person in this plant."

"We should have separate meetings for the pacer operators," says Toni. "They will get different instructions than the other people."

"Excellent," I say. "Now I'm not going to hold you any longer. There's a ton of work ahead of us."

CHAPTER 30

Saturday is a hectic day for all of us. On the way in, I notice the totes of many colors, piled high on the dock. I can see that the part-identifier labels are attached, as promised. When more than three hundred tote pans are all in one pile, it's a veritable mountain. We assemble in the cafeteria to enjoy the coffee and doughnuts that I've ordered from a local caterer, and listen to the instructions from MX. He divides us up into groups. I'm assigned to Vickie's team at the blue resource—the turret lathes. MX gives each team captain a kit consisting of routing sheets and baseball hats the same color as our tote pans. We have two hourly employees with us—Red, and a girl named Tara.

"The first thing that we've got to do is bring all of the blue tote pans to the turret lathe area," says Vickie. She's dressed the way she was the first day I met her—in blue jeans and a gray sweatshirt. Her blue baseball cap is set on the back of her golden hair.

We bring all of the blue tote pans to the turret lathe queue. "We'll be needing more storage racks at these pacer resources," I say.

"We won't buy any," says Vickie. "We'll just move racks from the non-pacer resources. They won't need them."

We match up the parts sitting in front of the turret lathes to the correct totes and put them in the queue rack. It hardly makes a dent in the pile of totes. Vickie looks at the router sheets. "We've only got two part numbers to worry about at this pacer. Larry, you and Tara take the G3's, and Red and I will take the M2's." She hands me a router sheet. "Follow the router backwards, and do the same thing that we just did with the parts we found here," she orders. MX must have put me in her charge on purpose. It's like him.

It takes us most of the morning to finish the task. We finally run out of totes, but there are still five operations left with parts that must remain in gray tote pans. I go find Vickie to help her, but she is about finished. She also runs out of totes before she gets all of the parts transferred. "Let's go and see how the other teams are doing," I say.

Shot blast and hand deburr are just about done, but the team headed up by MX has a long way to go. There are still about a hundred yellow boxes left. I laugh at MX. He's covered with grease and dust. He really gets into his work. "You're holding up the whole project," I say.

"I wonder if it has anything to do with the fact that twelve of the twenty parts go through this resource," he says. "It's going good, though."

"Do you think that we ought to break for lunch?" I ask.

"Why don't we all pitch in and get out of here early?" suggests Vickie.

Sounds like a good idea to me. At about one o'clock we are finished. The hourly people go home, and the rest of us take a final tour to make certain that nothing is amiss.

"Look, we can see how the parts flow," says Toni. "Just follow each color back through the line. It looks impressive."

"Why don't we color each pacer the same color as the totes that are heading for it?" says Vickie.

"That would be an excellent idea," I say. "The pacer resources are the keys, and they should be set apart from the other resources."

"Be careful that you don't do anything permanent, like painting the machines," says MX. "It could turn out that the pacer could shift in the future."

"Why is that?" asks Joe.

"If the product mix changes drastically, or some improvements to one of the present pacers decreases the time so much that it becomes a noncritical resource, then the pacer would shift to another location. You wouldn't want to be scraping and painting machines every time it happened, would you?"

"Work up something. I think it's a good idea to set the pacers apart," I say.

Vickie follows me back to my office. "That was a job well done, but it made me hungry," she says.

"Would you like to go someplace and get a bite to eat?" I ask.

"I'd love to, but the way we're dressed it can't be any place fancy —Wait, I've got an idea. Do you like ribs, Larry?—juicy, barbecued ribs?" she asks.

It makes my mouth water just thinking of them. "Love 'em," I tell her.

"I know a place a little bit north of here, that serves the best ribs in the free world. Come on, we'll take my car," she says.

A little bit north turns out to be ninety miles. It's a beautiful, warm April day. The Maserati flattens out the mountain road, and the scenery is awesome. It's a pleasant ride. We talk about many things—Toni and MX, Arthur and King Arthur, our new scheduling system, and the fun we had last weekend. We have an awful lot in common, Vickie and I. Before I know it, we're passing through the village of North Conway, called the Switzerland of America by some. It's right in the heart of the White Mountains, and we can see the snow still clinging to the higher elevations. A couple of miles north of the village, Vickie points to our destination, the Red Parka restaurant. She tells me that it's a favorite haunt of the ski crowd during the winter months. It turns out to be a cozy place, and the ribs are excellent, as advertised.

On the way back to Salem, we stop at a shopping center to pick up some wine and cheese before we get back to the condo at about nine. Vickie comes in to help me with the wine and cheese. We watch TV for awhile, until the food is all gone. It's pleasant just relaxing and enjoying each other's company. I feel drawn to her. I'm getting that feeling more and more lately.

We're both sitting on the sofa, watching TV, and she leans her head on my shoulder. "I'm tired and I've had too much wine, Larry. I'm in no condition to drive all the way back to Cambridge. Where are those pajamas I used the other night?" she asks.

Maybe it's the wine—I don't know, but I take her in my arms and kiss her. She responds by grabbing me around the neck and kissing back—hard. She forces my head against the back of the sofa, continuing to respond hungrily to my kiss. "What took you so long, Larry?" she gasps between kisses.

It comes out before I can think, "I love you, Vickie." Now she's really into it. She's got me down on the sofa, where we stay in each other's arms for a long time. We're starting to get hot and heavy and I've got to stop before it's too late. I roll her over and sit up.

"What's the matter?" she asks.

"I don't think we should go any further right now," I say. "It's a promise I made to Arthur last weekend."

She tries to pull me back down with her on the sofa. I give her a short peck on the lips and sit up again. She gives me a pouting look. "What kind of promise?" she asks.

"He asked me to look after you just as if you were my daughter," I answer. "I'm not acting like a father right now."

"That old fox. He knew!" she says.

"What?"

She laughs. "He knew this would happen, don't you see? Arthur trusts me. I've been away to college for more than five years, and I have never given him cause not to trust me."

"What would make him ask me to watch over you, then?"

"It's you. He's got you watching after yourself. Arthur's made his fortune by manipulating people. He could see how close we were getting, even better than we could. He knows your character—what you're made of—and that you're a man of honor. He's used your honor to insure the chastity of his friend's daughter." She laughs at the predicament we're in. "Now, what do we do about it?"

Now I know how victims of scams feel. I grab her by the hand, pull her from the sofa, and practically drag her into my bedroom. "I'll show him," I say. Her eyes widen in wonder at my uncharacteristic action, but she doesn't look frightened.

I open my dresser drawer, take out the spare pair of pajamas, hand them to Vickie, drag her back out of the bedroom to the bottom of the circular stairway leading to the loft, give her one more long, passionate kiss, and push her up the stairs. "I'll show him," I repeat, "—that he's a wise man. Good night."

She laughs, and her look melts me. "Good night, Larry. I love you, too."

I take a cold shower and go right to bed, but it takes me a long time to doze off. All I can think about is Vickie, up in the loft. I wonder if she's asleep yet. I feel good all over.

It's morning. I can hear Vickie rattling the coffee maker. I hurry out of bed and into the kitchen. I give her a kiss on the cheek. "Good morning. Did you sleep much last night?" I ask.

"I slept like a log after I took a cold shower," she says. "Did last night really happen, or did I dream it all?"

"What are we going to do about it?" I ask.

She looks happy as she says, "What do any two people who are in love do about it? They shout it from the roof tops—They get engaged—They——"

"Wait," I interrupt. "We've got a serious problem that other people don't have."

"You're not handicapped or anything, are you?" she asks in mock horror.

I laugh. "Don't be silly. Our problem has to do with who you are and who I am. You're the protegée of the head of one of America's top firms, and I'm a candidate to succeed him. I know that Arthur is a fair man, but it wouldn't look right, especially to Marty, if we were to announce our engagement right now, would it?"

Vickie sips her coffee and says nothing for a few minutes. She finally says, "You're right. We don't want to hurt anyone." She looks at me and smiles. "Arthur is so right about you, Larry. You really are a man of honor and integrity." She puts down her cup, comes around the table, and gives me a bear-hug. "We'll wait, but you're mine, and don't you ever forget it."

CHAPTER 31

It's Monday morning. Everybody is out on the factory floor to make sure that we get started on the right foot, so I've pushed the weekly staff meeting back to this afternoon. I get Les Walsh on the phone. "Les, can you get to all of my customers and find out if any of them will accept early shipments?" I ask.

"They'll think that I'm on something," laughs Les. "I'm usually calling them to tell them that we're shipping late."

"Good," I say. "The unexpected shock may cause them to be receptive to taking stuff early. Give it a try."

"I sure will," says Les. "I'll get back to you later this afternoon. Oh, while I've got you on the phone—How are my thousand rush S3's coming? The promise date is only two weeks away."

Damn! In the excitement of what we've been up to, I've nearly forgotten about that special order. "It looks good," I tell him. "I'll have an exact date for you when you call back."

"Fair enough," says Les. "I'll call you later."

Teresa Lockeridge comes in. "Got a minute, Larry?"

"Sure thing," I beckon her to a chair. "Come on in." She doesn't look too happy.

"The people in the stockroom and at some of the early operations are complaining. They think that management has finally cracked," she says.

"How's that?" I ask.

"For weeks now, they've been working all the overtime they can handle. Now, today they come in, and there's all kinds of work in front of them, but their foreman won't let them touch it because it isn't in those fancy tote pans. You didn't order enough of them," she says.

I laugh. "We explained all that to them last week."

"I know," she answers. "But words are one thing and action is another. They think the place is going out of business or something when you stop them from working on parts that are available."

I point to the large red INVENTORY that I've scribbled on my board. "See that."

"Yeah, it says INVENTORY," she says. "So what?"

I hand her the letter from headquarters. "Read this."

She reads the letter carefully. "They mean business with this inventory thing, don't they. What has it got to do with the people that have work, yet have nothing to do?" she asks.

"What we are doing out there in the plant is reducing the inventory," I tell her.

"Pardon me, but how in the hell does not working on something reduce inventory? We should work on it and get it out of here, shouldn't we?" she asks.

"We have a limited demand. If we had an unlimited market, that would be the right thing to do. The way we need to do it, is to reduce the manufacturing cycle, so that we won't need to start the parts so long before they are due to ship. It will only be a short time before we get the inventory adjusted to where we want it, and then everybody will have the same amount of work to do as they always did. Nobody is being deprived of a job. In fact, I'll guarantee you right here and now that nobody will lose any pay because of what we are doing out there," I tell her.

"I guess that none of us want corporate auditors climbing all over everything," says Teresa. "You've been fair with me so far. I'll talk to the people."

"How did it go this morning?" I ask, as staff commences.

"All in all, I'd have to say that it went very well. There was some confusion, and a lot of questions, but no major disasters," says Joe.

"We had one problem with priorities at the noncritical resources. We told the people to do work in the order that it was received, but today everything was there at once. We went in and made a rough sequence by dates. It was all right," says Ernie.

"We caught a couple of people working on parts in gray totes, but we stopped it," says Gary. "It may be a problem if it goes on too long. There's only so much cleaning we can do."

"Don't let them work on the parts in the gray totes under any conditions," I say. "I'd rather see them with coloring books and crayons."

"I want to propose the first change to the system," says Toni.

"Already? What is that?" I ask.

"We have that problem with all that extra inventory in the line after the pacers. What is the real bottleneck in our plant?" Toni says.

"It's the market demand," says Dean. "We all know that by now."

"Where should we concentrate our protection from Murphy—at the bottleneck, right?" she says.

"We've got all our protection at the pacing resources," says Joe. "We really don't have anything to protect us after the parts get through those resources, do we?

"Let's put a buffer right in front of the shipping dock. It will be easy. We've already got the inventory in the line. It can be a dynamic buffer, just like the others. We can get another color tote pan, and make up a week's rate of empty totes for everything that we ship, and just leave it right in front of the packing area. The packers will empty the totes, and the final check operators, just before packing, will refill them with parts from the gray totes as they work on them."

I see the tremendous value of her plan—protection against disruption for a week at the real bottleneck. "Theoretically, if the buffer is full, we'll be assured of the week's shipments when we come in on Monday morning," I say.

MX throws in his two cents' worth. "If the buffer in front of pack is always full on Friday, then you don't need it. It would mean that there is never any disruption between the pacers and packing, so you ought to cut it."

"That's theoretical," I say. "In reality, if the week's shipments aren't complete, we can see exactly what we need, and exactly what we need to fix. I don't expect that the buffer will be full often, and if it is, we can cut it back. It'll save us money in inventory if we do."

"I'll order some new totes. I think that the vendor had white and red left," says Gary.

"Get them both," says MX.

"Why do we need two new colors?" I ask. I envision all of the money that we are saving being spent on tote pans.

"We need to set up something for special orders—you know, rush orders and the like—orders that need to be given top billing at all times," says MX.

"How do we fold them into the new system, MX?" I ask.

"Simple," he answers. "Just start them through the factory in special totes—let's say red. Whenever an operator sees red, she makes it her top priority and works on it immediately after the batch she is running is complete."

"Sounds like the special orders will get through our factory pretty quickly that way," I say.

"I've done some simulations on it and you won't believe what I've found out," he says.

"How fast?" I ask.

"How does two weeks grab you?" MX says.

"That fast," I say. Everyone else is surprised too.

"It may even be faster, depending on how big the batches are. If they're small enough it may even be one week," he says. "Take any one of your parts and add up the actual time it takes to process it through all of the operations. You'll find that the average time is less than half a day. With checkpoint scheduling, the parts sat around idle for more than ninety-five percent of the time!"

"What the hell, get both colors," I tell Gary.

"Can anyone tell me where that special order for one thousand S3's stands?" I ask.

"It's going to go out just under the wire, in about a week and a half, I'd say," says Joe.

"Good job, guys. Now, I've got something I've been avoiding discussing with you since late last week. There's a big inventory reduction push on, and they mean business this time," I say. I read them the letter.

"No problem," says MX. "Your cycles will be a minimum of twenty-five percent shorter by the end of June."

"Will a twenty-five percent reduction in inventory get us under budget, Toni?"

"With room to spare," she says. "But we had better reschedule the incoming material soon."

"I'd hate to do that and then have the new system fall on its face. Gary, how long can we wait, before we reschedule June's input, to give the vendors enough time to comply?" I ask.

"We'd have to do it immediately, or the vendors will charge us rescheduling costs," he answers.

"Do it," I say. "We'll make this system work!"

"We have no choice now," says Joe. "You've just burned the bridges behind us. We can't go back."

I call Les to tell him that his S3's will be shipped slightly ahead of schedule. He's overjoyed and practically guarantees me that his customer will give us a big follow-on order. I ask him how he made out with my request. It turns out that none of the customers is opposed to shipping parts up to a month early. Most of them did say that they would not accept anything early in December. Their inventory targets must be pegged right at year's end, and they are loose during the rest of the time. That is not the way that the Salem division of ConnYankee is going to conduct business—not any more!

CHAPTER 32

Vickie and I are on the nine o'clock Eastern shuttle to LaGuardia. King Arthur is making his debut in the Big Apple at Belmont this afternoon. We've settled into a routine of romance and companionship, but I'm still bound by my promise to Arthur. It hasn't been an easy time for either of us—you know, so near and yet so far. Vickie spends half of her nights at the condo, and seems happy. I am too, but it's as though the year will never end.

I reflect back on the past two months. The new system is working well. There are continuing minor problems, but it is the system itself that is helping us to uncover and fix them.

There have been a lot of changes in just two months. There are the colorful totes and the flags—Toni and Vickie went out and bought some flags like the ones car dealers use when they have a sale. They had Dean mount them over the pacing resources. The biggest change of all seems to be in the attitude of the people. They seem to be enjoying their work more, and they consider themselves part of a team. The jacket awards program has taken off better than I hoped it would, thanks to Joe. He has a supplementary program going. If a person is a repeat winner, he or she gets a gift certificate and a patch to sew on the jacket they already have. The patch is a likeness of a drum. Joe calls our new system a percussion scheduler.

He says that the pacing resources bang the drums loudly, so that everybody else in the plant works to their rhythm. It has taken hold, and some of the workers already have three or four drums sewn on the sleeves of their jackets.

Vickie nudges me to snap me out of my daydream. "Arthur tells me that King Arthur has learned to change leads. I'm so anxious to see him run again."

"He hasn't been in competition for two months," I say. "I hope that he's tight enough."

"Mike Roberts says that the really great ones can run in their sleep," says Vickie.

I look at the newspaper that we picked up at the airport. "The handicappers don't know that he's that great yet. He's four to one in the morning line."

"That's because the New York handicappers consider him an outsider—an unknown quantity. They tend to favor the horses that have been running in New York. Besides, he has run only one race, and just barely won that one, remember?"

"How can I ever forget," I say, as I pat my billfold. "I've still got that forty-five hundred and it's going on King Arthur's nose today."

"Larry, you wouldn't!" she exclaims. "That's too much money."

"The way I look at it, it's two dollars," I say. "I've got only two dollars of my own money invested in this parlay—the two that I bet on that daily double. All the rest is winnings."

We meet Arthur at the track. He has that outdoorsy look about him, from working with the horses.

"Are you getting ready for the midyear business review?" he asks, during a lull in the action.

"We're working on it. I'll be ready." I say.

"I hear that you are doing some unorthodox things up there in Salem. It doesn't surprise me, knowing you," he says.

"They may be unorthodox, but they are working. Have you looked at our schedule conformance report lately?" I ask him.

"I sure have. We all have. Salem is number one when it comes to customer performance," he says. "Some of the other measurements look shaky, though. Are you working on them?"

"I'll give you a full report at the business review," I say, as I hear the call to the post.

In a few moments, after the horses leave the paddock and enter the track, Mike Roberts shows up.

"How's he look, Mike?" asks Arthur.

"He's fit as human hands can make him. He should run a big race today," says Mike.

I leave to bet my forty-five hundred to win, on King Arthur. When I return, Arthur is the only one in the box. "How has Vickie been doing?" he asks.

"She's doing fine," I tell him. "She spends most of her time up at the Salem plant, helping us and working on her thesis. Many of the ideas we're trying are hers."

"I know she's in good hands now," says Arthur.

I'll bet you do, I think, as Vickie and Mike Roberts return. The race is about to begin, as the horses are being loaded into the starting gate.

King Arthur is fractious. The handlers use the blindfold technique once more, to get him into starting position. This time they leave the blindfold on.

"I doubt if we will ever be able to get him used to that iron monster. He can't stand being cooped up," says Arthur.

"I'm trying something different today," says Mike. "The jockey will pull the blindfold off just a fraction of a second before the gate opens. If his timing is right, the horse should shoot right out of there."

I glance at the infield board. King Arthur is going off at odds of seven to two. My bean-counter mind quickly calculates the payoff for my forty-five hundred dollar ticket to be in the neighborhood of twenty thousand dollars. My heartbeat quickens as I stare at the starting gate. The world seems to stop. I love the feeling.

The crowd gives a mighty roar as the starting gate opens. The track announcer shouts, "They're off!"

It's a beautiful start. The horses are strung across the track in an even line, but not for long. One of the other horses shoots out to a commanding five-length lead over King Arthur, who is lying in second place along the rail. "Beautiful, that horse in the lead will burn out!" shouts Arthur.

"Whoopee, that blindfold trick worked like a charm!" says Mike.

King Arthur doesn't wait for the other horse to burn out. He takes off after him immediately. Before they've gone a quarter mile, he catches up and passes the other horse.

"The King can't stand another horse in front of him," says Arthur. "It's the same way on the farm."

"I hope he doesn't burn out too," I shout.

"The King is bred for distance and speed," says Mike. "This race is all over!"

By the time that the horses barrel into the final turn, King Arthur has a seven-length lead and increases it with every stride. The jockey looks like he's out for a ride in the park, just sitting there hanging on. As they straighten out for the run home, King Arthur stays along the inside rail as if he's tied to it. The jockey looks around to see where the other horses are. Now he knows that if he doesn't fall off, the race is his. They cross the finish line a city block ahead of the second-place finisher.

Vickie is jumping up and down. She grabs Arthur around the neck, almost knocking him over. Mike is stunned. "Wow! That is some impressive performance. Those were the best two-year-olds in training he was running against out there. We've got another Secretariat on our hands," he says to Arthur.

"What was the time of that race?" asks Arthur.

As if to answer Arthur's question, the track announcer blares forth, "Result is official. The winner is Connecticut Yankee Farm's King Arthur—running time for the six furlongs is one minute, eight and two-fifths seconds, a new track record."

"I think you're right, Mike!" shouts Arthur.

We all run down to the winner's circle for the picture session, where Arthur receives congratulations from scores of fellow owners, trainers, and officials. I take the twenty thousand dollar ticket from my pocket and show it to Vickie.

"Better put that in the bank. There won't be any good payoffs from now on," she says.

CHAPTER 33

The corporate business review left me with conflicting emotions, and it confused the hell out of the corporate staff, if nothing else. They're so damned set in their ways. Changing that condition will be one of my top priorities when I take the reins.

The humidity in the morning air gives promise of a scorcher, even for July. The heat waves rising from the macadam are visible already. When I enter the plant, the air conditioning feels good. So does the atmosphere.

The people are confident and productive, and they seem to be enjoying their work more. The jacket award program is paying big dividends. When Joe took charge, his first rule was that no member of management was to receive a jacket. He wants the jacket to be a symbol of something special, and feels that it would not be, with every supervisor and manager wearing one.

Helen hands me a memo as I pass her desk. Les Walsh wants me to get in touch with him as soon as possible. I wonder what he wants to pull in now, as I dial his number. He got his thousand S3's on time—actually three days early. Les answers the phone.

"Have I got a deal for you!" he begins. "It will knock your socks off."

"You sound like a carnival huckster," I laugh.

"How soon can you ship another thousand turbine blades to the same customer to which you shipped the S3's?" he asks.

"Depends on the type," I answer.

"It will be on the order of about a hundred each of ten different types. The customer wants to see how we respond to emergencies, and also evaluate our product line at the same time. Can you ship complete in eight weeks?"

I think about the week's buffer in front of ship, and the risk involved in depleting some of it temporarily. It's a matter of priorities and the reward involved. "What would it mean to us if I could?" I ask.

"They are disenchanted with their present vendor, Larry. This customer is a major producer of turbine engines. They want to change vendors when their present purchase order runs out. If we can demonstrate on-time delivery, with high quality, at a competitive price, they will give us all of their blade business for next year. I've taken care of the price, and now it's up to you to come through on quality and delivery."

"How sure are you that we'll get the order?" I ask.

"I've got nothing more than a verbal promise from their corporate manager of materials, and this first commitment to buy the thousand, but I get positive vibrations," he says.

"How much does this guy spend on turbine blades in a year?" I ask.

Les pounces on the question. "Twenty-five million dollars! One hundred thousand blades altogether!"

When I get over the shock, I go through some quick mental gymnastics. I know that we're making about a quarter million blades now, with a two-shift operation. We could go to three shifts by the first of the year, if we hire and train about a hundred people. I'll go for it! "I'll take the order for the first thousand. You say that you want them when?" I ask.

"Eight weeks or sooner, but eight weeks will be fine," he says.

It's my turn to use the shock treatment. "How about if I ship them in four weeks?"

You'd think that he's just won a million dollars in the state lottery. The reply rings through my ears. "You ship those damn things in four weeks and the order is ours! I can guarantee it!" he shouts. "Do you really mean four weeks?"

"Give me the order, and the parts will definitely be shipped in four weeks, or less," I tell him.

We go through the usual measurements to start off the weekly staff meeting. Output is right there. Overtime is way down—hanging in at about five percent. Inventory has made a significant drop, but I tell them that we can do better. The quality measurement is terrible, but I'll talk about that later. Pacer performance is in the high ninety percent range. I want to use the meeting to go over the corporate business review with the staff.

I preface the review with the fact that I'm not sure what the executive officers thought of us. I put the first slide on the screen—Schedule Performance.

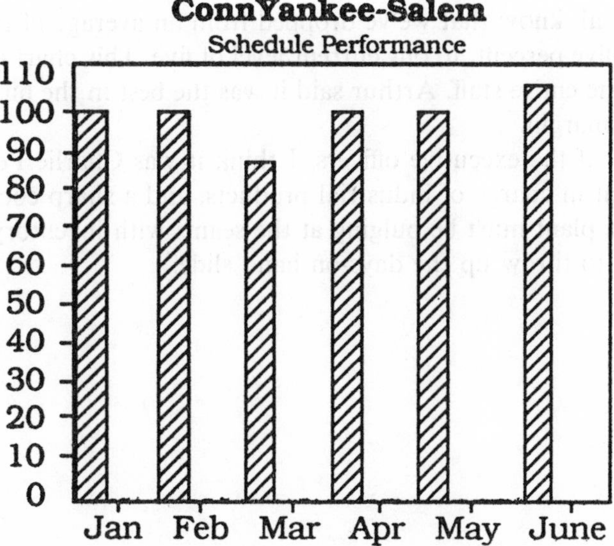

"I wanted to get off on the right foot, so I went with my strength. Those guys forgive an awful lot if output is good. When they saw that we've been on schedule all year, except for that month when we had the laser problem, they were impressed. In fact, one of them mentioned that nearly everybody else has been having trouble with output lately.

"I continued my display of strength with the overtime chart—"

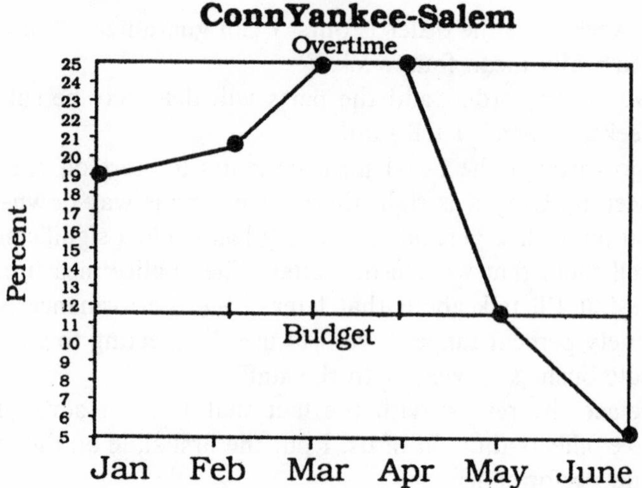

"You all know that we've dropped from an average of twenty to twenty-five percent, to our current level of five. This chart got a rise out of the entire staff. Arthur said it was the best in the business by quite a margin.

"One of the executive officers, I think it was Charlie Pearl, vice president in charge of industrial products, and a sharp cookie, said that our plant must be bulging at the seams with inventory. It was my cue to throw up the days-on-hand slide."

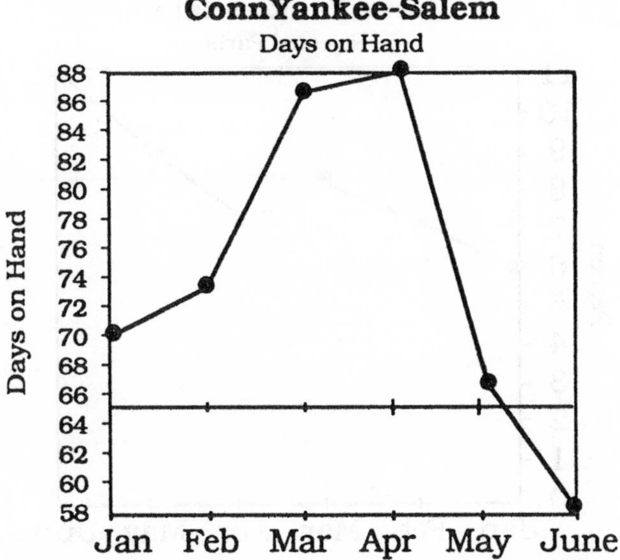

"I'll tell you—that brought Charlie up short. Our inventory, which was ten percent under budget at the end of June, is also the best in the business. I could see that I had them, but it didn't last long. Unfortunately, I had to show them the rest of the slides.

"When I got to the quality chart, they had their first chance to jump all over me, and they did."

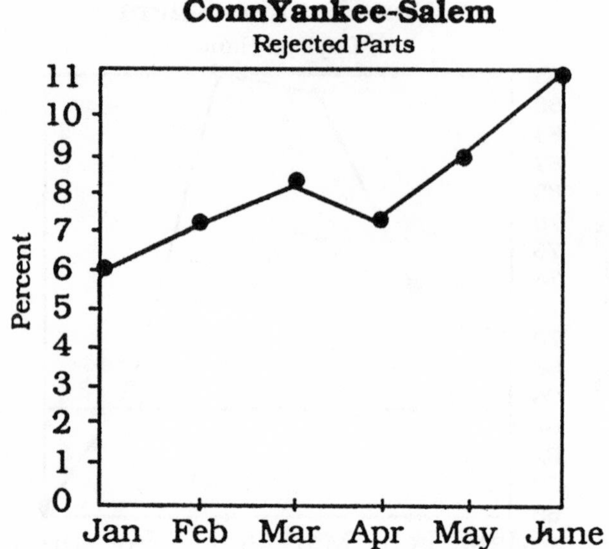

"Did you tell them that we haven't really gotten that bad—that the problem is we don't have the inventory base?—You know, twelve percent of our present work in process is fewer parts than seven percent of what we did have," says Ernie.

"I couldn't tell them that, Ernie. We need to do a better job and improve this number. With our low inventory scheduling system, we just cannot afford to have as many bad parts lying around as we once had."

"We are getting better," says Ernie. "It's just that with the start-up and all, it's coming slow."

"It might make sense to use some of the idle time at non-pacing resources to do rework," I say. "Of course, first-run parts would always take first priority, but work something out. Be careful that you don't sacrifice the flow to fix bad parts, whatever you do."

I put up the efficiency chart.

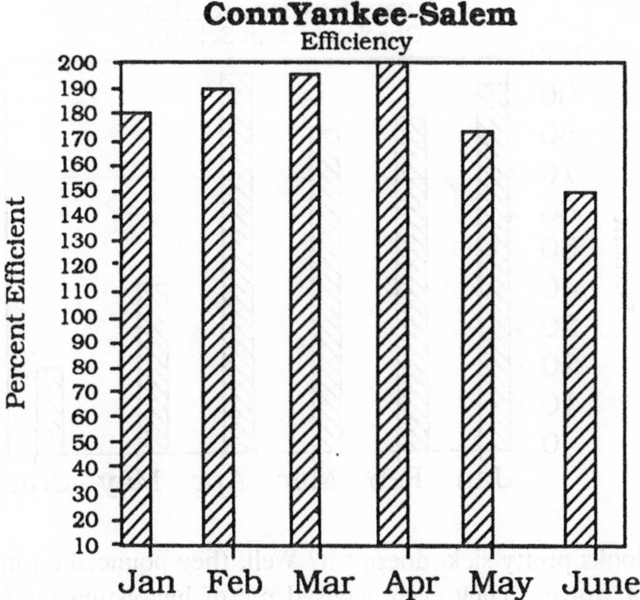

"This one really got them going," I say. "Charlie Pearl called it the worst-looking efficiency chart that he's seen in years, and most of the rest of the group agreed with him. It's exactly the reaction that I wanted."

"Did it work to your advantage?" asks Toni.

"I told them, 'Look back at the rest of the charts, gentlemen. My output is up, my overtime is the lowest in the corporation, and inventory is way under budget. I haven't hired any more people than I had when my efficiency was over two hundred percent. The measurement is counterproductive.' "

"Are they ready to throw out efficiency as a prime measurement?" asks Gary.

I shake my head slowly in disgust. "They remind me of Pavlov's dog. They've been conditioned to react negatively to curves that bend the wrong way. They told me to get my efficiencies back up where they belong."

Even though we haven't been keeping track of checkpoints, I had a "what-if-we-were" chart made up for the review. I put it up on the screen.

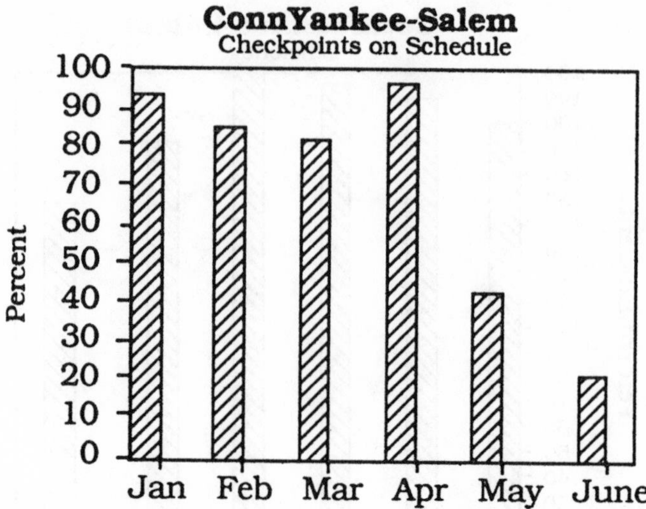

"It looks pretty sick, doesn't it? Well, they pounced on me like a pack of wolves. They even accused me of harvesting the business just to make the other charts look good. They are sure that Salem is heading for a disastrous second half of the year, because there is just not enough work in process to maintain flow. What a joke!"

"Did you explain the percussion system to them?" asks Joe.

"Each plant manager is only allotted thirty minutes. I did the best I could with my time running out. I pointed out the fallacy of getting on checkpoints, by explaining that overtime and inventory are in conflict with the schedule. I didn't get the message across that way. I asked them a question that they could not answer, 'How does getting on checkpoints help a business that already makes shipments on time?' I explained to them that if a business can ship on schedule, the fewer checkpoints that are on schedule the better. I guess that I gave them credit for being smarter than they are. It seemed to go right over their heads."

"That's tragic," says Toni. "Did any of them understand what you were trying to tell them?"

"I think Charlie Pearl did, and I know that Arthur King is interested in hearing more. In fact, he is going to pay us a visit in a couple of weeks. Better get the place spruced up a bit, Dean."

"What happens if they don't like what we're doing up here?" asks Joe. "We could be blown right out of the water."

"What was it that Admiral Farragut said in Mobile Bay?—Damn the torpedoes. Full speed ahead!"

I switch the viewer off and turn my attention to the conversation I had with Les. "I've got some tremendous news. I just got off of the phone with Les Walsh, up in marketing. There's a damned good chance that we can get an order for one hundred thousand more blades for delivery next year."

"They must be going to close Murfreesboro," cracks Gary.

"No, nothing like that, it's a new customer. All that we have to do is ship one thousand assorted blades that we don't yet have the order for, in four weeks," I say.

"Wow! That's a tall order," says Joe. "I put a tracer on several totes recently, and they are running through the plant in an average of five and one-half weeks. Knowing that, and adding the fact that the vendors have been squeezed tight to get the inventory down, I doubt if we can do it."

"I accepted the challenge, Joe. We should get the order on the telecopier this afternoon. We took only twenty-five percent out of the cycle for the purpose of scheduling vendors. That's seven and a half weeks' material cycle. We should have plenty of material. We'll use the red tote pans for this order. Remember, red is top priority all the way through the plant. There's a lot at stake."

Joe looks as if he wants to say something, but hesitates. After a few moments he says, "Damn, four months ago, I'd have told you that you were a melonhead if you took on something like this, but—we can do it, can't we?"

"I'm planning on it," I say. "In fact, we could ship all thousand pieces at the end of this week if we want to strip them from our shipping buffer, but I want to prove that the system is solid enough to respond to our needs. I want to get them from scratch in four weeks or less."

I drive all the way back to Lynton for the night. Mom called me a couple of times, checking up. I've been staying at the condo almost exclusively lately, but Vickie has gone back to Lexington for a week or two. The condo's a lonely place without her.

CHAPTER 34

The plant is new, it's always clean and tidy, but the difference is amazing when I enter the parking lot. The grass is mowed, the bushes around the building are perfectly manicured, and the lines marking the parking spaces are freshly painted. There is a large area roped off in the parking lot and marked with a large white cross, to give the helicopter pilot a target. Arthur King is due to arrive from headquarters within the hour.

I take the weekender bag into my office. Arthur has invited me to return with him to Saratoga Springs. King Arthur is running tomorrow in the biggest race of the season for two-year-olds, the Saratoga Special, and Arthur King has borrowed a chalet for the week end.

The usual tour of the plant will be followed by a debriefing in the main conference room. Arthur has heard about our percussion system. Vickie has made certain of it. I'm hoping to do a little maneuvering of my own.

When I enter the office, Toni is sitting in my chair. Her smile is a yard wide. "I couldn't wait to show you this," she says, as she jumps up and holds her hand out to me. On her third finger is the biggest rock that I've ever seen. "MX gave it to me last night. Isn't it gorgeous?"

"Congratulations, Toni." I give her a hug and kiss. "He's one lucky son of a gun."

"I'm the lucky one," she says proudly.

Joe and Gary come in to announce that everything's in order for Arthur's visit. Toni throws us a curve. "I hope that Arthur hasn't seen the shop cost report for last month. The costs are really going through the roof."

"I have the right to say this, Toni, because I'm a member of the royal order of bean-counters too. The financial measurements that this company uses are no damned good!"

Toni laughs. "You know it and I know it, but Scott Crotty doesn't know it, and I doubt that Arthur King does. We could be in for a long, difficult meeting."

"I hope that it does come up. I can handle it," I assure her. "There's a big advantage when dealing from strength."

We go over the details of the tour, step by step, to be certain that we haven't missed anything.

The unmistakable, intruding noise of the helicopter gets me moving out of the building toward the landing area. I watch as the powder-blue chopper settles onto the parking lot and Arthur emerges. "Welcome to Salem, Arthur. Did you have a smooth flight?" I greet him with a hearty handshake.

"Smooth as silk, Larry. I hope that our trip to Saratoga is as good," he says.

We enter the plant through the front door and Arthur drops his briefcase in my office. I take a page from MX's book and begin the tour in the stockroom, then follow the parts flow.

Joe explains the color-coding system as we follow along the route. I notice that all of the red tote pans are through the pacers already.

We stop at the yellow resource—my pride and joy, the grind center. I point out that we are inspecting parts before grind to increase throughput. Arthur watches the teamwork involved in making a setup, and I tell him that the machines run even when the workers take breaks and lunches. He is visibly impressed. He notices the change from color-coded totes to gray, as the parts pass through the pacing resources. Arthur spends a lot of time on the tour, asking questions about setups, lot sizes, and priority determination. This guy knows manufacturing. The tour takes about twice the time we've allotted for it—a good sign.

When we return to the conference room, the coffee is ready, thanks to Helen, and Arthur's briefcase is on the table. The next item on the agenda is a show-and-tell detailing the workings of our system, but Arthur wants to talk. He laughs. "I've seen a lot of factories, but I've never seen one like yours. I like it. It's solid."

I go through my pitch and I notice Arthur nodding constantly, absorbing every aspect of what I'm saying.

When I'm finished, Arthur says, "I see this system as your version of the Japanese Just-in-Time systems. They fascinate me, but every time I read something about them, the author adds a disclaimer, to the effect that the Japanese culture differences make it work for them. I almost believed that bullcrap until today. You people are making it work right here in Salem, USA. You're not done yet, but you've got quite a system in the making. In some ways, your system is better than the Japanese. You run with less inventory than they do, and your system is a combination of push and pull scheduling. Their's is one hundred percent pull."

I keep underestimating this guy. He knows a lot about our system —as much as we do.

Arthur continues, "Since the business review, a couple of weeks ago, when Larry tried to explain the fallacies in the way we measure manufacturing, I've been thinking about some of the points he brought up. Do you think that the measurements are wrong from a financial standpoint, Toni?" he asks, taking the ball right out of my hands.

Toni is taken by surprise, but only for a second. "The financial measurements prevent us from making money!" she exclaims.

Arthur takes a paper from his briefcase. "This is your monthly shop cost report. It's pretty sick. Can you tell me how this measurement prevents ConnYankee from making money?"

I told her that I would handle it, if it came up, but Arthur has changed that plan. It doesn't seem to bother Toni. "Let me review the way we accumulate shop costs," she begins. "Workers report their time against a particular part number, in the form of work done on the parts, or setups on a machine. These inputs are accumulated and used to develop shop costs. An overhead rate is established from our salaries, heat and light, premium for overtime, and other things. This is factored into the shop cost scheme as a multiplier to the labor and setup numbers. Material costs are added, to come up with a final cost. For example—" She goes to the board and writes:

Overhead Rate	250%
Material	$225.00
Labor	$50.00
Setups	$10.00
Shop Cost	$435.00

"The shop cost is calculated by adding material cost to labor cost and setup cost. In addition the labor and setups costs are multiplied by a factor of two hundred fifty percent, which is added to the total, making the final cost the four hundred thirty-five dollars that you see.

"Suppose that we cut the batch sizes in half. The setup time would double to twenty dollars, making the final shop cost go up to four hundred seventy dollars."

Arthur nods his head. "That's the way that it's supposed to work. Theoretically, when that happens, there are supposed to be other places where the setups are reduced to compensate for the time lost, all things being equal."

"If what you say is true, some of our shop costs would go up, and some of them would go down, don't you agree?" asks Toni.

Arthur takes a quick look at the report in front of him. "I see what you're driving at Toni. All twenty of your shop costs have gone up dramatically in the past three months. Interesting."

"It's the way that we accumulate costs. In order to drive the inventory down, we need to cut cycles. Cutting cycles without working excessive amounts of overtime can only be accomplished by running smaller batches," she says.

"There's the Japanese philosophy again," says Arthur.

Toni continues, "Running smaller batches means more setups, which drives shop costs up all over the place."

"If you're making more setups, then your shop costs should go up, shouldn't they?" he asks.

Now Toni's got him. She's like a matador playing the bull. "We are shipping parts to our customers on time—in fact, this month we will be shipping some parts early."

Arthur nods in agreement.

Toni continues, "We are working far less overtime, with less inventory investment, and we have not hired any additional people. Where are those additional costs, that your report shows, going?"

For the first time since I've known him, Arthur is speechless.

Toni presses her advantage. "We incur costs—a negative—and we generate income—a positive. If the difference between the two is positive, we make a profit. If it's negative, we lose money. It's as simple as that, when the window dressing that we call shop costs and efficiencies is removed. With our lower inventory, lower expenses, and earlier shipments, we are making more money for ConnYankee, and the financial measurements are lying to us."

Arthur laughs, "Well put, Toni. I thought that you'd be easier on the old man than your boss, but I was wrong. If what you say is true, what do we do about it?"

I get the feeling that Arthur was convinced by a certain blonde, long before he got here. I take over. "What we must do is categorize things differently. I want inventory to be all of the things that we buy that ultimately go out the door as finished goods. Everything else, including labor, will be pooled as overhead—operating expense is a better word," I say.

"How will that help?" asks Arthur.

"Our present system assumes that we have a perfectly balanced plant, that everybody's time must be accounted for one hundred percent. If we do have a perfectly balanced plant—that is, if all of the people have exactly enough to do to keep them busy for forty hours, no more, no less—we might be able to use shop costs and efficiencies, but it wouldn't make any difference, because a perfectly balanced plant cannot function."

"Vickie explained the theory of perfectly balanced plants to me the other day," says Arthur. "I know what you mean."

"By lumping all operating expenses into the overhead pool, we can account for all of the time, both productive and nonproductive. The only really important numbers will be the bottom line—the profit and loss statement."

"You can't use the profit and loss statement when you're dealing with Joe, Gary, Ernie, and Dean," says Arthur. "You can't tell them to go out in the factory and make you some money. They make turbine blades."

"That's right," I say. "The measurements that equate to making money will still be used. We must still measure output, overtime and quality the same way as we always did. We will continue to drive inventory as low as we can, by using the system, but it will be in terms of material only. We will no longer keep track of efficiencies and checkpoints. Instead, we will measure throughput at the pacing resources," I say.

Arthur makes some notes before answering. "I'll digest all of the information I've heard here today, and I'll let you know." He looks at his watch. "Thank you for a most enlightening day. It was well worth the trip. I like what I see here. Keep up the good work."

It was the standard exit routine that I've heard a thousand times. I get the feeling that my people expected more—a medal, maybe. But men in Arthur's position always take the conservative approach, never making hasty remarks or decisions. It all boils down to whether we've done our homework. If we have, we'll get what we want.

CHAPTER 35

Helicopters are not my favorite mode of transportation, and Saratoga is at the outer limit of the chopper's range, but we get there without incident. The chalet turns out to be a rather large estate, set in the hills. I notice Vickie standing there as we circle the house, and I want to jump out before the chopper is on the ground. I stifle my urge and let my host deplane first. The natural instinct is to take Vickie in my arms, but I settle for a polite kiss, in deference to Arthur. She whispers, "I love you," and leaves me to walk to the house with him.

The first chance we get to be alone is when I take her out to dinner. We do a little cuddling in the car, to make up for lost time, before we end up at what is reported to be the best restaurant in town. It's called The Firehouse, and that's what it is—a reconverted firehouse. We both order salad, baked potato, and filet mignon. It is excellent, and Vickie catches me up on the news while we have an after-dinner drink.

"King Arthur has a good chance for the Eclipse award, as the two-year-old horse of the year, if he runs big tomorrow," she says.

"That's quite an honor. Is there anything in the race that can beat him?" I ask.

"All the New York horses that he beat at Belmont, and a couple of nice colts that have just started racing, are here. He's a big pre-race favorite, according to the morning line."

"Toni was showing off her engagement ring this morning. Did you know that she and MX got engaged last night?" I ask.

"Yes, she called me this afternoon, after you left the plant. Oh, I forgot to tell you. Toni and MX are flying in and will join us at the track tomorrow. Toni wants me to warn you that MX is bringing that infernal computer of his. He's got a new scheme worked out that is going to make him a fortune, so he says." She laughs, and shakes her head.

"How did Arthur like Salem?"

"He seems to be impressed, but he's hard to read," I answer.

Vickie laughs, "I can read him like a book. He gives everybody the opinion that he doesn't make snap judgments, but that's a façade. He wants to project the image of a proper conservative executive who thinks things over and studies every angle, so he lets people stew. The truth is, he's always made better decisions when he makes them at the speed of light, like a prize fighter throwing punches. If the fighter stops to think about the best angle and the proper leverage, he'll get knocked on his bottom."

"Well, I'll be damned!" I say. "He's really a gambler at heart, isn't he?"

"That's why he likes the sport of horse racing so very much. Everything about it is a gamble," she says.

When we return to the house, Arthur is sitting on the front deck. "How was your meal?" he asks.

"We went to The Firehouse for filet. It was excellent," I tell him.

We settle into the deck chairs with him to enjoy the late evening air. After a few minutes, Vickie bids us goodnight, saying that she has a slight headache.

Arthur asks me to wait and goes into the house. In a few minutes, he returns with a pitcher of plantation punch, laced with rum. He pours us each a tall glass. "Larry, I think that you've got the makings of a successful operation up there in Salem. I learned a lot today," he says.

"We believe in what we are doing, and those measurements are getting in the way," I tell him.

"That too," he continues. "But that's not what I was thinking about. I learned something even more valuable."

"You mean, something you saw?"

"Yes," he says. "For years, I've been pretty damned successful running ConnYankee, and I'm proud of what I've built."

"You should be. Few people can boast of building something from scratch, like ConnYankee," I say.

"Larry, what do you think my biggest problem has been over the years?"

I think for a few moments. "I can't even begin to imagine," I say.

"The toughest problem any manager has is handling change. When you're as far removed from the trenches as I am, the problem becomes monumental. I knew pretty much what you were trying to do at your plant, and that's not the real reason I went there today, although I must admit that your system looks intriguing. I wanted to see first hand how you were handling the change aspect of what you were trying to do."

"I never thought about it as much of a problem, really. I showed my people the weaknesses in the checkpoint system and created a desire to find a better way," I say.

"Yes, I heard all about your little debate. Nice touch, but there's more to it than that. I've tried the motivation technique many times. I get expert consultants in to present new ideas, and the people seem to understand and agree with everything the experts say, but when the presentation is over, they go back to their jobs and continue on their merry way, doing the same old things that they always did." He refills his glass from the pitcher. I do the same. It's a smooth drink.

Arthur continues, "I work on the idea that in order to achieve change, my managers have to want it. I never force change down the throats of any of them, and I think that they use the same philosophy on their people. It's a slow process, when it works. Too many people in this company are carrying around the anchor of the past."

Arthur goes into the house to get another pitcher of punch. He returns and fills our glasses to the brim.

"Boy, this is good stuff," he says. "Where was I? Oh yes . . . as I was saying . . . Change is a slow process, but the change that you made, from checkpoint scheduling to your . . . what did Joe call it? . . . percussion system . . . was accomplished almost overnight. Larry, that is a significant change. I wanted to see what you did that was different from what I would have done."

"I don't think that I did anything different. I showed my people the better way—made them want it."

"You did better than that, Larry. You didn't give them a choice. You made it clear up front that it was going to happen, and then you got right down in the mud and worked side by side with them to make sure it did," says Arthur.

I take some more punch. "I never thought about it that way, but you're right—that's what I did. It seemed so damned important for me to be a part of it."

"Your participative form of management may be the best way to effect sweeping change. Thank you for the lesson. Here, help me finish off this punch." He fills both of our glasses.

We enjoy the last of the punch. It's getting late, but my bottom feels like there's a lead weight tied to it. I look at Arthur and he's staring at me with a silly grin. "We are both drunk," he announces.

"I do feel a bit light in the head," I tell him.

Arthur looks at me. "Poor Larry, I've got you in a box, haven't I?"

"What do you mean?" I ask.

"I know, Larry—I know! And it's this competition that's keeping you from telling me, isn't it?"

Maybe it's the punch, but he doesn't make sense.

He continues. "You're in love with Vickie, and she's in love with you. I know—just as her own father would know."

That will sober me up, if nothing else. "I guess that we should have told you, but it wouldn't look right at this time," I say.

"You're too honest, Larry. Anybody else would use all of the weapons they could get their hands on, if they had the chance you've got. It really won't change my decision one iota, you know."

"I know that," I say. "It's just that Marty might not appreciate it."

"I've known Marty for a lot of years, and if that's what's worrying you, forget it," says Arthur. "He knows that what is written on that paper in my wall safe will determine who gets the job, and nothing else."

"I don't know what to say. I just want you to know that my intentions have been nothing but honorable all along and I—"

He interrupts. "I know that. No need to explain. I trust you both completely."

"Is that why you asked me to look after her like a father?" I ask.

"Just a little insurance, that's all. Pretty clever of me, wasn't it?" he laughs.

Since the cat is out of the bag, what the hell. "Sir, since you have taken her father's place, may I have your permission to ask Vickie to marry me?"

"I'd be honored, Larry, but can you hold off on the wedding for a while? You know, there are preparations to make. This will be no ordinary wedding."

"If she'll have me, I'm sure that you and she will work it out."

He struggles to his feet and staggers forward. I do the same, with a great deal of effort. We clasp hands. "I know Ed Barlow would have been honored to have you as a son-in-law and I feel the same way—but one more thing," he says. "You must stop this drinking until all hours of the night."

CHAPTER 36

A loud rap on the bedroom door awakens me. I feel as if I've just gone to bed. I struggle to my feet, and throw on a robe. It's Vickie. "Are you going to sleep all day, lazybones?"

I take her in my arms and kiss her. "What was that for?" she asks.

I want to tell her all about last night, but it's got to be candle light and soft music. "Oh, nothing . . . just wanted to start the day off right."

"I appreciate that," she says. "Come on down, or you're going to miss breakfast. Arthur's already left for the track, and we've got to meet Toni and MX pretty soon."

Somehow, I manage to sweep away the cobwebs and get dressed. Soon Vickie and I are at the airport. MX has already landed, and he and Toni are waiting for us. As promised, MX has the trusty laptop computer under his arm. "I've figured out the system that will make me a bundle today," he says.

"Is it like the last one?" I ask.

"As a matter of fact, it is, but I've made some significant improvements. It's going to work, you watch," says MX.

Vickie admires Toni's ring. "I'm jealous, Toni. That's beautiful," she says. "Congratulations to the both of you. Have you set the date yet?"

"No," she answers. "It'll be some time in the spring. MX wants to take a Windjammer to Bermuda for the honeymoon."

I laugh. "Leave it to you, to think up something like that."

MX is anxious to tell me about his new system to beat the races. "Let's get back to my system. When the selection comes up on the screen, it will carry with it a rating number on a scale of one to one hundred. It is the relative strength of the winning selection as compared to that of the opposition. I'll start with a bankroll of one hundred dollars and will wager according to the rating number."

"Sounds complex to me," I say.

"No, let me give you an example. Suppose that number three is the computer selection in the first race. My bankroll is one hundred dollars and the rating number is thirty-two. I would bet thirty-two percent of my bankroll on the three horse, to show—in this case, thirty-two dollars."

"I thought that your system picked horses to win."

"That's the beauty of it. It picks the horse to win, and I bet it to show. It's giving me the edge, because if the horse comes in first, second, or third, I cash," says MX.

I shake my head and wish him good luck.

Saratoga is a beautiful old track. It operates only during the month of August, when the New York horsemen have a kind of vacation away from the hustle and bustle of New York City. The state racing commission puts up extremely large purses for the winners.

We settle into Arthur's box before the races. It's a bit early. The girls have gone to do whatever it is girls do. "I've been working with the scheduling system, trying to make my algorithm fit it," says MX. "It's working pretty well, but it wants to keep varying the amount of parts that go into a tote pan."

"That's interesting," I say. "If your algorithm is sound, there has to be logic that is causing it to happen."

"There is. We've got batch sizes that vary according to the order in which the totes are received at a resource. We are controlling the process quantity. That's all right, but it doesn't take it far enough," MX says.

"What are we overlooking?" I ask.

"In your factory, you have two different kinds of batches running together," says MX. You have the process quantity, which is the amount that you run between setups. We have figured out a way to vary that quantity, and it has worked well and helped shorten the cycle tremendously, but it's not enough. The other batch is the quantity that you pass from operation to operation, the transfer batch. You have fixed that quantity to be always fifty pieces, by the size of the tote pan."

"That's a restriction placed on us by the size of the tote," I say.

"That's just it. We don't want to schedule our factory around the size of a tote pan. It restricts the flow. We would get better synchronization if we could vary the quantity in each tote. The computer can do it. We should be able to do something with the percussion system."

"What if we find out which parts are arriving late, and put more totes in the line, but keep the same buffer size?" I ask.

"I was thinking along those lines," says MX.

"Let's say that a part's buffer has a history of being filled two days late. We could add about forty percent more totes, but put only thirty pieces in each one, creating a forty percent reduction in the transfer batch."

"Yes," says MX. "You would be increasing the speed forty percent, so the buffer should be filled faster, and the problem should be evident earlier. You could start there, watch what happens, and adjust accordingly. The setup frequency should not be affected, but you can watch that also."

"That's right, and the better flow should decrease our inventory again."

The girls come back, and we turn our attention to the races. MX enters all of the data for the first race. His selection is number seven, and the rating is fifty-two. "I'll bet fifty-two dollars to show on number seven," he says as he leaves to make his wager.

The number seven horse loses the first race, but only by a nose, in a photo finish. The show payoff is four dollars. MX cashes his show ticket, which is worth one hundred four dollars. His bankroll is now one fifty-two.

His selection in the second race is number two, and the rating is a whopping seventy-five. The horse wins the race, and pays four twenty to show. In two races, MX has increased his bankroll to two hundred seventy-seven dollars. "Beautiful system. It works like a charm," he says as he enters the figures for the third race.

"That's only two races," says Toni. "The last time you tried your system you were doing great after two races also."

"This time, with the enhancements, I'll sustain it," says MX. "I'm going to have to bet on number four in the third race, and the rating of sixty-five calls for a one hundred eighty dollar wager."

The race is run and the four horse finishes third, but MX is a winner once again. His bankroll is now nearly five hundred dollars.

MX wins the first seven races, and his bankroll stands at four thousand dollars. "See that big diamond ring on Toni's finger?" he says. "I'm paying for it today, with my winnings." He's high.

Arthur joins us after the horses enter the track for the feature race, the Saratoga Special. Mike Roberts is with him. "This is the one we want," says Arthur. "We've got an offer from a syndicate for twenty million dollars, if he wins today."

"You're not thinking of selling my baby, are you?" asks Vickie.

"Not on your life," says Arthur. "We'll make a deal to get into the breeding business after his three-year-old season. We still keep possession of the King, but the syndicate gets the biggest share of the stud fees. It's good insurance."

Arthur notices the computer in MX's lap. "What kind of a chance does that thing give my horse?" he asks.

"I just put in the data—watch."

The computer blinks a few times before the number five comes up on the screen, with a rating of one hundred. King Arthur is the five horse in the race. "The computer pegs King Arthur as a sure thing. I've got to bet four thousand dollars on him to show."

The horses are led into the starting gate. King Arthur gives them the usual hard time, but the blindfold trick works again. The track announcer's familiar "They're off!" calls our attention to the track. King Arthur is away from the gate in good shape, once again, well up with the leaders. The jockey is content to ride along in third place until they hit the top of the stretch. Mike Roberts says, "I want to see what he's got. I told the jockey to hold him until right about now, and then touch him with the whip to see what kind of move he could put on."

We watch as the jockey reaches behind him with the whip and

flicks it at King Arthur. He reacts as if he's shot out of a cannon. Before I can blink, he's past the two horses that were in front of him. The jockey hits him once more before resuming his hard ride. By the time he reaches the finish line, he's a good fifteen or twenty lengths in the lead.

Arthur turns to Mike, and they shake hands lustily. "Welcome to the big leagues, Mr. King," says Mike.

"Big leagues is right!" exclaims Arthur. "The success of Connecticut Yankee is assured for years with the syndication money, no matter what the King does from now on."

Vickie says, "I won't think of it as a success until King Arthur wins the Kentucky Derby."

We all leave for the winner's circle. It's getting to be a habit. After the usual ceremony and round of congratulations, we are ready to leave. Although there is one more race, it is anticlimactic. "Wait! I've got to see my system through to the end," says MX. King Arthur paid two twenty to show, and MX won only four hundred with his four thousand dollar bet.

"Be satisfied with forty four hundred dollars," says Toni. "You've proven that your system works."

"It's got to be for a whole race card," says MX.

He has his way. We wait around for the last race. The horse selected is a ninety-five rating, making MX's bet just about four thousand dollars. A ninety-five rating is a pretty damned good horse. The race begins.

"Look at him go," says MX. "He's got a two-length lead right out of the gate."

MX's horse keeps his lead until well into the homestretch. "It's like eating ice cream," shouts MX, as he watches his horse galloping. Suddenly, for no apparent reason, the jockey is trying to hang on to the horse's neck to keep from falling off. The saddle is slipping under the horse's belly. Before the horse has taken two more steps, jockey and saddle are deposited into the dust of the race track. The horse continues on to win without a rider, but is disqualified.

"That's fate," says MX. "I'm convinced. At least I've still got four hundred left, enough to pay for the laptop computer."

As we leave the track grounds, MX stops where a paperboy is selling his wares. "Do you like computers, kid?" He asks.

"I sure do, mister. That's what I'm saving up for," the boy answers.

MX takes a paper and hands the boy the laptop computer. "Stop hanging around the race track, kid. Go home and play with this thing," he says.

CHAPTER 37

Two weeks have gone by since I had that session with Arthur and the plantation punch. I haven't asked Vickie yet—waiting for the right opportunity. We went to Saratoga again this past Saturday. King Arthur ran in the Hopeful Stakes. The distance was slightly longer, but he won impressively again. Arthur had been planning to run him only one more time this year, in the Breeder's Futurity at Keeneland in October, but the syndicate wants to run him again in California in November, in the Breeders' Cup races. They say that a victory would double his stud fee.

After lunch I call Gary and Joe to my office. "Did we get the thousand-piece special order shipped on Friday?" I ask.

"It went out complete and right on time," says Joe. "But we needed to borrow a few pieces from the shipping buffer to make it."

"That's what it's there for," I say.

"We can work overtime to get the buffer filled up again," says Gary.

Joe interrupts. "That won't be necessary. Remember how our system is set up. Every resource, including the pacers, has extra capacity. We'll just let the buffers fill gradually and avoid the overtime expense." Joe has adapted to the system enthusiastically.

"How do you slow down again when the buffers are refilled?" I ask.

"We don't need to do anything," he answers. "The only surplus work in process is in those red totes that didn't make it all the way to ship in four weeks. When they do get to ship, we'll transfer the parts into the buffer tote pans and put the red totes away. It's like repaying a loan."

"Hell of a nice job, but there's no rest for the weary. You've done such a great job that I'm certain that we will get that big order for next year. Has either of you made any plans to man up for it?" I ask.

"We've got it scoped out," says Joe. "There's room for a lot of the additional people on the first and second shifts, but I don't like overloading like that."

"Won't it save us some money?" I ask.

Joe looks at me as he ponders the question. "What we save would be the ten percent night shift bonus, but factory flow might be adversely affected by the imbalance between shifts. Our system runs much better when the shifts are even. I think that we should pay the night shift bonus and keep the workforce as evenly distributed as we can."

"I see what you mean," I say. "We don't want to add any wait time that we could incur if parts waited for an operation that wasn't covered on the off shift. Sometimes it might be necessary, but we shouldn't force it. Good idea, Joe. Do it."

Gary says, "I've already got some preliminary quotes out to the vendors, so we'll save some time when we get the final details."

"Stay right on it. Visit those vendors, if it will help. I don't want to be waiting for parts."

"Our short cycle system allows us to give the vendors more lead time. We'll be all right," says Gary.

"Joe, you'd better start the preliminary screening interview process now, so we can line up hiring and training as soon as the order is official," I say.

"I'll get right on it," he answers.

"Have you done anything with that flexible transfer batch scheme?" I ask.

"We put it in but had problems at first. Some of the operators were filling the tote pans before passing them on. We finally solved that by getting some wooden blocks and filling the empty slots with them when parts are issued. It's working now, and I can already see the improvement in the buffers," says Joe.

"Stay right on it," I say. "It's got to be a continuing process. Buffers and batch sizes must be looked at constantly."

"We did find an instance—I think it was the S3's. A drilling operation was not yielding enough good parts to fill the buffer on time," says Joe. "Instead of reducing the batches, which would have done nothing for us, we got Ernie and his crew to look at the problem. They ended up improving the holding fixture to give us tighter tolerances, and we improved the yield. That's what our system does for us. It uncovers problems. It steers us in the right direction. Reminds me of draining a swamp—the alligators have no place to hide. Excess inventory was our swamp."

Things look too good to be true, and they are. By the end of the week it becomes apparent that we are going to miss a shipment for the first time in months. We try everything, but two hundred B7's are not on the truck when the week ends. I call a special Saturday morning meeting of Gary, Joe, and MX.

"What happened out there?" I begin.

"I think that we've found a flaw in the system," announces Gary. The remark gets MX's attention.

"Why do you say that?" he asks.

Gary continues, "I don't believe that our system can handle emergencies as well as it should."

"I didn't know that we had any emergencies this week," I say.

"It really started last week," says Gary. "We needed to strip the entire B7 buffer of two hundred pieces to get out that special order. When we came to work this week, we couldn't see any B7's in the ship buffer. It made us uneasy."

MX asks, "What did you do about it?"

"Like any good expediter, my guy took a long hard look at where the nearest two hundred pieces were. They had a long way to go." Gary goes to the board and draws a flow diagram.

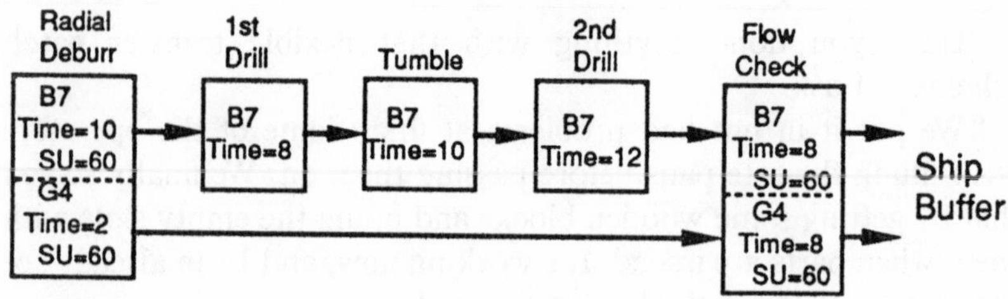

"All two hundred pieces were waiting at radial deburr. Actually, there were ten tote pans in queue, five B7's and five G4's. They had arrived there in this order." He writes the sequence of totes on the board.

G4 G4 B7 G4 B7 B7 G4 B7 G4 B7

"The expediter knew that B7's go through five tough operations to get to final packing, while the G4's go through only two of them. He looked at shipping and found that the G4 buffer was already full, that the week's shippers were already there. He went back to the radial deburr queue and saw that the G4's were in the way of the B7's," says Gary.

MX drops his pencil and holds his head in both hands. "What did he do?"

"He did what any good expediter would do," says Gary. "He reshuffled the sequence of tote pans at radial deburr so they looked like this." Gary writes a new row of numbers on the board.

B7 B7 B7 B7 B7 G4 G4 G4 G4 G4

"Why did he do that?" asks MX.

"Simple," say Gary. "All of the G4's for the week were already at shipping, while the B7's had a long way to go. He gave them top priority—greased the skids, so to speak."

MX has turned his attention away from Gary and is busy making entries on a scratch pad.

"Why didn't it work?" I ask.

"It would have if it weren't for that damned Lennie Seboy. He insisted on working the flow-check parts in the order that they arrived. When my expediter tried to reshuffle the parts once again, Lennie threw him out of the area," says Gary.

Joe laughs. "Lennie is dedicated. He has been told to follow a certain sequence, and he will. I can't fault him for that."

"He blew it. It cost us a shipment," says Gary.

"If your expediter moved all of the B7's to the front of the line at radial deburr, why didn't they remain there? What happened?" says Joe.

"I can show you exactly what happened," says MX as he heads toward the board with his scratchpad.

"How can you possibly know what the hell happened out there on the shop floor? You weren't even around the plant all week," says Gary.

"You're right. I wasn't here all week, and the first I heard of the problem was just now, but I'll bet you lunch at the Red Carpet, for everybody in this room, that I can show you what happened," challenges MX.

"You haven't spoken to anybody about this?" asks Gary.

"Nary a word," answers MX.

"You're on," shouts Gary. "But I've got to warn you that I eat big on Saturdays."

"And every other day too," mutters Joe.

MX writes numbers on the board as he speaks. "We work two forty-hour shifts at all of the operations involved in Gary's diagram. That equates to forty-eight hundred minutes working time per week. The numbers I'm writing down represent the start and stop time for each batch at each resource for the entire week. This is the best case." In a few minutes MX has created a matrix of numbers.

Batch	RadialD	1stDr	Tumble	2ndDr	FlowCh	Ship
B7	0-500	500-900	900-1400	1400-2000	2000-2400	50
B7	500-1000	1000-1400	1400-1900	2000-2600	2600-3000	50
B7	1000-1500	1500-1900	1900-2400	2600-3200		
B7	1500-2000	2000-2400	2400-2900	3200-3800		
B7	2000-2500	2500-2900	2900-3400	3800-4400		
G4	S2560-2660	X	X	X	S3060-3460	50
G4	2660-2760	X	X	X	3460-3860	50
G4	2860-2960	X	X	X	3860-4260	50
G4	2860-3060	X	X	X	4260-4660	50
G4	3060-3160	X	X	X	4660-	

"The letter S means a setup is paid," continues MX. "You can see what happened. The first two batches got to flow check first and were processed through with no problem. By the time that the third batch of B7's got to flow check, all five batches of the G4's were already there. Lennie Seboy followed the sequence as I've shown here, with the result being that the G4 buffer was filled once again, while the two hundred order of B7's could not be filled. Is that how it happened, Gary?"

"That's exactly right," says Gary. "But if it weren't for Lennie Seboy being so uncooperative, we would have made it."

Joe interrupts. "You lose the bet, and I eat big too."

"All right, but if my expediter hadn't pushed those parts through radial deburr the way he did, we would have had a real disaster on our hands," says Gary.

"I'll make the bet more interesting. I say that if your expediter had stayed home all week, we would have been better off. If I'm wrong, I'll buy the dinner and drinks. If I'm right, you do the same," offers MX.

"You mean to tell me that if we had done nothing, that we'd have been better off? That's a sucker bet. You're on again," says Gary.

MX erases his figures from the board. "Suppose that you had as much faith in the system as Joe and Lennie. What would happen if you did not allow your expediter to expedite?"

"The parts would have gone through the operations in the original sequence," answers Gary.

MX writes a new sequence of numbers on the board. "This is the schedule that would have taken place with the original queue."

Batch	RadialD	1stDr	Tumble	2ndDr	FlowCh	Ship
G4	0-100	X	X	X	100-500	50
G4	100-200	X	X	X	500-900	50
B7	S260-760	760-1160	1160-1660	1660-2260	S2600-3000	50
G4	S820-920	X	X	X	920-1320	50
B7	S980-1480	1480-1880	1880-2380	2380-2980	S3520-3920	50
B7	1480-1980	1980-2380	2380-2880	2980-3580	3920-4320	50
G4	S2040-2140	X	X	X	2140-2540	50
B7	S2200-2700	2700-3100	3100-3600	3600-4200	4320-4720	50
G4	S2760-2860	X	X	X	3060-3460	50
B7	S2940-3440	3440-3840	3840-4340	4340-		

"The parts would have arrived at flow check in the following sequence," continues MX.

G4 G4 G4 G4 B7 G4 B7 B7 B7 B7

"As you can readily see, even though you would have made a great many more setups, you would have shipped the entire two hundred B7's as well as getting more G4's. You must let the system work. It's designed to do the job for you."

Joe never lets an opportunity slide by. "You melonhead. Your expediter screwed things up—not Lennie Seboy. You owe him an apology, and you owe us all a treat at the Red Carpet."

Gary looks bewildered, but I can see that he gets the point. I intervene. "It's never good to miss shipments, but the lesson learned here today is much, much more valuable than one missed shipment. What have we learned?" I ask.

"We must always look at the entire plant when we make decisions out on that floor. If we don't, we can't know if our decision is correct," says Joe.

"That's exactly right," says MX. "Setting priorities by looking at only one resource is nearly always disastrous."

"I can think of another thing that we've been trying to avoid," I say.

Gary knows. "It's the big-batch syndrome. At the first sign of trouble, both the expediter and myself made big batches out of little ones. We actually extended the cycle time, didn't we?"

"That's right," I say. "From now on, expediting must not change sequencing of parts in any queue unless it can be shown that productivity of the plant as a whole will be served. Now let's go to lunch on Gary."

CHAPTER 38

The foliage that covers the White Mountains in late September is dazzling. Reds and yellows of the maples, blended with the variegated browns of the oaks, and the evergreens, paint a spectacular display around North Conway. It's between seasons in the mountains. The summer tourist crowd has left, and the ski bums have yet to make their appearance. I pull the Maserati into the empty parking lot of the Red Parka. We have the restaurant to ourselves. We order ribs and get our salad from the abundant salad bar.

"MX told me about the nice luncheon that Gary bought for everyone a couple of weeks ago," says Vickie. She laughs aloud. "Imagine MX telling him that the plant would have been better off if the expediter had stayed home! That's precious."

"It was true. We actually would have been better off if the expediter had not intervened," I say.

"When I heard the story, I added a chapter in my thesis about expediting," says Vickie. "The expediting function, as we know it today, is a roadblock to synchronized manufacturing."

"It was for us," I answer.

Vickie continues, "If a manufacturing facility is small enough so that one expediter can handle the entire plant, expediting could possibly be an effective production control tool. Problems arise when more than one expediter is needed."

"It becomes a question of who has the loudest mouth and the quickest feet, doesn't it?" I ask.

"That's right. In fact, my theory is that expediting, as an effective production control tool, is inversely proportional to the number of expediters one has."

I smile. "Every manufacturing guy that I've ever met thinks that a topnotch expediter is worth his weight in gold."

"What an effective expediter is supposed to do is make sure that the correct parts are being run so that schedules are optimized. He really can't determine what is best for the entire plant, so he pushes parts. He is like a snowplow, pushing the pile closer and closer to the ship point. What he actually does is cause people to change from one part to another, or not to, depending on what he's trying to push."

"Yes," I say. "The expediter in the push environment actually determines batch sizes."

"Correct," she says. "Expediters have a lot to do with the bottom line—profit. When they direct a changeover, they cause a lot size to change as well as cause a setup to be made. When they decide to do nothing, they cause lot sizes to increase, buffers to get larger, and inventory to go up."

"That is an awful lot of responsibility to give to one person," I say.

"The problem with it is that increasing inventory between operations makes an expediter's life a whole lot easier. There are parts everywhere, just in case they are needed," Vickie says.

"If it weren't for the stockroom issuing parts to a preset schedule, the expediters would fill every available space with inventory," I say.

"Our scheduling system prevents this, but in the conventional system, production control establishes static cycles that are long enough to insure extra inventory, just in case," says Vickie.

"That's the way it was with the checkpoint system, and that's the way it is throughout the the rest of the ConnYankee organization right now."

"Isn't it exciting?" says Vickie. "You may just have the opportunity to do something about it very soon."

Her statement brings me up short. The task seems insurmountable.

Vickie continues, "When an expediter pushes hard to make a date, he is usually shortening cycle time. When he does this, the law that for every action there is an equal and opposite reaction takes place. Something else gets long-cycled. This assures the expediter that he will have something to expedite tomorrow. The fires never go out."

"What bothers me about this whole subject is that the average expediter spends most of his time messing around with the crucial, or pacer, resources in the plant. When an expediter upsets a lot size on a crucial resource, he is causing an extra setup to be made on a resource that can only make schedule if setups are kept to a minimum. He is solving a short-term problem by actually decreasing the throughput of the entire plant, and losing money for the business," I say.

"In a pull-type system, like the percussion system, the expediter is invisible. It's a transparent rope that ties the parts to the pacing resources and pulls them along," says Vickie.

"I'm going to take a long look at the expediting function in our plant," I say. "But, right now, I wish that I had an expediter to send into the kitchen to push our ribs along. I'm hungry."

The ribs arrive, succulent and messy. I get as much on me as I do in me, but are they ever good! Vickie is sipping Irish coffee when I take the ring box out of my pocket. I slide it slowly across the table toward her as I stare directly into her eyes. I can see that she is stunned. When the box sits directly in front of her, I open it, and the lights catch the facets of the diamond. It's a beaut—cost me damned near all of the money I won on King Arthur. Vickie is visibly shaken. I can't help noticing how beautiful she is at this moment, as tears fill her eyes and she gasps. I say nothing, taking her left hand in mine while I remove the ring from the box. I slide it gently onto her finger. The moment is so perfect that I don't want to spoil it with words. I wait a few moments, holding her hand tightly as we stare at each other. Finally I say, "I've said this a couple of times in the past, Vickie. I love you very much."

"I love you too, Larry." She leans across the table and kisses me. "Can we leave now?" she says.

"You bet we can," I say. It's a beautiful evening in the White Mountains. I never want it to end. We stop a couple of times along the mountain road, to hold hands and walk. The ride back is the end of a perfect evening—and the beginning of something better.

CHAPTER 39

It's Breeders' Futurity weekend, and as we drive through the entrance to Connecticut Yankee, Vickie gets as excited as I've ever seen her. "Oh Larry, I'm so anxious to show Arthur my ring." She snuggles up to me and holds her left hand at arm's length, showing off the diamond.

The limousine pulls up to the front door of the main house, to a waiting Arthur King. Vickie jumps out, almost before the car comes to a halt. She rushes to Arthur and I feel like a forgotten man as I watch them embrace. When Arthur notices me standing there, he extends his hand. It is a warm handshake. "Welcome, son," he says. It's corny, but he has never been noted as a warm, outgoing individual. That evening in Saratoga showed me the real Arthur King. I liked what I saw then, and I like what I see now.

"I've had lunch set out. Let's go inside. We've got a lot to talk about." We settle into the dining area as Arthur continues, "First things first. What plans have you two lovebirds made?"

Vickie answers, "None yet. We can't make up our minds what kind of wedding we want. If Larry has his way, we'll elope to Nevada and get married in secret. If my parents were alive, though, I'd want what every girl dreams of—a big church wedding with all the trimmings."

Arthur takes her hand and shows a slight smile. "Larry is like me in a lot of ways. Cynthia and I had one of those small weddings, and she always felt that she had missed out on something. It was different in those days, though. We were scratching to make ends meet. That's certainly not the case now. Vickie, I want your wedding to be the wedding that your own father and mother would have wanted for you—as lavish as I can make it—something special. Do you mind, Larry, if I meddle a bit?"

I laugh. "I'm outnumbered in the camp of the enemy."

Arthur continues, "Is the first week in May of next year too soon?"

Vickie and I both say it together. "No."

Vickie continues, "No date is too soon for us, but why then?"

"It's the biggest time of the year in these parts," Arthur says. "It's Kentucky Derby week. Everybody who's anybody will be here for the Derby. We can really do it up brown. King Arthur will win the Derby on Saturday, we'll have a victory party on Saturday evening, and the wedding and reception will take place the next day. It will be the biggest social event in the entire country. I'll rent the whole Marriott for the invited guests. Maybe the President can come." He's getting carried away with the idea.

I whistle softly. "The President, huh? Just a modest affair."

Vickie gets out of her chair to jump up and down before throwing her arms around Arthur's neck. "Oh, Arthur, you really are like a father to me—thank you! It'll be perfect. There's so much to do. We'd better start making plans right away."

It's apparent to me that I have no say in the matter, so I say nothing, resigned to my fate.

"Good," Arthur announces. "It's all set, then. I'll get the announcements out within the week and hire a professional firm to handle the whole thing." I must look worried as Arthur looks into my face. "Don't fret, Larry. I promise you that I won't meddle after this. Just let me do this for you and Vickie—and myself."

"I'm not worried, but I guess I didn't expect all this."

"That's the price you pay when you marry someone Arthur King cares very much about," he answers with a grin.

"Let's change the subject. Let's talk about your plant. Vickie, you don't need to stay, unless you want to."

"I'll stay," she says. "The plant is a big part of my life right now."

"You're the talk of the company," Arthur continues. "That big contract you got for turbine blades is worth more than twenty-five million—the largest single order that ConnYankee has ever received. Congratulations."

"Thank you," I say. "We're really excited about it. My managers are right out straight—what with the day-to-day output considerations and ramping up for the new business. It's an exciting time in Salem, New Hampshire."

"I can well imagine," says Arthur. "It's times like this when I wish that I could be involved more in factory life. You've got yourself a really fine staff, and if anybody can do it, they can."

"One thing that you said, way back when you set this competition up, has stuck with me. It's the best piece of advice that I've ever received," I tell him.

"What was that?"

"You told Marty and me that people were what would make the difference for us. Truer words were never spoken. If I didn't have the right people, change could never have taken place—at least not the kind of change we've accomplished."

"As you go on to new challenges, always remember that, Larry. The people always make the difference, which reminds me of something else that I wanted to talk about. Have you thought about who your replacement is going to be? You'll be out of Salem in two and a half months," says Arthur.

"I've thought a lot about it. I've got two really outstanding individuals working for me," I say.

"Let me guess," says Arthur. "Could it be Toni and Joe Leonard?"

"You're very astute," I say. "That's right. Toni comes out on top, but her lack of experience prevents me from naming her. I'm going to go with Joe."

"Wise move," says Arthur. "You would be throwing Toni to the wolves. There's plenty of time for her."

Vickie interrupts, "Don't be too sure of that. You know how it is between Toni and MX. He is going to influence her life, you know."

Arthur laughs. "I'd hate to have MX influencing my life. He's completely unpredictable, but smart as they come. By the way, how is your system coming along?"

"The best answer I could give you would be that we got the big order, but the positive results that you saw in the last business review are even better now. Inventory has settled in at about forty-five percent of what it was with checkpoints. Overtime is down to about three percent, and we hope to get it even lower. Deviated parts are a lot less than they were. With our system, we can't afford the luxury of having parts sit around waiting to be reworked. We make rework our second priority. The only thing that comes before it is first-run parts. Joe says we run lean and mean. Our output numbers are there for everybody to see. We stay on schedule and are actually doing a lot more special orders for marketing without adding resources. It's got to pay off on the bottom line," I say.

"I'm glad to hear that. I've been toying with the idea of setting up a task force to look at our entire company and the way we schedule our production," says Arthur.

"That is the best action you could possibly take to improve the business. I'm all for it," I say.

"Good. You will definitely be involved deeply in it, one way or another," Arthur replies.

"There's one other measurement that has surprised the hell out of us," I continue. "It's the efficiencies."

"I thought that you'd abandoned them," says Arthur, a look of surprise on his face.

"Scott Crotty kept harping about them so much that I continued to track efficiencies, to appease him more than anything else. Do you remember the terrible dip that my review chart showed?" I ask.

Arthur chuckles, "I can't forget that. Charlie Pearl called it the worst-looking efficiency chart that he's seen in years. Has it continued to deteriorate?"

"On the contrary, our efficiencies are right back up where they were at their highest point. The dip was a temporary thing, caused by the reduction in cycle times and inventory. There wasn't a whole lot of work to do for awhile. Once the inventory was positioned where it needed to be for our new system to work right, everybody had as much work to do every week as they always had. In fact, because of the smaller batches, the flow is smoother, and the efficiencies are slightly better than they ever were," I say.

"That makes sense. Do you intend to reinstall the measurement on an official basis?" asks Arthur.

"Not on your life," I say. "Efficiencies go up by doing the right thing. The things that we do to shorten cycles, lower batches, and pace the plant to our constraints cause the measurement to improve, but if we used efficiencies as a driver, the trend would be reversed. Inventories would go up again! We can't afford it!" I sound emotional.

"Sorry I asked," laughs Arthur.

We finish our coffee and Arthur looks at his watch. "We'd better get going if we want to see King Arthur run."

"How does he look?" asks Vickie.

"He's in fine fettle. The only question is the distance of the race. It's a mile and a sixteenth, but he should win, given a fair share of racing luck," says Arthur.

We make the short trip to Keeneland and watch the horse take command of the race from start to finish. The fans give him a round of applause as he is led into the winner's circle. It certainly looks as though King Arthur and I have a date with destiny during the first weekend in May.

CHAPTER 40

People have been hired, the first castings have just arrived on the dock, and the buffers have been recalculated. It's been a hectic month at the plant, and the staff needs a slight respite. Six weeks from now, it will be the beginning of a new year, and the end of my tenure in Salem. I've invited the entire staff to the condo to celebrate our victories, and at that time I'll name my successor. They all know that I'm leaving, but only Joe knows who will take over when I do. MX is there also. It's impossible to separate him from Toni these days, so why try? Vickie has gone to California for the Breeders' Cup race, which is scheduled for today. It will be the first King Arthur race that I've missed, but it was impossible to get away. It's on national television though, so we will all see it right here. The TV is already tuned to the channel with the sound turned off.

Everybody has had one or two drinks—enough to get them in a relaxed mood—so I begin. "Folks, I've got a couple of announcements to make. First, you all know that Toni and MX are planning a wedding in April. They have asked me to be best man and Vickie to be maid of honor. They've agreed to return the favor in May, when Vickie and I will take our vows." The group stands to give us a round of applause.

I continue, "Thank you for that. May I add that I hope each and every one of you, together with your families, will pay us the honor of being guests at our wedding."

Toni interrupts me long enough to say, "That goes for MX and myself as well."

"The reason that I've brought you all together today is to make an important announcement, but first let me say that each of you has done an outstanding job during the past year. We've had our ups and downs, but you are the best, and I mean that sincerely. As I go on to a new assignment in six weeks, the one thing that I will regret more than anything else is the fact that I will no longer be working with all of you people. You're winners."

They give me another round of applause. "Are you going back to corporate headquarters?" asks Ernie.

"Yes, I am," I answer. "I'm not at liberty at this time to tell you exactly what it is that I'll be doing, but you will be the first to know when the time comes." I don't think that it's appropriate to tell them that I don't know.

"And now for the big news. At this time I'd like you all to meet your new boss. As of January the first, the manager of the Salem facility will be Joe Leonard," I say.

"All right!" exclaims Gary. The others seem to be overjoyed as well. They rush to Joe to congratulate him.

Dean says it best. "We were worried. We thought that it might be somebody new to break in. Joe deserves it—he's worked harder than any of us to make the plant go."

"If he gets the same support from all of you that I've received, he'll be home free. Joe, would you like to say anything?" I ask.

"You've said it for me. I'm looking forward to helping the business grow. I want everybody to fill their glasses to the brim, so that I can propose a toast," he answers.

Everybody does as he requests. "Here's to Larry Jones, the best damned boss that anybody ever had. Corporate's gain is a big loss for Salem. You've left me a big pair of shoes to step into," Joe says.

Everybody clinks their glasses together in toast.

I'm moved by Joe's action. MX saves the day by turning our attention to the TV. He turns the sound up as the rundown of the two-year-olds Breeders' Cup race begins.

"Is it true that the race is for a purse of one million dollars?" asks Toni.

"Yes," I answer. "The winner's share is six hundred thousand. If King Arthur wins, it will put his total winnings for the year over a million. Not many two-year-old horses have accomplished that feat in the past. It will also clinch 'horse of the year' honors for him."

"The announcer seems to think that there's a California horse in there with a chance to upset him," says Ernie.

MX says, "That's why they have races. If it was a sure thing, there wouldn't be a need to run. There are no sure things in horse racing. Believe me, I know."

"I can vouch for that," says Toni.

As the horses are led onto the track, King Arthur comes into view. "Look at the jockey on King Arthur. He looks like he's got on one of the Salem jackets," says Gary.

"If you belong to ConnYankee you will either keep moving or you will definitely be painted powder blue," laughs Dean.

The cameras pan into the box where Arthur and Vickie are seated. My heart gives a quick jump as Vickie appears on the screen. Everybody in the room gives a loud cheer when they recognize her.

The horses are led into the starting gate for the long race. As usual, King Arthur acts up, but they're finally all in line. A quick flash of the final odds shows the King as a prohibitive favorite. The gate opens as the announcer says, "They're off!" King Arthur is away well and settles into fourth place along the rail as the horses wind their way around the clubhouse turn and straighten out for the run down the backstretch.

"He's in great shape," says MX.

The jockey has the horse under tight restraint, waiting for the proper time to ask him to run. Suddenly, the horse directly in front of King Arthur bobbles and goes down. King Arthur swerves to the right to avoid the same fate, and somehow manages to stay on his feet. The horses behind him, not being as close to the mishap, are able to stay in close to the rail and avoid losing too much ground. When King Arthur straightens himself out again, he is in last place and seemingly out of it.

"Oh, my goodness!" exclaims Toni. "What a shame!"

"That's what I mean about no sure things in horse racing," says MX. "But I know this horse. He won't give up."

As if he heard MX, the jockey settles down into the saddle and uses his whip to get King Arthur's attention on the task before him. There's about three-quarters of a mile left to run as the King gets into his tremendous running stride. I'm thinking that no horse can go all out for the last three-quarters of a mile of a long race, but maybe he can get up for second or third.

"Look at him go," says Ernie. The gap between him and the back of the pack is dwindling rapidly.

"He'll run out of gas at that rate," says Gary. King Arthur swings wide around the tail end of the pack to get back up into fourth place as the horses head for home.

The jockey is pushing and shoving and whipping. "C'mon King Arthur! You can do it." We're all screaming at the top of our lungs.

He's third, then second. The horse in the lead, the California bred, is cruising along with a five-length lead as he passes the sixteenth pole. The jockey thinks that he has the race in his pocket and chooses not to use the whip. King Arthur is close in along the rail as the other jockey looks over his right shoulder to see where the opposition is. He cannot see King Arthur, who is moving like a fast freight down along the rail. The announcer is as excited as we are. "Here comes the King down on the inside!"

The jockey on the California horse senses the challenge too late. He looks to his left just in time to see a blur pass him as they cross the finish line.

Drinks are being spilled on my rug as everybody is jumping up and down. "It's unbelievable, but that horse will not be beat," shouts MX.

The TV cameras pan to Arthur and Vickie, who look more excited than we do. Later, in the winner's circle, the announcer interviews Arthur. I feel as if I'm there with them, as I look at Vickie standing beside him.

"We had a bit of racing luck out there today," says Arthur.

The announcer speaks into the mike. "When a horse can do what yours did today, luck or no luck, he's a great one. He's got my two dollars on him in the Kentucky Derby next year."

"I hope you win," says Arthur.

CHAPTER 41

With just two weeks left in the year, Vickie and I are taking Toni and MX out for a night on the town. At least we thought we were, until MX had one of his bright ideas. After a short plane ride over the Berkshires, we find ourselves in the Catskills at the Concord Hotel, the crown jewel of the borscht circuit. MX wants to see his idol perform.

MX manages to persuade, or should I say bribe, the head usher to seat us at center stage. We get our drinks and prepare for the curtain to go up. "I'd like to make an earth-shaking announcement tonight," says MX. "My goal to adjust the algorithm so that it can schedule all of manufacturing has been achieved."

"Congratulations," I say. "But there are so many different kinds of manufacturing conditions. How can you be sure that you've covered all of the bases?"

"We've been doing some extensive testing under all kinds of constraints, and we haven't been able to find a condition that we can't model with it. It's like Just-in-Time in the computer," says MX.

"There are thousands of manufacturing facilities in the world. You can't possibly have covered them all," I say.

"That's what keeps me going—looking for the situation that I can't model. It's early in the game, but indications are that it will be difficult to find such a case. You're right when you say that there are thousands of different ways to manufacture things, but are they really all that different?" says MX.

I think about it for a minute. The three big B's pop into my head. "I guess that as long as Bottlenecks, Buffers, and Batch sizes exist, they will be the dominating influence on any manufacturing facility."

"That's absolutely right," says MX. "All of the other things are considered secondary problems, and that makes them easy to solve, although it takes some innovative thinking sometimes."

"Interesting," I say. "I take it, since Salem was your beta site, you've got us in your computer model."

"Yes, your site was the basis for everything that followed."

"Well then, what does your system do for us that the percussion system doesn't?" I ask.

"It would adjust your buffers automatically to make both short-term and long-term output, while holding inventory investment at a reasonable level. All you would need to do is load in the master schedule and watch your resource utilization. It would fluctuate batch sizes to fine-tune synchronization throughout your plant, and enable you to cut lead times a bit more. It would also enable you to get rid of those fancy colored tote pans."

I laugh. "I've grown fond of them. They add color to the place. Powder blue can get boring. Would it enable me to make more money?"

"You've got a hell of a system already. It fits your kind of environment, and I wouldn't mess with it. The small payback you'd get by going to computer-aided scheduling might be less than the cost of the new problems you'd introduce. There's no free ride," says MX.

"What do you mean?" asks Vickie.

MX continues, "Your factory is fairly straightforward. The manual system gets the job done fantastically well in your environment. It doesn't depend on super-accurate data to function, and there aren't any really complicated manufacturing conditions to contend with. Oh sure, a computer would do a better job of scheduling, but the cost could be more than the payback."

"How much are you going to charge for your system?" I ask.

"I haven't even thought about that as yet. It's not that kind of cost I'm considering here. The cost of data maintenance is what I'm referring to. You must have extremely accurate records to feed into the scheduling system—things like work-in-process inventory. The computer needs to know where everything is. Planned times must be the same as real times. Setup times must be accurate. Rework details need to be considered in the model. You get the idea. A computer needs a whole set of data that had better be accurate. Some things need to be more accurate than others, but the bottom line is, the more accurate all of the data is, the better the schedule," says MX.

"Are you saying that computer-aided scheduling is not always the best way to go?" I ask.

"That's right," he says.

"Give us some examples of the kinds of factories that could use a computer-aided scheduling system," says Toni.

"The more complex a factory is, the better a computer scheduling system will work compared to a manual system. Most factories are a lot more complex than yours. The conditions that exist make it nearly impossible to schedule manually with much success."

"Factories have been around for hundreds of years. Computers are babies," says Toni.

MX laughs. "Remember how you used to schedule Salem? Imagine the chaos that must exist in a manually scheduled factory that is many times more complex. I've seen a few of them. They run in a panic mode all of the time. The late Ollie Wight used to call manual systems 'order launch and expedite'."

"Give us some examples of the kinds of things that you've encountered that make for complex modeling," I suggest.

"There are many. I'll give you a few that come to mind. Take the case of special orders where there are varying degrees of priority. In your factory, you'd have a tough time getting enough different colored tote pans if you had very many special orders. Imagine a business that has several hundred or several thousand products, with variations. My system allows one to set any number of degrees of priority to orders."

"I can see how that kind of tool would be valuable in some of the electronics industries," I say.

"You get the idea," says MX. "How about this one? Suppose that a factory used fixtures that traveled with a part through several operations before they got released. With a manual system, it would be impossible to synchronize the arrival of parts and fixtures. My system has the capability of scheduling them both to arrive at the same place simultaneously."

"That would be a dog to schedule manually," says Vickie.

"How about the case of a furnace, where scores of parts are baked at varying temperatures. The setup time would vary, according to what was in the furnace to begin with and what was going in next. Time would be a function of temperature differential," says MX.

"That sounds like a bag of worms to me," I say. "I'd probably set all setup times to the longest one and forget it."

"That's what is done with a manual system. If a schedule could be developed forward in time that foresees the changeovers, it could schedule the times accurately and improve throughput. Mine does just that. Here's another one. Suppose that you had a product that could be made two different ways, and you had two different routings. My system can handle alternate routings so that the best alternative is scheduled every time."

"How about alternate machines?" asks Toni.

"Piece of cake," says MX. "I can schedule alternate resources and even provide for the difference in times between those resources."

"Very impressive," I say, but there's more.

MX notices that the MC is about to come onto the stage. "There's lots more, like uninterruptable processes, consumable resources, minimum batch sizes and maximum batch sizes, enforced delays, disassembly operations, different working days for different resources, future considerations where resource quantities vary for any number of reasons, fixtures that do many different things, and on and on."

"Then most factories need a computer-aided scheduling system, don't they?" I say.

MX nods his head in the affirmative as the sounds of the orchestra drown out any effort at further voice communication. The MC comes to the center of the stage to introduce MX's idol. "And now, directly from Las Vegas and points west, the Concord Hotel is proud to present the chairman of the board, Mr. Frank Sinatra."

The show is spellbinding with full choreography and colorful sets. Frank is in his best voice. The audience is captivated—that is, all except MX. He seems to be showing some impatience. Just before Frank goes into his grand finale, MX jumps up and shouts, "Sing 'My Way'!" The audience supports him with a thunderous round of applause.

Mister Sinatra obliges and brings down the house. "That's my song," says MX. "I do it my way."

During the return flight to Boston, the conversation turns back to MX and his algorithm. "Now that you've got something to offer, what do you intend to do with it?" I ask.

"I'm going to start a consulting business. All of the details haven't been worked out yet."

"The market is glutted with them," I say.

"Mine is going to be different. My firm will offer seminars where we show prospective clients the tremendous productivity improvements that can be accomplished with what you call the three B's—Bottlenecks, Buffers, and Batches. We will offer to go into a factory, make a study of the facility, and recommend the kind of system that is best."

"Would that include both manual and computer considerations?" I ask.

"Yes," replies MX. "If a manual system is best, we will actually design one that is custom fitted for the facility. If the factory is complex, we will offer the computer system complete with education and backup assistance to install it. There is no facility in this country that cannot be improved by one of the three services we will offer—seminars, manual and computer systems, as well as continuing education and support. There's a big market out there."

"I like it," I say. "ConnYankee may very well be your first and biggest customer soon."

"I'm counting on it," replies MX. "I hope that I don't alienate the company by what I'm going to tell you next."

"Here it comes," mutters Vickie.

"When Toni and I return from our honeymoon, she will be leaving ConnYankee, to become my partner in business as well as life."

CHAPTER 42

I experience mixed emotions as I wander through the factory on the last day of my tenure as manager of the Salem facility. This factory will always hold a special place in my heart. I make it a point to see every employee and say goodbye personally. Damn! Everybody keeps telling me what a great guy I am. I'm starting to believe it.

I'm proud—damned proud of what we've accomplished. The added business has even been phased in without a hitch. No matter what happens tomorrow in Lexington, I know that what we've started here is a wave that must sweep over all of ConnYankee's factories, if we are to remain competitive in the near future and beyond.

When I get back to my office, the entire staff is waiting for me. They usher me into the office to my seat, and close the door. Ernie produces a bottle of champagne and pours us all a glass.

"Here's to you, Larry," says Dean as they raise their glasses toward me. "Wherever you go and whatever you do, we all want to wish you the very best of luck. You will always be a part of this plant. We'll miss you."

Toni hands me a package, neatly gift-wrapped. I open it to find a quartz desk clock made in the shape of the state of New Hampshire.

There's a bronze plaque attached to the wooden base. I read the inscription, "Good luck to the world's best boss from his staff." The names of each of them follow.

I'm filling up inside, but I manage to say, "Thank you. This plant, and you people, will always be a part of me. This has been the best year of my life in so many ways." I clam up. That's all I can manage at this time.

Later, Helen manages to get me to the cafeteria between the first and second shifts. The entire workforce is there, and I'm greeted with a mixture of applause and cheering as I enter. Teresa Lockeridge is waiting for me with a large package in her hands.

She begins, "Larry, you promised us that if we went along with your new ideas eight months ago, good things would happen for us. We chose to trust you, and you sure didn't let us down." A round of applause supports her statement. "All of the employees want you to have this." She hands me the package.

I open it and remove the contents. It's one of the powder blue jackets that we've been awarding the hourly employees. Both sleeves are lined with little drums. I put it on, as the employees applaud. Teresa continues, "We have always taken great pride in the fact that these jackets would never be awarded to members of management. We're breaking the rule for you, Larry. You are one of us. We want you to wear it proudly."

Somebody in the crowd shouts, "It's the only one that any member of management will ever wear." That brings out another round of applause.

I'm moved. "When I took this assignment, I was told by Arthur King himself that people would make the difference. Now I know what he meant. I love you all."

Words are not enough. I kiss every woman and shake hands with every man in the place. Both my lips and my hand are numb when I leave the plant and head for the airport and Lexington.

There's no snow in Kentucky, a definite change from the white landscape of southern New Hampshire, but it's just as cold as I take an early morning walk with Marty Connolly, my rival and friend.

"I'll be glad when this is over. How about you?" I ask.

"I'm sorry to see it end," he answers. "It's been great to get back into harness and smell the lubricating fluids again." He's not nervous, or at least he's not showing it.

"I've really learned a lot about manufacturing life in the past year. It's really where it's at," I say, trying to cover up my extremely nervous state.

"I've heard a lot about what you've been doing up there—pretty unorthodox," says Marty.

I laugh and clap him on the back. "I had to do something different. I could never hope to beat the old pro at his own game, could I?"

"I should hope not," he answers. "I had one hell of a good year, and I've left the Murfreesboro plant with a bright future."

We walk by King Arthur's stall. Marty says, "Did you see that horse run in the Breeders' Cup? That really was something. He just won't let anybody get the best of him—lotta heart there."

"Yes," I say. "He reminds me of Arthur, with that tough competitive heart. It will take a super horse with a lot of luck to beat him."

As the meeting with Arthur begins, I'm getting more and more nervous. On the other hand, Marty seems to be getting more and more relaxed. He's in an extremely happy mood. I wonder if he knows something that I don't. During the preliminary round of drinks, Marty and Arthur joke back and forth while I'm unable to say much of anything. It seems apparent to me that I've lost. A song keeps going through my head, "Turn out the lights, the party's over."

Finally, after what seems to be an eternity, Arthur goes to the wall safe and removes the large envelope. "Before I open this, I want to say that the both of you have done an outstanding job. The Salem plant and the Murfreesboro plant are both way ahead of all of the other plants by every measurement. Of course, I would have been disappointed if it had been any other way. When I put my two top executives on a project, I fully expect spectacular results."

It sounds like what I've been fearing all along is about to happen. He's going to use all of the old measurements to determine the winner. Damn! Why doesn't he use the only measurement that means anything? I don't see how Marty could have made any more money than I did.

Arthur continues, "Just so you will both know, I kept track of the traditional measurements. Marty, you had better efficiencies and much better schedule adherence numbers. You both shipped product pretty much on time, although Larry, you did make more special orders. Larry, your inventory levels are way below Marty's. The overtime worked was about the same for the first half of the year, but as Marty's increased toward year end, Larry, yours went down and stayed down."

Nothing definitive yet, I think.

"I looked at the bottom line. Isn't that what you wanted me to do, Larry?" asks Arthur.

I nod my head. There's a slight glimmer of hope.

"Marty already knows this. You absolutely wiped him out. Salem made several million more dollars for the company coffers than Murfreesboro did. It wasn't even a contest after the middle of the year. Larry, you've showed us all something spectacular up in that little plant of yours."

I turn my attention to my rival, but he isn't bothered in the slightest by this turn of events. "That's what my goal was from the beginning," I say. "The only reason that the plant is there is to make money—measurements be damned!"

I feel triumphant until Arthur brings me back down to earth. "That's not what I based my decision on, though." He fumbles with the envelope and tears it open to remove the paper.

No wonder Marty is relaxed. He already knows the result.

Arthur says nothing, but turns the paper around so I can see it. In large black letters I see the final words—LARRY JONES, CEO.

It hits me like a ton of turbine blades. I've won! Marty is the first to congratulate me. He's still smiling. What a guy! I'd have slashed my wrists in his place. Arthur offers his hand and does the usual damage to mine.

I'm still in a daze, but I've got to know. "What did you base your decision on?" I ask.

Marty laughs aloud. Arthur smiles. "There never was a competition to begin with. Marty and I rigged this thing up to get you some valuable experience down in the trenches. Why do you think that the old warhorse is so happy today?" He points to Marty.

"I was wondering about that."

"Marty has been around a long time. He's done an outstanding job for a lot of years, but he's going out to pasture as soon as this meeting is over, and with a hell of a pension, I might add."

Marty says, "My retirement was in the works when we first met. Arthur asked me to stay on another year to play this game with you. I'm glad that I did. You've really come up with something there in Salem. You see, I'm fully knowledgeable of everything that you've done. Vickie has taken care of that duty for both Arthur and me."

Vickie knew it all along. Wait until I get my hands on her.

"It was all a complicated scheme," says Arthur. "I've realized for a couple of years that the Japanese competition will eventually put me out of business if I don't change. It's a deadly game we're playing—a fight for survival, and winner takes it all. Vickie being at Harvard, the plant being in Salem, and you running it—it was all a setup. I wanted you for CEO of ConnYankee, and I want a Just-in-Time system. I decided to kill two birds with one stone."

No wonder that ConnYankee is so successful. "How did you arrange MX?" I ask.

"That was Vickie's idea," says Arthur.

"I've got to hand it to you," I tell him. "You have full control at all times. I hope that I can fill those big shoes of yours."

Arthur laughs as he takes me by the arm. "For the next year, that's just about where you'll be—in my shoes. You and I are going to be like Siamese twins. We will be inseparable. By the end of that time, you can be sure that you will be the best damned CEO there is."

"You're not coming on my honeymoon, are you?" I laugh.

He jerks my arm hard as he leads me into the next room, the dining room, where I find another surprise. There's a big cake that says, "CONGRATULATIONS LARRY JONES." The cake is surrounded by Vickie, Toni, and MX. I rush to them and embrace them all at once.

After the excitement of the day is over, Vickie and I are sitting by the fire with Toni and MX. "It has been quite a year, folks," I say. "But next year will be really something."

MX says, "Two weddings, my new company, the education of a top CEO, the Kentucky Derby—it really will be something. We could write a book."

"I can give you plenty to write a book about. Don't make any plans for your new company until you see me," I tell him. "I'll probably need you exclusively for a couple of years. We've got a lot of plants to look at, and each one has a different story to tell."